SLASH

SLASH

JEANNETTE C. ARMSTRONG

THEYTUS BOOKS

Canadian Cataloguing in Publication Data

Armstrong, Jeannette, C. 1948-
Slash

Rev. ed.
ISBN 0-919441-29-7

1. Indians of North America—British Columbia
Fiction.   I. Title.

PS8551.R7635S4 1988 j813'.54 C88-090114-4
PR9199.3.A74S4 1988

Cover photo: August Armstrong
Cover design: Richard Gray

Published by Theytus Books
Penticton, B.C.

Printed and bound in Canada

For Tony

Words were always easy for you
You played with them
in long chains
or little piles
People laughed at your stories and were happy
for a few moments you would be too

Then you would return
to that cold and wordless place
where the only sounds
were those of an always new beast
waiting just in the shadows
where emptied bottles
spoke of the battles now lost

All we have of you now
are echoes of words to make us laugh
and we are poorer
but the war you fought alone
is ours too
already our people gather
to choose their weapons

We all walk in the shadow of the beast
so we will step lightly
All the stories you used to make laughter
will be told around the tables of your people
And we will be rich with weapons

TABLE OF CONTENTS

Foreword

SLASH is a gently written novel, dealing with a brutal theme. It is a story of colonialism in Canada and the rest of this continent. Colonialism over the aboriginal peoples, with its own special quality of cultural and physical deprivation and a legacy of racial genocide. It is a story of one personality attempting to find a way out of this living death by way of prison, spiritual confirmation and active political struggle.

Through the wanderings of her hero, author Jeannette Armstrong traces the outlines of an emerging will for liberation and self-determination, beginning with a challenge to self-doubt. Her hero muses: "I know there is more than passive discrimination in the schools and everywhere else for that matter. The only time there is less is if you dress up like Jimmy does and change your voice to a higher pitch and use different English with big words mixed in, and even then there is some. That in itself, to me, is more than passive discrimination. It is and insult to a whole race of people thousands of generations old. And that kind of discrimination does more damage, overall, than any cops kicking the shit out of a drunken Indian. I mean, like that's the main trouble why that Indian was drunk. Why a lot of Indians are drunk. I get real mad inside that our people seem to be looked on as if we were less than just different.... "

These are difficult realizations, struggling even for linguistic metaphors to reach a simple truth that the dominant culture appears to have removed from reach. The hero of this story has to find the resources to fashion a means of survival. It is slow going, yet he cannot rise quickly from his slowness or his confusion. Such things were imposed on him and his tattered culture. They were not of his choosing. That they persisted into the restless '60s and '70s reveals how thorough was the assault of colonialism on the aboriginal peoples.

Capitalism introduced into North America was merciless in its quest to secure resources. Using military forces, traders and priests as the shock brigades of colonial power, capitalism swept through choice flatlands and secured the base for a mighty agricultural economy which, to this day, is world foremost. But the architects of this capitalist empire did not stop there. To feed the engines of developing industry, they secured resources in energy, metallurgy and forestry for exploration far into the future. That the lands their social system over-ran were traditional homelands for aboriginal peoples living there was merely a problem of conquest. Using poor whites as military fodder, these lands were taken by force. Treaties and formal agreements of conquest became so much archival paper. Often using religion and alcohol as mind-altering drugs, the preserved history and traditions of the original peoples were ruthlessly eliminated from memory or turned into objects of scorn and humiliation.

Oddly, these conquered peoples were not systematically trained as producers and consumers in a capitalist economy. What was left of their lives and cultures was frozen into permanent patronage under the auspices of the public sector of the state. This resulted in contradictions which created a revolutionary condition on the Indian reservations throughout North America in the 1960's and subsequent decade.

Fueled by activists like the imaginary Slash Kelasket, of whom Jeannette Armstrong writes, the reservations became hotbeds of growing cultural awareness and political sensitivity. The people re-connected with traditional lore and social and community practices leading to unity. The young and the old began to translate social relationships within and outside the reservations into new alliances, for it was soon discovered that modern capitalism is most democratic in its exploitation of *all* disinherited peoples-be they blacks, poor whites, women, youths or the aboriginal civilizations. Life on the reservations did not improve, but the promise of change was heady.

Jeannette Armstrong is not blinded by narrow idealism or romantic illusions. She is an unflinching observer of political realities, even when such observations are painful. Herself a veteran of the movements of the '60s, and an intelligent analyst of national liberation struggles in the Third World, she recognizes the pitfalls of faulty revolutionary theory, of leadership tempered by opportunism, of one sided accommodation born of exhaustion, of scars too deep to heal easily. She recognizes, even as she gives passionate argument otherwise, that a revolutionary struggle for self-determination is not simply a struggle for return to some idyllic past that is again vulnerable to conquest. She recognizes, also, that relationship of people to land, of man to woman, of family to community, of collective will over personal gesture, must be resolved before the next and most meaningful campaign of all can be launched.

Her hero and her heroine, at the end of the book, do not rest easily with activities which appear to meet the needs of the day. There will be more deaths and mutilations of the spirit, as well as betrayals. For it has been a time of arousal to action-a time of preparing. The tempering of the will through struggle is yet to come.

In recognizing this, the book becomes both a testament and optimistic promise. For the boundaries of race and economic inequality do not isolate a shared revulsion by ordinary people of violence, war and genocide against aboriginal peoples by corporations and government agencies protecting such practices through deliberately corrupt legislation and abuses of power. Any defeat to such practices brings liberation to all who are oppressed by such cruel exploitation of earth and people.

— George Ryga, March, 1984

Prologue

As I begin to write this story, I think back. I search my background, back to when, as an almost man, things seemed so simple. I look at that child and find him a stranger and yet he is nearer to me, as I am now, than when I became a young man full of a destructive compulsion to make change happen.

Yet I must examine how I changed and what caused the changes. I must understand it and, understanding it, I may understand what changes our people went through during those times and what we are coming up against.

It is crucial because I am an Indian person. As Indian people, we each stand at a pivot point at this time in history. We each have the burden of individually deciding for our descendants how their world shall be affected and what shall be their heritage.

The characters in this novel are fictitious. Any resemblance to persons, living or dead, is coincidental.

The events are based on actual events but are not meant to be portrayed as historically accurate.

CHAPTER ONE

The Awakening

School started that morning with old Horseface hollering at everybody to line-up. Boy, it was cold! My ears were hurting. I shoulda took my toque, I guess. I poked at Jimmy next to me. "Hey, wanna bet Horseface has on long wool bloomers?" Jimmy rolled his eyes and said, "Shit, how you gonna find out?" I leaned over to him and whispered, "Why don't we unscrew one of those light bulbs like last time? We'll hold the ladder and just look up her skirt." Jimmy kicked a rock and made a snorting noise, "Jeez, I wish she'd hurry up and let us in. We could eat those damn goof-balls inside."

Mrs. Hosfah must've heard Jimmy because she hollered, "Jimmy Joseph and Thomas Kelasket, please stay at lunch for talking during line-up for vitamins." A couple of girls and the do-goody guys snickered.

We filed into the one big room and went to stand by our desks. The little kids in Grade One were closest to the big oil stove. Us grade sixers were by the windows. It was coldest there, but in spring or fall it was okay because you could look up at the trees and hills and at the sun setting.

Well, anyway, we sang some songs like "Robin in the Rain," which was my favorite song, and "God Save the Queen." After we prayed Our Father and ten Hail Marys, we sat down and started to do our work.

Sometimes, the days were so long before we went home, especially when Horseface was busy with the other grades more than us. Sometimes, she would let us read if we finished our numbers fast. I liked reading a lot. I could imagine all those places and things just like I was there. Jimmy thought that was kind of sissy-pissy, but I didn't care. Besides, my Dad said boys like Jimmy, who didn't know how to do right things, like skinning a deer, were really the sissies.

After school, the kids that lived close by went home. Us kids who lived up the hill waited for the bus; some kids stayed and played ice-rock. We lived way outa town in the hills where there was more snow than down at the school. It was already dark when we got home. This was the middle of January and everything was frozen solid. Around the trails, stiff thorn trees spread black crooked branches looking like frozen webs. They glistened with silver, and thick gobs of blue-green ice piled up behind rocks and drift logs in the creek.

I knew feeding the horses and cows was going to be a cold job. My older brother was home. He was out of school already. He was past Grade Six. Our school only went as far as Grade Six. Anybody who went to school after that went to residential school, where they lived right at the school. Dad never let Danny go. I knew I wouldn't go, either. Dad said we would just learn how to steal and lie at that school.

We had an older cousin, named Joe, who had gone there. He was a quiet man that came to help Pops during haying. He was working to buy a horse. He was a good storyteller. He used to sit up with us boys in the summer tent and tell us about his days at residential school. His mother had died of T.B. when he was little, leaving him and his two brothers and three sisters. They all went to residential school too, because of that.

He told us a story about him stealing a piece of raw bacon skin and hiding it under his shirt to chew on when he went on barn duty. He remembered being hungry all the time, so this piece of bacon rind tasted good and he was chewing on it in the barn while he was supposed to be feeding the pigs. It was bitter cold and he was sitting under the feed bin chewing the bacon, with his hands freezing, when Percy, the barn hand, caught him. Percy was half-touched; all the kids knew. He came after Joe with a pitch fork and the only thing that saved him was one of the priest brothers was in the barn. Still, he was punished for stealing, with a strapping across his bare back and his head shaved. He was given an extra month of barn duty too, for not working like he was supposed to.

Joe told us that we were lucky Pops wouldn't let us go there because it made people mean inside from being lonely, hungry and cold. He said kids were even beat up for talking Indian. He told us some other stuff about what happened to some of the girls that was really bad. I was sure glad Danny didn't go there.

Danny was already feeding the horses when I got out there. "Hey, Tommy! Hurry up, okay! We got some visitors. Looks like old Pra-cwa from over the hill." I hurried with feeding, slinging shocks of loose hay with the pitch fork over the fence to the cows. "Dad wants us to sit around and listen," Danny hollered over his back.

I walked toward the house. I saw the lamp, yellow-bright, shining through the window. The snow all around looked like soft yellow butter, fresh made. Inside I saw my Grandpa, my Uncle Billy, my Dad and Pra-cwa all sitting at the table. My Mom, my Aunt Shu-li and my older sister Josie were all walking around the stove. I smelled fried deer meat as I walked in. My Mom took a pan of biscuits from the oven. Boy, I liked the feel of the warm and the smells. It sure wasn't the same smell at school. At school we had to push around this green stuff called dust bane, on the floor, with wide brooms. It stank awful. So did the oil in the stove.

My Dad said in Indian, "Shake hands with your Grandpa Pra-cwa." I walked over and said in Indian, "Hello, it is a good night." Pra-cwa said, "Yes and you are a big man now. What did you do at that writing place? Did you learn to write?" I looked at him and said, "Yes, that is what I learned." "Good," he said, "Now you can read this paper for your Dad. He said you were good at that. Danny isn't too good." I looked at that paper. It was an awfully long paper with a lot of words. I began to read. Most of it I couldn't really understand because some of the words were too long, but Shu-li helped with them. She was real smart. She went to school a long time ago in the States.

The paper seemed to have said something about Indians going to vote for a government. It said that some could and some couldn't, but those that could would be equal. I think it talked about voting somewhere else besides at our community hall, where all our people voted for who was going to be Chief.

Pra-cwa then asked my Dad to tell it to him in Indian. I listened for awhile as Dad explained that some Indians, from then on, could go to the town and vote for who was going to be the white man's leader. He said Diefenbaker was the leader.

Pra-cwa listened and said, "Why would we want to do that? We wouldn't want them to come and vote for who was going to be our Chief. We live different than them and they live different than us." My uncle said, "But some Indians think it's okay. Some of them in the North American Indian Brotherhood want to vote. They say it'll do some good. They say maybe we would get a better deal on our lands."

"I don't know," my Dad said, "I think they just want to be whites." Pra-cwa said, "They don't really know what they are doing. They could be getting ready to sell us out of our reserves and make us like white people. You see that last one about paying tax. That's what I mean. I don't like it. I don't agree. You tell the rest not to agree."

Pra-cwa was a headman to all the people who still talked Indian. He was like a Chief even though he hadn't been voted on. He was smart. I listened to them talk and talk late that night while Danny snored beside me. Pra-cwa was visiting all the houses of people like us in the whole Okanagan. Finally, I must have slept because next thing I knew, Dad was waking Danny and me up to milk cows and feed the horses.

Pra-cwa was still sitting at the table. His long mustache drooped and his thick grey hair stuck out every which way. Every time he laughed, all his wrinkles shook. I knew that they had stayed up all night talking. The good stories came out towards morning. I sometimes stayed up to listen.

Once I heard a story, in the early morning, about a woman named Hightuned Polly. She had a dog that she babied like some white women do. She carried it around and made little skirts for it. One time, Hightuned Polly was at a celebration in Omak, during the Stampede Pow-wow. She was staying with some friends in a pow-wow teepee. Her dog got in heat. So all day, there was a big troop of dogs following her wherever she carried her dog. They even sneaked into the teepee under the flaps, while she was inside. Everyone was teasing her as she walked around with fifteen dogs trotting along. Finally, that night, she decided to sew a buckskin pant for her dog, to keep the other dogs from getting to her. Well, in the morning, Hightuned Polly found her dog with many visitors and a hole chewed right through the buckskin.

Pra-cwa and Dad agreed that someone had best talk at the big meeting coming up in Kamloops of all the Indian tribes in B.C. He said that the Chiefs especially should think before they did what the white government asked. Pra-cwa was going to talk to the Chief of our Band.

I thought about that. Our Chief was a quiet man. We visited him sometimes. We used to go down in Dad's big old flat deck hay truck, with the whole family. We would visit for a

whole week sometimes. At those times, I got to walk to school
and play with the other kids around the village.

I remember hearing all the strange sounds at night, when
we stayed at the village which was near the town. The trains,
the airplanes and cars never seemed to quiet down, even at
night. And the sky always seemed to be lighted up so you
couldn't see the stars very clearly. The people here could just
walk to town. They did, too. We seen them towards evening.
The young men mostly. Also the people here always seemed
to have store-bought foods like sliced bread and bologna and
things.

Later on that year, I heard my Dad talking with some other
men, while we were visiting with my cousins who lived in the
village. They talked about schooling of the kids. Many of
them did not want the schooling to be changed to make us
go to town school. I don't know why. They also argued about
whether or not it would be good for Indians to go to beer
parlours and drink and buy beer and other stuff like that. I
guess they couldn't go into town and buy beer or drink it
there either. But I knew some people bought it anyway.

Jimmy was there when they were talking. When we went
outside to play Jimmy said, "Did you ever taste beer?" I told
him, "No, but a cousin of Dad's, named Edward, came to visit
us and he was drunk. He talked and sang real loud. Then him
and a man named John fought. I was real scared."

I said, "I hope they don't agree to buy that stuff." Jimmy
laughed and said, "Oh hell, I tried it with my older brother
Kenny. We sure felt funny. It was fun. When I grow up I'm
going to drink it and have fun all the time, because there's
nothing to do around here anyway that's fun."

I just looked at him and thought about what my Dad had
talked to us about. He said that drinking was bad and that lots
of people didn't care about working or anything once they
started to drinking. He told us not to ever let anyone change
our minds.

I wondered why they were talking about it. "Can't Indians

buy it or not?" I asked my Dad. He said, "Indians can't buy it. It's against the law. Now they want to change the law so they can buy it without going to jail." He said, "It's no good stuff. It's better if nobody could buy it. But they would find a way to get it anyway. So that's why I say, just stay away from it, even if they change the law. The law don't mean much on paper. It's what's in your head that's the real law. If you learn good things and think good, no paper laws are needed for you. That's how we believe."

By the time spring and summer came I forgot all the talks during the winter. I just hurried home from school to help with the planting and weeding and haying. I liked being in the big gardens of fresh growing vegetables. Sometimes I sat and looked at the new green stalks, row on row, melting together far down the field into soft green gold. I felt like a big warm lake was flowing around the fields and all around me and I was in the middle of it and it poured soft sounds like a long slow drum song over me. I guess everybody in the family felt it because they all liked to work out there. Those were fun times. Everybody would work in the fields until dark.

In the evening there would be a huge meal, under the dense green cover of thornberry trees, while the oil lamps threw shadow people around. My special Uncle Joe came to stay with us and help. I went with him everywhere and he told me a lot of stories of old times. He told me about a long time ago, how our people used to live. He sure made it sound like fun. Especially the part about when young boys were allowed to go on long hunting trips for weeks way up in the mountains. We only went hunting one day at a time.

I went hunting ground-hogs with him almost every week that summer. He liked to eat them. I thought they tasted pretty good too. We went to the rocky places at the base of the hills away from the fields. It was hot among the big black boulders. Brown weeds, sage and yellowed cheat grass spread soft colors over the dry shady spots between grey shale banks and cactus patches. Uncle Joe liked to eat the fat little animals. He said they were clean animals which only ate alfalfa and clover flowers. Uncle Joe showed me lots of stuff about hunting deer and other things, too. He always bragged about me to my Dad and other men when we got home. Sometimes we would walk from daybreak until after dark. Other times we would camp at a nearby relative's if we were far from home.

One time we went hunting grouse. He said, "This time we only take one .22 bullet apiece. That way we have a contest. Whoever misses gets a kick in the ass from the other one, okay?" "Well," I thought to myself, "I'll let him shoot first, that way if he misses I'll get to kick him." I said, "Uncle Joe, you are the Elder. I will respect you and give you the first chance to shoot."

He looked at me, "So, I see you are a fast learner." Finally, we saw some grouse way up on a big pine tree. Uncle Joe took careful aim while I held my breath. Crack! We both waited for the grouse to fall. It didn't. I started laughing and said, "Okay, bend over!" Just as he laid his gun down the grouse fell to the ground. He laughed and laughed. Guess who bent over that day!

Uncle Joe was known as a medicine man among our people. He showed me lots of plants and things for curing sicknesses. We walked all over the hills. Birds and squirrels were always singing and chattering around us. Sometimes the pine trees sounded like they were moaning, especially late in the evening when the coyotes began to call with shrill voices across the sage-smelling dark. Uncle Joe sometimes sang the Coyote Song while he drummed on Dad's hand drum. His voice sounded like those trees in the soft night filled with fresh smells and Coyote Song.

I learned a lot of good things that summer with my Uncle Joe who was my mom's brother. He came from a place to the south, in the States. A place called Nespelem. I sure missed him when he left.

When it was starting school time again, my Dad called us

together: Danny, Josie, me and the smaller kids, Jenny and Wayne. He said, "I want to talk to you kids about school. This year the day school is going to close because the Indian agent wants all the Indian kids to go to town school. You are going to have to go to school with white kids. It's going to be hard, because you're different. They will probably treat you mean and make fun of how you talk and how you dress and how you look. Now I want you kids to go to that school and don't listen to them. Be proud that you're Indian. Don't worry about your clothes or your looks or how you talk. We are the people who have every right to be here. We ain't sneaking in from somewhere and pushing our way in. Remember that everytime one of them says anything bad to you. You know who you are."

So the next day we all got on the bus and headed downtown. Everybody was real quiet. Even Danny and Josie were with us. They had grades higher than Grade Six at the town school. When we got there all the kids from the village stood together in a big knot. Everyone was quiet. We didn't know what to do or where to go. All the white kids stayed away from us. We all noticed their shiny bikes and brand new clothes and shoes. They screamed and ran around all over the place too.

Finally, some teachers came out and a loud buzz came from the school. The teachers told all the children to go to the gym. We just followed all the white kids inside a big hollow room with bright lines and circles drawn on the floor. That was the gym. We all sat on seats above the floor while the teachers sat at tables on the shiny floor. One by one, white kids names were called and they went to stand in line with a teacher. I never seen so many kids together all at once. It was scary.

After all the white kids were gone, just us from the reserve were left. The man they called the principal talked to us for awhile about rules. There was so many I can't remember, but one thing I do remember; he said, "You Indians are lucky to be here. We'll get along just fine as long as you don't steal from the other kids. I want you all to wait here while the nurse comes to check your heads and ask you some questions. Then I will assign you to classes."

I wondered what he meant about stealing and checking our heads. I thought maybe he wanted the nurse to look at our hair color or something, because everybody else seemed to have blonde hair. The only kid I knew to steal was Leonard. He got marched into the old school by his grandma who shamed him in front of the whole class. He stole a comic from one of the richer kids that time.

The classrooms we went to had high ceilings with rows and rows of lights above. The teachers told everybody to sit in desks that were shiny with bright green legs. They sure were different than the old wooden desks we had at the res school. We had a different classroom and a different teacher for everything. Boy, some of us were lost all the time for a while. Especially, since we wouldn't ask where we were supposed to be, once all the kids disappeared from the halls and the doors were closed. The halls were a quiet and terrifying place to wait until some teacher noticed one of us.

I never knew, until a long time later at school that year, what the principal had meant. The white kids began to get used to us and they sometimes teased us and talked dirty but not all the time. One boy, a big fat kid in Grade Eight named Humphrey, said, "You frigging Injuns are nothing but thieves, full of lice, everybody knows that!" Jeez, old Monty, a grade sevener, but older than some grade nines, was really mad. He kicked Humphrey's ass. Monty didn't come back to school after that. We heard the principal kicked him out for good, but Humphrey, who started everything, didn't even get detention.

I guess it wasn't all bad going to school but sometimes I sure hated my looks and my clothes, especially when I wished I could join in some of the lunch hour or after school games the other kids played. They never would ask us to play with them though. We had to be asked before we joined in anything. It was proper. All the Indian kids acted proper that way. It seemed that white kids were different in a lot of things.

Gradually, I started to learn to make new friends, but mostly we Indians stuck together. We just didn't talk or play the same as them. There were lots of things they didn't know, too. They mostly thought we lived like the Indians of the movies, with feathers and tomahawks and all that. Even some of the teachers were like that. They acted scared around us. Most of the Indian kids talked English different too. That was hard on us. We got mostly E's in Grammar and everything else that we used English in, which was just about everything. So, I guess we mostly got E's in everything but P.E. and Woodwork.

One time, we were all talking and this one skinny white kid named Don Evans, with real thick glasses, was with us. He hung around us a lot because the other kids didn't like him. They bullied him too much, too, I guess. But anyway, he asked, "Hey did you watch Bonanza last night? Boy, that was a good shoot-out huh?" All of us just looked at him. I asked him, "What was that, a movie?" "Naw, you know on T.V.," he answered.

We all looked at him. Jimmy said, "You mean you got a T.V. in your house?" "Sure," he said, "Doesn't everybody?" Well, that's how things were at the new school for the next few years.

Sometime, maybe the next year or after, some of the people in the village began to get new houses built with Indian Band money. We didn't. Some others didn't either. My Dad and others said it wasn't good to take hand-outs like that even if it were the Band's.

I told that to Jimmy once, when he said, "Why don't you guys get a new house with electric lights and a bathroom inside?" I told him how Dad and them talked about it with Pra-cwa and some other Indian-talking people. I told him that Pra-cwa had said, "Ever since those young people went to school away from home, they are changed. They don't like our ways. Maybe it's because they only know English. They are ashamed of everything Indian. That's why they take stuff like Band houses and other things, like leasing their land for money to white people. They got no pride. Everything was given to them at that school and they got to liking to live like white people in white painted rooms with electric lights and shitters inside their houses."

Boy, Jimmy was mad at me. He cussed and said, "Bullshit! You guys up-the-hill is just stupid and old-fashioned. Nobody needs to talk Indian anymore. My Dad and them are smart. They are up-to-date. We are gonna get a T.V., too. My Dad is working at the sawmill now. He is gonna buy me a bike, too."

I felt pretty rotten for awhile after that. I kinda felt maybe, just maybe, Jimmy could be right. Why were my Dad and them so stubborn about new stuff anyway? I sometimes thought about it late at night when I was all alone. But somehow I understood my Dad and them. I was proud lots of times because I knew there was lots learned because of talking Indian that the other kids missed out on. A lot of it had good feelings tied to it. Like when Uncle Joe and me talked about the hills and all the animals and plants, their names and the legend stories about them. Pra-cwa's early morning stories with the other old people were like that too. At the same time, I also felt ashamed at school because we didn't have T.V. and a new car. Heck, I didn't even have new clothes, let alone a bike.

Lots of things changed them years while I was going to school in town. Danny quit in one year. He just couldn't work in school. He wanted to be outside all the time. He never even tried to get at least C's in anything. I guess he liked horses too much. Josie quit, too. She went and got an old man. They lived with us at home.

Clyde, her old man, was okay. He didn't know much about living up-the-hill but he learned okay with Danny showing him how to hunt and how to harness the horses to cut hay and stuff. Danny rode bucking horses too. He was pretty good at it. Everybody always went out to the corral to watch him break a new one in. Pops always shouted, "Stay with 'em, son!" and everybody would cheer. Clyde liked doing that too. Him and Danny hit it off real good.

A lot of new Band houses were being built on the reserve. It seemed like everybody was busy working at the sawmill or something so they could buy T.V.'s and fridges and cars. Lots of people still went to Oroville and Omak to thin apples and pick them, too. People could make more money down there.

We went once when Dad said we were going to buy a tractor. The whole family lived in a little cabin in Tonasket, Washington.

We picked apples for three weeks solid. All our food was bought, like loaves of bread and peanut butter and wieners. Not like at home where we mostly ate deer meat, fish, potatoes and vegetables we grew. At home Mom used to make all the bread, too. So it was different to us kids. We had fun but the work was really hard. Every morning, Stadler, the boss, used to come by and talk with Dad. He was okay, just plain white folk. Once he let us pick raspberries for supper, from his garden.

Dad got a tractor when we got home. He was all excited and so were we. We all took turns learning how to drive it around and around. We got some new clothes and shoes, too, from what was left. I felt almost good when I went back to school that time. But things didn't change much there.

It was that year that we went to a pow-wow at Inkameep, near Oliver. The Chief had a feast and old-time stick-games were played. The old people said that it was the first time in many years since we ever had one in the Okanagan on this side of the border.

I remember watching old Eneas playing stick-games and listening to the drumming. It sounded pretty good and it almost made me feel like when I was with Uncle Joe and he was drumming and singing, teaching me Indian songs. It was fun, with lots of laughing and visiting. Dad was all dressed up in his buckskin vest, beaded with red and yellow roses. Everybody there was Indian and they played baseball as well as stick games, each reserve against another.

Not too long after that we heard on the radio about the Indian agent, saying that pretty soon there wasn't going to be reserves anymore. He had talked to townspeople. My Dad, Uncle Billy, Pra-cwa and a lot of others went to talk to the Chief about it. Pra-cwa told him, "I told you that's what was going to happen. Ever since you accepted voting and liquor rights and sent our grandchildren to white schools, I have been scared. Look at all the Band houses and all the people taking welfare and all the people drinking and forgetting how to ranch and hunt. Look at it. Is that good? Now the government wants to end reserves. How are the people going to pay taxes? They will lose their lands. They will be skid-row people. Now what are we going to do?"

The Chief just listened and said, "I do not tell them how to live. They tell me what they want done. I try my best. They only want to live good. I am worried, too. I wish things were different like in old times but now the people think different. I can't change that. Only some of the people think like you do. This new priest we have here now, he wants to help. He wants to get the women and young people doing good things. Why don't you work with them and help our poor people? We might have an Indian Days like at Inkameep to help the people feel good."

Pra-cwa sat for a long time and nodded. "Yes, I guess that is how things are, but for us, we like doing things for ourselves. We like to live free. We don't want that to change. We want our Indian rights always but we will help as much as we can, with the Indian Days and other things, too."

I had heard of the new priest but I hadn't met him. I was afraid of any of them. I had known the old priest and he was mean with the little kids. Somehow, he looked almost not a person, especially with the black suit he wore all the time. The church was right outside the school and sometimes after school he would call us in his house to listen to his catechism. The classes were always boring because we couldn't understand them. If we tried to run away he grabbed us by the ear and twisted hard, so we had to listen.

One day, near Christmas, all the little kids were having a party put on by the white community. The radio station people were going to be there and a lot of other town people, too. My little brother and sister wanted to go. They said to Mom, "Can we go? Everybody is. They are going to show us a movie, too."

After Mom and Dad talked about it, Dad said, "Okay, you kids can go. You know the town people put on this party because they think you kids is so poor that you don't get candy and presents. They want to give you presents because that's what Christmas means to them. You know we also respect that time of giving. We also respect anybody who wants to give. So we give each other presents and have a big feast at that time. Now you kids go to that party and accept the presents given to you. You got to take some presents too. Your Mom is going to make a few things for you to take."

Boy, were the kids happy! Of course I had to go to watch Jenny and Wayne, so they wouldn't shame us. It was kind of exciting, anyway. I met the new priest there. I didn't even know he was a priest. He talked and laughed and played with the little kids. They really liked him. I did, too.

A lot of other big kids, thirteen and fourteen years and older were there. They were looking after their little brothers and sisters. I had heard some of the white ladies worrying about it near the kitchen. One of them had said, "My goodness! Looks like the whole tribe is here. They said only twenty-five children under twelve years old. We brought food and presents for that many."

Some mothers and dads had gone, too, because they had little kids and no older kids to send to watch them. The whole tribe hadn't gone either; just almost the whole reserve, except for some parents and old people. Well, those ladies didn't need to worry because us older ones hadn't expected presents. We all shared sandwiches and candy and oranges, like we did

anywhere else. It was fun, even though the white ladies really
looked worried all the time, because the little babies crawled
around all over, dragging ribbons and their oranges through
everything.

When it came time for presents, the radio station man called
out names and all the little kids went up and said, "Thank
you, sir." My little sister, Jenny, walked up to the radio station
man and said, "We brought you some presents too, for you
and the priest and the ladies that cooked." She looked real
proud when she said, "My Mom made these buckskin coin
purses for you." They didn't know what to say. The ladies
looked funny like they were ashamed to take the presents.
The radio station man was happy. He said, "My, feel how soft
this is. Tell your people thank you very much." The priest
smiled and explained real loud that our people like to give
things, not just take things. He said it showed a deep respect
for the white club who wanted to put on this party.

I looked at the priest and thought, "What a good man. It
seems like he is different from all the other priests the old
people in my family talked about."

My parents and grandparents weren't church goers. They
said the priests maybe didn't understand that the Creator was
all over. You could talk to Him anywhere but mostly in your
heart. They said you only had to go to church if you done bad
things and couldn't face it.

The priest talked to me that night. He said, "Hi! You must
be Tommy Kelasket. It's good you kids came tonight. How
are you getting home? Can I drive you?"

I told him that we were riding in back of my cousin's
pick-up because they lived past us. He said, "Oh, well, that's
okay then. I bet it's fun. Not too cold tonight." He looked at
me for awhile then said, "I heard you were a fine student,
Tommy. What are your plans?"

I looked at him and said, "I don't know what you mean. I
guess I do okay in school. I like it. There are lots of things I
want to know. I read a lot. Do you have to have plans for
going to school?"

He laughed and answered, "No, I guess you don't. Love for learning is never planned. Why don't you join the Youth Club on the reserve. Would your Dad let you if you had a ride home?" I said, "I don't know, I'll ask."

I asked and Dad talked with Pra-cwa about it. They told me it was okay because I would be helping doing things the way they talked over with the Chief.

It was fun at those Youth Club meetings because we talked about all the news and stuff on the radio. We called these "Current Affairs Discussions." We also had dinners and recreation things for the members. The priest was always there. We even organized a talent show with his help. We did many things like that.

That was the year John Kennedy got killed, and all them black people were burning cities all over the United States. I guess black people had it almost worse than Indians. I read that they couldn't even pee in a white man's toilet. I had sure hoped they won whatever they were fighting for. I thought it must have been more than peeing in white toilets, but that sounded close to what it was all about.

Lots of stuff was on the radio about nuclear war and bomb tests. Some people said that radiation just melted people's flesh. I read that too. We talked about it in "Current Affairs" and tried to make sense out of it. My Dad and other people talked a lot about it all the time, especially about the Negro Civil Rights fight. Uncle Billy said, "Someday, all the dark races will fight together against the white people for all what they do. That is a story from long time ago." I wondered if that would happen. I wondered if Indian people would be joining together. I sure hoped not. It sounded ugly. I had seen pictures of dead Negroes.

Sometimes though, I knew what it felt like to want to do something, when white kids sneered at me. Sometimes, I used to lie awake at night, wishing in the morning I would wake up and all the white people would have vanished so nobody would have to do anything about it. I turned fourteen that year.

CHAPTER TWO

Trying It On

"Come on, Tommy!" Jimmy hollered at me. "We're going for a ride up the creek in Johnny's car." We were all down at the old school talking at the youth group meeting when Johnny got there. Johnny John was from another reserve. He was a little older than us and he had quit school to pick apples in Oroville, Washington.

We stopped by and picked up some of the girls. I had hoped Candy was going to be there. She was really pretty. She didn't hardly notice me but I liked just watching her. When she laughed or walked her bumps jiggled under her blouse. I liked that. Sometimes I hated Jimmy when he teased Candy. He didn't care what he did. Once he chased her around and knocked her down and put some angle worms in her blouse. Boy, she screamed but she didn't seem mad. Jimmy was like that, but nobody could be mad at him long.

We went with Johnny in his new car roaring up the res with the radio turned on real loud. Johnny was seeing a girl named Deena. She was okay. We stopped at a place up the res called Elderberry Road. Everybody sat there in the dark smoking and talking and kissing around. It was real cold and

still outside, but there was no snow, even though it was
January. Candy was squeezed between me and Jimmy.

Pretty soon Johnny said, "Hey, you guys know what?
There's Sasquatch around here. I heard last week that Wall-
eye and some of the older men were up here having a few
beers and they seen one." Jimmy laughed, "Shit they were
probably having the snakes." "No," Johnny said, "It walked
out right over there in broad daylight."

I felt kind of funny because my Dad and them told me that
there really were such things. He told me that they had seen
them. But I knew these guys would only laugh like some of
the white kids did about anything they thought was "superstition," while at the same time, things like angels and the devil
weren't superstitious to them.

While I was thinking all this, one of the guys said, "I know
a better place further up where my Dad says they come all the
time. Let's go find out." "Okay," said Johnny, "I don't really
think there are such things, but I hear some of the old people
say there are."

We drove to the other place where there was a big pointed
rock. We shut the car lights off, lit cigarettes and sat real quiet
for awhile. It was pretty dark because of the big trees all
around us and the steep high side of the mountain next to us.

After awhile everybody started talking again and we had
almost forgotten why we were there, when all of a sudden,
Jimmy said, "Shut up! Listen!" Everybody stopped real quick.
We all heard a shrill, deep-throated whistle, almost human-
like, way up the mountain. Everybody said at the same time,
"Did you hear that? Was that a bird or what? Maybe it's
somebody." Just a minute after that, it whistled again; this
time definitely closer down the mountain. I got this real funny
feeling like everything slowed down, even people's voices. I
couldn't seem to move but I heard everybody yelling at
Johnny, "Let's get the hell out of here! Dammit, Johnny!"

Johnny must have been scared shitless because he started the
car with such a helluva roar that we just jumped ahead and

stalled. While he started it up the thing whistled again, this time only a couple of hundred feet away. It seemed like I heard it echo up and down my back and inside my head for a long time. Finally, Johnny got started and he put the lights on and peeled out of there real fast. We drove down to the village in a great big hurry, everybody breathing real loud.

We never talked about that to anybody. I never even told my Dad and them because they would have lectured me about parking around in places we shouldn't. Most of us just wanted to forget it. It didn't make sense to most of us, I guess, because we knew it didn't fit in with what you learn in science books about animals and things that exist. So we didn't talk about it, even amongst ourselves.

Later on that year, about the time we heard about the black leader named Malcolm X getting shot in New York, the priest had a big meeting with the Youth Club. Him and this older lady, who was on the council, asked us how things were at school. They asked us about discrimination and stuff. They said they were going to make a speech in town. They told us that some group in Ottawa did a study on Indian criminals to find out why they ended up in the slammer. They also talked about the civil rights marches in the States. They said that it wasn't right for whites to discriminate and that they mostly did it because they didn't know anything about other people.

We told them about how a lot of teachers and kids thought we lived in teepees and wore feathers on the reserve. We told them about Monty getting kicked out for fighting with Humphrey even though Humphrey started it by calling us "Injuns" and "full of lice" and stuff. We told them about all that but there were some things that we were too ashamed to even tell. Like all of the white girls laughing at Tony when he asked one of them to dance at the sock-hop. He quit school after that. Also how none of the Indian girls ever got asked to dance at the sock-hops because us guys wouldn't dance with them because the white guys didn't. Another thing we never told them is how we always felt, like we just weren't good enough to mix with the white kids. I mean with things like using wrong words and laughing at the wrong times and we always felt shabby and poor because we couldn't talk about new styles and things with them.

We left out the fact that sometimes out of "good manners" they would talk to us. We knew that it wasn't because they liked us or wanted to be friends with us. We left out why that was worse than not talking to us.

I thought about that new American President's speech, where he talked about a "Great Society." He talked about "progress without strife and change without hatred." At the same time he also said to "reject any among us who seek to reopen old wounds and rekindle hatreds." I wondered if everybody realized what he was talking about, and how white people, even here in Canada, went by that. I mean about rejecting people and stuff. I knew he talked about the blacks or any people that upset the fake idea about a "Great Society." I thought about all the history books and stuff at school and in movies. How it was all like that, a fake, while really the white people wished we would all either be just like them or stay out of sight.

I thought to myself that it was probably good for white people to hear about them things even if they didn't like to. The priest and the old lady were doing something right by making speeches like that.

I felt good that somebody understood, so I spent some time talking to the priest after that. He said, "How come you don't come to church, Tommy?" I sat there for a long time wishing I could say, "Sure I will", just because I liked him. Finally I said, "I don't because I ain't a Catholic. Dad, Mom and my grandparents all don't either. Not because they are bad or anything. They pray a lot, all the time, in Indian way. They say we got to pray all the time no matter what we're doing. They say the whole world is our church and we go to church all the time." I looked at the priest for a long time; he never answered. Finally he asked, "Do you believe that?" I said,

"Yeah, I do. I feel good when I pray Indian." I didn't tell him about praying in the sweat house or at the winter dance because I knew he might think it was wrong.

He said, "Tommy, don't ever change your way. You know, you are my good friend and you can visit me anytime at my home, if you need to talk or ask questions about school or about anything. Now, about church, some people really do need it because they don't see things the way you do. They need to feel good and clean sometimes and they feel they can only do that in a place like the church."

I knew what he meant but I wondered why all our people didn't think the same way as my Dad and them. Of course, I thought that a lot of them went to church, too, because of the priest. Mostly because they liked him.

Ever since the new priest came, more and more people seemed to go to church and other stuff they wouldn't do before. Like all the new clubs and organizations for adults, women, teens and kids. Seemed like everybody had a club they could belong to. The new priest had a certain way about him that everybody liked. He never talked hell-fire and stuff like the other priests. He didn't wear his black clothes, only when he was having church. He also played ball, sang and played guitar, drank beer, told jokes and talked serious politics with the men. Sometimes some of the Elders commented on these things saying, "He sure don't look like a priest." I knew what they meant. The only thing was, nobody liked to criticize him because they liked him too much. Besides, if he said things were alright then they must be alright, because he was a priest, wasn't he?

I did a lot of thinking about them things that whole year, but I couldn't seem to straighten things out in my head too good. At school things got worse and worse. Most of my friends were quitting school, one by one, as they turned fifteen. I liked school but I didn't like the classrooms and stuff. Mostly I went to the library at noon or walked downtown all the way to the lake and back. I felt stiff and cramped sitting in a desk too long. I was too used to running and hard work, that's why.

The schools stank something awful, too. I hated the smells of some of the other kids too. They used all kinds of strong smelling junk. I sometimes felt dizzy by lunch time. I wished sometimes I were outside with the horses or cows. They sure smelled better. I would sometimes think of walking high up near Flint Mountain where the fir and pine smells mixed with the sage; soft wind darting and dancing through the yellow grass and far away the "heap" "heap" "heap" sound of the blue grouse. Then the teacher would yell at me, "Thomas Kelasket! Quit day dreaming and get to work. You have to work hard to keep up. You have no time to waste."

It wasn't true that I had to work hard to keep up. I mostly took a few minutes for any work assigned. I spent most of my time reading and doing stuff I was really interested in. Even tests I didn't have to study and study for. Seemed to me if you read something once or are told it once, that's all you need to know it. Anyway, that's how we were taught at home. Pops or Uncle had always said, "Watch close now. We show you only once. After that you know." If we forgot it, then we had to find out on our own or never learn. I didn't like not learning so after I'm told once, I know about a thing.

It's like old Grandpa Cashmire said, "You got a little box with a cover. You open it just right so only what you want goes in and not a lot of other junk. When you want to take that thing out again you open the box, just so, and there it is, all by itself, same as when you put it in. That's how you keep things."

Sometimes, I think the teachers really got mad at me because I always knew all the answers. Sometimes I knew it was because they didn't like an Indian to do better than some of their favourite white kids. Most of the time, when I got into a new class the teacher would automatically think I was dumb. I knew that by their remarks. Like one teacher, who explained what she wanted in slow Hollywood talk. She said, "You fix'um little story, Tommy, about how you live." To the other kids she had asked, "Please prepare a short biographical sketch of yourself." Man, that time everybody in the class looked sick. You can guess how I felt. After writing my first test, or answering questions okay, I had to work to keep good marks because some teachers liked to find stuff wrong. Mostly my wrong stuff was about things I couldn't know because I lived on the reserve. Sometimes I put half wrong answers just to keep everybody happy.

I used to read the Reader's Digest a lot so I could learn about town stuff and town people. I answered a lot of questions just from that. There were one or two teachers though that were really good. They made you feel good to learn. Those teachers didn't care if you were Indian. They encouraged you and helped you. Mostly they understood you didn't want pity, just a fair chance. Without them I couldn't have stayed in school. Them teachers made you understand that whites are human too.

At home, things were pretty much the same. I went out in the mountains quite a bit with Uncle Joe. He sure was fun to be with. He told me some pretty good stories about old timers. I thought he was probably the smartest man in the whole world. He taught me what he called "Indian medicine ways."

Once when an old woman came to him for some Indian medicine he talked to her for a long time. I heard him explain about sickness sometimes happening because of store-bought food. He said that the white people sometimes put things into foods that weren't good for people. He also said that a lot of stuff that's dirtying the air is no good for people. He said, "You got to quit eating them kinda foods. You eat berries and roots with wild meat. It don't have stuff in it to poison you. You got to sing more too and go out where the air is clean to get food. You'll be happy and you'll get lots of moving around. When you're happy your body doesn't get sick. Good clean food, and working to get it, will get you well. I'll make a medicine that will clean out them poisons but I can't help you if you don't listen to my advice."

What he said sure sounded like some of the "new ideas" some teachers talked about in science and guidance and health classes about psychology, nutrition and pollutants and daily exercise. It made me wonder just who exactly knew what was what.

One time, while we were going to an art class at the old school house, we were visited by a lot of men and women from other reserves. A white lady artist was working with us at the old school; actually she was there as a sort of materials provider and encourager and she got along with us real good. The people who visited us were all in town for a leadership meeting organized by the new priest. These men and women came in and looked at everything and talked with all of us. They spoke to us about school, about "progress" and lots of other things. Also they talked about stuff like "Red Power." We didn't know anything about that stuff. We had heard about "Black Power" because it was on the radio a lot. "Black Power" was about people who had kind of organized to fight against discrimination.

We had heard from Johnny John that some young Indians from Vancouver had talked about forming an organization like that for Indians. I guess that's what they meant by "Red Power." The men and women must have talked about it during the meeting which the new priest had helped set up. We told them that our Youth Club was really not for that. We told them that it was really organized because there was nothing much for us to do together on the res. The arts nights were for that too. We would do art stuff and be together and tease and joke with the girls and each other.

It seemed funny that these men and women from all the reserves were together talking about such things, including us. An "Indian Affairs Committee" had been put together for that, with the help of the priest. Only younger men and women were on that committee, not any of the old people. I wondered why. It seemed to me the old people always had the best advice about a lot of things but people said that wasn't so anymore.

One time me and Tony and Jimmy talked about it. Tony said, "Did you notice how all young Chiefs are getting elected in all the reserves? Well, maybe now things will change. What we need are young Chiefs and Councils to try out new stuff. Like in Inkameep, now, they're going to grow grapes to sell. Lots of people will be able to work and the Band will get richer." "Yeah," said Jimmy, "I heard that in another reserve they are thinking about turning the reserve into a city-like, you know, part of it anyway." "What do you mean? Are you talking about the houses they want to build and lease out to white people?" I asked. "Yeah," Jimmy said, "My Dad told me that they are gonna do something like that here, too. We are going to build something for all kinds of animals and all of the Indians can work there and those that don't can grow hay and grain and corn and stuff to sell there for the animals to eat."

It didn't sound like a bad idea to me. I thought to myself that jobs were what people needed. Jobs would help because I knew a lot of people lived on welfare and a lot of people drank a lot more, too, since they opened up the beer parlours and liquor stores to Indians. There didn't seem to be anything to work on and stay home for because most people weren't farming or ranching anymore. People mostly picked apples. A few worked in the small sawmill on the reserve run by a white company.

Old Pra-cwa and some old men talked about it with Dad and my uncle in angry voices whenever they got together. The schooling the Indians got away from home was blamed for most of it. It was said that none of the young people wanted to work their land anymore to raise cattle and crops because they didn't know how, being away at school all the time. Also many people leased their land to white ranchers so they could get money once a year. Drinking was blamed for a lot of people not wanting to work their own land.

My Dad talked to Pra-cwa, his voice quiet but angry sounding. He said, "First it was the schooling, then it was the welfare and Band housing, then it was the beer parlours and land leasing and now it's development. Pretty soon, Indians don't have to do nothing but get money and spend it drinking. They got nothing to get up for in the morning, nothing to occupy the hours in the day. It's too easy. It's no good. Lots of our people are going to die. Already lots are dead from drinking. Good young people, that might have had big families. Seems like the more Indians try new things, the worse things get for them."

Old Pra-cwa nodded his head slowly, his heavy eyebrows jiggling. He said, "Yes, that is how I think and a few others of us, but you know our people are two now. There is us and there is them that want to try all kinds of new stuff and be more like white people. They don't even think like us anymore. What can be done? I just don't know. I don't like to feel sad and worried and ashamed of my people. I like to feel proud of them. I like to see them like long time ago; working and happy, strong and healthy, not selfish, lazy and weak." He sighed heavily, "I know they get mad at me and close their ears, because what I say hurts. They answer back in anger that if it wasn't for us stupid old people giving up in the first place and allowing many things to be done to us, things wouldn't be bad. They don't understand, we kept arguing against new stuff and we kept losing because more people wanted to go to schools, more people wanted to forget our ways, more people wanted to take welfare and Band houses and open beer parlours and all them other things. It was like that from way back and it's how it is now. It's how it will be for a long time. Our people are two now, that's why we have bad feelings at them Band meetings."

At the old school, during Youth Club, I had heard a lot of talk about it and other things. Mostly about the "old fashioned people" or "hill-billies" and how they were just against everything no matter what.

I listened one night to a young man who had been away living in Vancouver for most of his schooling. This guy looked so neat, almost like a white man, with his grey slacks that had sharp iron creases and a pink button-down shirt and blue polkadot tie. His hair was cut in what we called white wall style. We all had our hair in long duck-tails and mostly wore blue jeans and sweatshirts. His shoes were pretty crazy. They were shiny, like glass almost, and pointed so much they kind of curled on the ends.

He spoke to us about how "we were living in the twentieth century," and how "we have a lot of catching up to do." He mentioned that young Indian people who were educated were now ready "to shape the future." He spoke about many things happening across Canada and United States. He said, "We must take our equal place in society. We no longer need to sit back and be forgotten, second class people stuck on reservations, living in the dark ages." He said, "We must learn to use new ideas and open up our lands to development, because lack of money is at the bottom of all of our social problems." He talked about making changes to the Indian Act which "would reflect changing conditions on reservations." He spoke about how reserves would change to be part of municipalities and how that would help "open up opportunities for Indian lands." He also spoke about how the liquor law was being changed to allow liquor to be served on the reserve.

All the while he talked, I had this terrible urge to laugh. He kinda looked ridiculous, like a parrot does when it mimics a person. At the same time as I listened to him talk, I felt really scared at some of the things he said, although he made it sound right. I knew that a lot of young people there agreed with him. I knew a lot of them thought he looked pretty sharp too. Some things he said, though, made me feel really bad. I could see what old Pra-cwa talked to us about wasn't being thought about. I really felt confused. I agreed with the young man but I also agreed with Pra-cwa.

I told that to Jimmy, outside, after the talk. I said, "You know, Jimmy, I don't know who is right anymore. I get real mad when white people make fun of us, but, at the same time I feel ashamed when I go to town with Dad and Ma and they

get stared at. I know they ain't dumb and dirty. They're smart
and kind and treat everybody good, even the ones that treat
them ugly. In school it's like that, too. The only time you are
talked to is if you dress and talk like whites and act real smart
and rich like that guy at the meeting. I found that out. Do you
think that guy is right? Would things be better if we looked
and acted rich and tried to change our reserve to be like town?
How come we have to do that? My Pops and them live good.
They're happy. None of them cares about clothes and fancy
stuff. Why is everybody else all of a sudden saying things are
no good, that we are not happy? Seems to me the ones that
ain't happy is the people who try too hard to get stuff like
new clothes and cars and want to be in town all the time.
They drink lots, too. What do you think, Jimmy?" I guess I
really wanted him to say that my Pops and people like them
were right to be the way they were and everybody else wrong.

He looked at me funny then he put his head down. "Shit, I
don't know." He said, "All I know is, I like to feel good. I feel
good when white friends of mine talk and joke with me as if I
were like them. They only do that if I wear smart pants and
shoes and have money to play pool with. I don't like them to
think I'm like the rest of the Indians. I wish our people were
like them. They have big clean houses and lots of stuff to eat.
Not macaroni like us. Their dads make lots of money and they
buy anything they want. They go to lots of places, like
Vancouver, and see lots of neat things. Shit, my Dad works
but he gets drunk and spends all his money. Even his new car,
he smashed the door and the front up so now it looks ugly.
And my Mom, she gets drunk now, too, and the house is never
clean, it stinks. Her and my Dad fight and argue and there's
beer bottles all over and all we eat is bologna and macaroni.
You know I never did get a new bike, so I went and stole one.
I hate being an Indian. I hate Indian ways." Then he looked at
me kinda defensively and said, "I know how you guys live up
there. That's okay, because your folks don't drink and they
work and all the kids in your family do stuff but down here, it

ain't like that. Somethings got to be done down here. Seems to me, the only thing that can be done is what that young guy talked about. That's what I think."

I sat there smoking a cigarette and thought about what Jimmy told me. I really felt let down, like he slapped me or something even though I had to kinda agree with him. It left me with a bitter feeling inside.

"Yeah, I guess so." I said. "But why don't they want to live like us up the hill?"

"Because it's too damn Indian, that's why." he said. Then, looking ashamed, Jimmy said, "Hell, let's go get old Donald to get us some beer. I feel shitty. I don't even want to think about it anymore."

We got Donald to get us some beer. Donald was a strange guy. Some people said he was the smartest guy on the res. He always had some scheme or another going. I know of one time that he outsmarted some businessman from the States with a scheme. That time he sold my Dad's horses. Dad had these two really good-looking matched pintos he had raised. Well, Donald had brought some guy in a Cadillac to "look at them." At least that's what he told Dad in Indian. A few days later the guy showed up in a truck ready to haul them away. He had given Donald a big down payment and had brought the rest of the cash that day. It took Dad a while to explain that the horses were his, not Donald's and he knew nothing about a deal with Donald for them. Boy, that was one mad man. He cussed at Dad something awful. Dad said, "It wasn't my doing. You should have checked on what you buy. Somebody could sell you a bridge next."

Nobody saw Donald for a good three months after that. Donald didn't have much morals. He didn't mind buying beer and stuff for us young guys, if we gave him a couple.

Jimmy seemed to be pretty sure of himself. He told Donald to get us some beer and we would meet him at the old barn behind Jimmy's uncle's old place. Jimmy told him, "If you take off with our money, I'm gonna tell Maggie what you been doing. You come back with it and we will give you some, okay?" "Okay," Donald said, "How come you don't trust me? You know I wouldn't cheat. Maggie's my only aunt. She told me never to do bad stuff. I'll be back."

It was the first time I drank beer. It tasted awful but I wanted to see what getting drunk was like. Every beer I drank I thought, "Hell with everything! I don't care!" Pretty soon, I started feeling really light and bouncy and everything seemed funny and all right. We laughed and told each other stuff about girls and sang, "It's Been A Hard Day's Night" real loud. That was a Beatles song and we thought it meant a whole lot.

Jimmy laid back against the weathered logs of the barn and shivered a little. He turned to me, his eyes burning and said, "You know what I'm going to do? I'm gonna go to school and be different. I'm gonna move to town when I finish and get a real good job and get everything I want and be just like the people on T.V. Maybe guys like that one at the meeting can shape everybody up here. Hell, the ladies are starting to dress more like white women ever since the priest came. They even are having teas and stuff like them. Maybe they will learn and the dads will work steady and not drink and stuff."

I just drank some more and sang "It's Been A Hard Day's Night, and I've been working like a da-awg." Finally, I must have gone to sleep or something because I woke up at Jimmy's the next day. I felt awful. My stomach and head were weak and my tongue was furry and ugly tasting.

I went home that afternoon, but I was kinda scared of what Pops would say. Sure enough Pops must have smelled me because he said, "You been drinking. That's why you didn't come home. How do you feel?" I felt real bad because he had a real hurt look in his eyes, and even though he was talking quiet I knew he was mad. I said, "Yeah, I tried it. I feel real sick now, but when I was drinking, I didn't. I was mad and it made me feel happy. I didn't do anything."

Dad sat there and said, "You're too big to whip. But I'm

going to talk straight to you. You listen real hard. I don't know why you were mad, but I can guess. There are lots of us feeling mad. I feel like saying, "Hell with it!" sometimes, and joining all the rest of them down there. Sometimes, I used to, when you guys were small. But everytime I drank, I would have to face the next day, when I ran out of money, or I woke up in jail. Then I felt real awful because of you kids. You kids needed what little money I could get my hands on, and I would spend it in one night. The bad thing about it is, pretty soon you get to want it all the time to make you feel good. You can't feel good about anything, unless you got that drink in you. Then you're good for nothing. All you'll work for is that booze, and you'll feel empty inside all the time. Now you tried it. I guess everybody has to, but that don't mean you have to carry it on."

I felt pretty bad after that, but I saw what my Dad meant. I saw it in Jimmy's parents and lots of people like that. But I saw how they felt, too. I went to bed that night and thought about Jimmy stealing a bike and probably other things, too. I thought about him bragging about his new radio and phonograph player to some white kids. I thought about the older ladies getting all dressed up in lady suits and white high heels and gloves, and getting a taxi to town to have tea with white ladies, and how at home their kids got clothes from the Salvation Army and macaroni to eat. I thought about how some didn't do that either, just drank and let things go. I felt like I wanted to cry or holler or beat up somebody. I couldn't figure out what was wrong, and if there was anything anybody could do.

Along towards the end of that year, the development was voted on and it was passed. I guess I really hoped that jobs and things would really happen when it was passed, even though my Dad and them voted "no" on it. For awhile some guys did work there, building fences, but nobody got full time jobs there.

Pra-cwa and Uncle Billy and old Harry and lots of others

had gathered to talk about it. They agreed that it was no use arguing with our people about them kind of things. It just split us up too bad.

Old Pra-cwa said, "From now on, we will let them do what they want without too big of a fight. All we can do is tell them what we think and hope they listen. If it comes to the time when it means our own lands and losing all our rights then we will have to stand up and talk for whoever thinks like us, but for now we will let it go and hope they will somehow make better decisions. Maybe they need a new way all their own to be able to live good again. Right now, they blame us for holding things back, and we can't seem to help them in any way. We all know we will never again be as one. They lost their language, their ways and are no longer interested in farm or ranch work. They have nothing to depend on except a hope that things will be better if they do things the white way."

He looked so sad and defeated when he talked. I felt that he was in pain as he went on to say, "I feel sad in saying these things, but they are true. Like this vote they want to have to let liquor be served at our community hall. Maybe I can't understand right but I wonder how that will make things better for us. The priest and the Council wants it. They said it would make Indians more equal, and that Indians would learn how to use it right if they had social drinking and dancing at the hall. They even said some of that in the newspaper. Seems to me, they ought to be against that. I guess our thinking is so different, we can't even understand one another anymore. Everything is changing too fast, even priests."

The only thing exciting that happened that summer was that a big feast and celebration was put on at the reserve park. We painted down there on the roller rink sides. The roller rink was brand new. Somebody from Indian Affairs had a bright idea, I guess. According to the Council, the Agent decided that Indian kids needed recreation to help them live better. So they spent lots of money levelling some land and blacktopping it, then put sides on it. The roller rink was really nice, everybody on the reserve said so. Only thing wrong was nobody had roller skates or even knew how to roller skate. We decided to put some paintings on the sides to dress it up and make it useful to look at anyway. I heard almost every reserve got one just like ours, but nobody's was going to be painted up like ours.

I did a lot of art work and things, just to get my mind off hard feelings that bothered me about all that kind of stuff. Me and Jimmy both liked to paint. We used to go to the white woman artist's place all the time to paint.

Later this guy named Dave, from some university, came to study our ways. He used to come to the reserve a lot. We found him to be really different; weird, kind of. He didn't seem to mind how we lived and he drank beer and talked to us a lot. He told us a lot of things going on all over the country. He also showed us some magazines that had a lot of girlie pictures. We used to read them and look at the pictures. One story I remember was about a professor, named Timothy Leary. He talked about a new drug that made people have visions and things.

I knew that some kids from school in town were smoking a drug called marijuana. They said it was pretty neat stuff. I asked this guy Dave about it. He said, "Yeah, I use marijuana. Lots of university people do. I won't give you guys any though. I need to keep my act clean here. It's against the law. Besides it don't do much that's different than alcohol, so forget it."

Me and Jimmy talked about it. Jimmy said, "Why don't we try some? Hell, if Dave smokes it, it can't be bad, Dave is real smart. Besides, it ain't like them other drugs our Dads tell us about, you know, the ones where they use a needle and then you can't go without it."

I thought about it. I knew Jimmy would try it, so would others, but it seemed to me that the other drug called LSD was much more exciting. Mostly because of the visions people were said to have. I was real interested in that because some of the old people claimed to have visions without drugs. We had been hearing a lot too about the flower-power people in San Francisco. Drugs seemed to be at the center of their power more than the peace and love which they talked about, from what I read.

I read a lot, whenever I could buy new magazines and stuff. I kept myself up on that stuff. I borrowed a lot of books from Dave, too. I thought a lot about crazy stuff that I sometimes read about. Things like self-hypnosis and occult were really interesting to me.

One of the things that really took my interest was a book about a girl who remembered a past life when she was hypnotized. I did a lot of reading about that. I wondered just what this world was all about. I sometimes thought about the old people talking about spirits and the spiritual world, and wondered what they meant. I knew they really believed in something that had to do with stuff other people called superstition. I wanted to know who was right. I needed to know. That's why I read a lot of crazy stuff, and maybe later why I did start trying the drugs too.

We tried marijuana on the reserve. The first time we did was crazy. Jimmy got some from somebody. He wouldn't tell me who, and acted like it was a really big secret. It was a pretty big crime to be caught with it at that time. One afternoon he whispered to me in the hall at school, "Wanna meet Mary Jane?" "Sure," I said, wondering who she was.

"Meet me at my uncle's old barn tonight after school, okay?" he whispered and looked over his shoulder. I walked on down the hall wondering what the hell was with him.

When I got to the old barn that night he motioned me inside. "What's going on, Jimmy? What kinda girl you got in there anyway?" I said kind of hesitating. He just shook his head and said, "Come on, man." He pulled out a little plastic package as soon as we got in there and said, "Here she is. Mary Jane. Marijuana. You ready?" He started to roll up a long, skinny looking cigarette out of it, then he lit it up and took a long puff and held his breath, handing it to me. I took a drag, like on a cigarette and handed it back. "No, man, you got to hold it in. Jeez, don't be so square all my life," he wheezed as his breath came out. "Okay. You sure this'll work?" I asked and took a drag. After a few more long drags like that it was gone and he rolled another. "You feel anything yet, Tom?" he asked, "Maybe we have to smoke this whole bag before it works good." "Yeah, seems like nothing is happening." So we smoked the whole bag, one joint after another, in about ten minutes.

We got done, and somehow it seemed like we had been sitting there a long time. I said, "Its been too long now to be working, I guess I'll just head home. God, I'm hungry though." "Yeah, me too," he answered, "How long we been here anyway? Hey, how come you look so funny, Tom?" And he started laughing and laughing, and that got me started, even though I wasn't sure what was funny. I laughed so hard that I fell on the floor holding my stomach, and I got scared inside thinking what if I die laughing, and somehow, that was funnier than anything. Somehow, after a long time we finally ended up at his house and ate a whole loaf of bread, because that's all he had to eat there, but it was the best tasting bread I ever ate.

Later on, me and Jimmy used to walk into town and go to this place called a coffee house where we could get more stuff to smoke. Lots of kids played guitar, toked and sang folk songs that made you mad about everything; like wars, bombs and working. We toked whenever we could afford it. Everybody seemed to accept us pretty equally, when we were high. But I guess nobody really cared much about anything either. It was neat being there and listening to young people talk and talk about changing the world, and everybody feeling mellow, saying we needed to make love not war. We did that a lot, too. I was sixteen then, in Grade Eleven.

Somehow after that, I let everything slip away that I used to like. None of it seemed important or good anymore. School was definitely the last place I wanted to be, after a long night getting high and talking about protesting against the establishment. After a few hassles with some teachers who used to give me looks that made me proud, I quit. At home, too, Dad walked around looking grim and I wouldn't meet his eyes much.

He only talked to me once, but I knew, without his repeating, exactly what he was saying with his looks. He said to me, "Look at you, Tommy. You're a smart boy. What's the matter with you? You could do all that school stuff easy, but you quit now. You know how to work on the ranch, too, but you don't anymore. You don't have anything to make you sad or mad. What's happening with you? Look at the morning and the birds singing. Look at the green grass and the mountains. Just clean and waiting to make you feel so light and happy inside that you could fly. Everything is good. We are free, Tommy."

"Maybe that schooling wasn't good for you. Maybe you're spending too much time down in the village. Maybe you want more and more to be like some of them boys down there. Maybe you think they are happier than you or that they are luckier than you. Well, that ain't true. They are pitiful because they have nobody to teach them good things. Their moms and dads are all pitiful. They got broken spirits from going to residential school. Lots of them died when they came home, from drinking and T.B. sickness. The ones that made it okay, made it by learning how to please the priests and nuns and rejecting everything Indian. They were praised for that. That's how they are. They put the white man way up high above Indians and listen to them, and try to please them. We pity them. You quit school. Now you have to do your share of work here at home. You understand?"

To me that sounded a lot like he had meant, either I could work if I was not in school, or could go out and support myself.

I resented that but I was ashamed, too, so I tried for awhile to help out, but I didn't get a lot of work done at home. It seemed like they couldn't understand that I had to go to them places where there was talk about doing something. Just working and living didn't seem to accomplish anything. I wasn't sure what I wanted to accomplish or what was being done at these talks but I went again and again, night after night. Anyway, I couldn't really feel good, unless I had a toke or two a day.

Talks happened on the reserve, too. Especially after an action committee was formed. Chiefs from other reserves were meeting with our Chiefs of the Okanagan, to talk about changing the Indian Act and things like that. I never went to them meetings much.

The times I went to interpret for Pra-cwa, people there seemed to try to impress each other about how well they could talk English, and how much they could look important with business suits and all. They didn't seem to worry too much about what was really wrong on the reserves, but they passed a lot of fancy worded resolutions. I never could understand what good a resolution was. Other than words on paper, it didn't seem to do much. The old people were mostly ignored at these meetings. After awhile they stopped going and so did I. I had other reasons though.

Me and Jimmy started drinking a lot when we didn't have weed. It just seemed natural to take a beer that was offered instead. So, between long nights, beer parties and hangovers, I didn't exactly do any work for Dad anymore. We went to other places where Indians were, like Omak, Spokane, Vancouver and Seattle. We mostly went with Johnny John because he seemed to have friends all over; Indians that were sort of doing the same thing hippies were. Toking and partying a lot and having youth meetings where they talked about everything.

One of the things talked about was some report that came out about the death rate of Indians being on the rise. It seemed that the cause of its rise was attributed to a lot more young

Indian men and women dying from suicides, and deaths that were related to drinking and drugs.

We went to Vancouver quite a few times to listen to some young Indian people having meetings. We even went to a demonstration they had. It was the first demonstration that I was ever involved in. I had watched a few by black people in the States. In those everybody seemed to be so smart. Like they represented something. At that Indian demonstration where young people talked about Red Power, lots of people acted the same. Everybody looked important, and I guess I felt that way, too. It's a strange feeling to be walking down a street carrying a sign. You're just a face in a bigger body that somehow is stronger than any one person in it. Everybody walked along chanting the slogan and it was like one huge voice saying, "We'd rather be 'Red' than dead." I hadn't been sure what that meant but it sure sounded good when everybody said it at once.

Around that same time a play came out about Indians in the city. While we were in Vancouver some of the chicks were pretty excited about seeing it. They got some tickets for a few of us, for free, and we went. I guess I didn't think too much of going to see a play. The only kind I seen were at school and they were silly. This was different. It was a play, sure, but it was like real, too, by what it does show. It talked about what happens to Indians like us. It kind of looked inside us, I guess. At that time it seemed like everybody was interested in us Indians, in one way or another. Few of them were as honest as that play.

I learned quite a bit during the meetings that I went to, but I never talked much. Seemed like everybody was so smart and already knew everything. If anybody asked questions, they were always looked at as if they were retarded or something. I didn't like that because there were a lot of us retards that did care. The know-it-all attitude that some of our people got was a turn-off, though, especially on the Red Power trip, but I picked up a lot of jargon from them. Besides, the parties after were always real good. During them times, there was always booze, weed and girls; "chicks" as everybody called them.

I kind of left home during them times. I came home maybe once a month. Everybody would be glad to see me, but they always looked at me with a big question in their eyes. I couldn't explain anything to them, so I would just turn away and pretend I hadn't seen. I usually took off as soon as I could.

One time, I tried talking with Uncle Joe about it. He had been visiting Mom when I showed up. I must have looked awful, my hair shaggy and dirty, and my clothes all rugged from sleeping anywhere in them. He looked at me long and level and said, "Come on, Tom, I'm going to take a sweat bath. Looks like you need one awful bad. You stink." I sat there for a while. When I looked up at him, it seemed like I didn't even know that man. Like he wasn't real or whatever. What did he know about Indians outside the res anyway. I knew what he talked about wasn't my clothes or my body.

I said, "Uncle, I don't want to sweat. You see, I'm doing a lot of finding out, and sometimes it's not good stuff I'm finding out about. I guess I don't feel the sweat is a place I can go in right now because it don't make too much sense to me anymore. In the cities it's a dead end. I seen it. I can't understand it. It's like that for quite a few people. I got to know what it is."

"Lots of us are like that, Uncle. We don't seem to be able to find any answers or fit in anywhere. We keep moving and looking though. Look down there on the reserve now. With all kinds of fancy clubs for everybody to become more like white people. Clubs for learning how to talk in public and stuff. What's the reason for learning that stuff, I ask you?"

"It's things like that some of us don't actually like. At the same time, we don't seem to be able to live like you guys either. We don't care too much to do some of the stuff that they are trying at the Band Council level. You know, community committees for welfare, education and stuff for doing things the way Department of Indian Affairs wants things. I know our people are trying their best to do better with all those 'Help Our Natives Help Themselves' projects. What it's all about, it seems to me, is that those things really mean 'Help Indians become more middle-class Whites.' But look where that takes Indians. Right to skid row like Rita Joe."

Uncle Joe looked at me long and hard. He said, "Tommy, I don't really know who or what you are talking about and where you picked up them words, like 'middle-class.' It's good to travel and find things out. I did that a lot. Yet you are unhappy. Why? Why do you show up in places stoned or drunk? Then you come up and tell me these fine things like a speech. What is it, Tommy? I want to know because you are right. There are a lot of you like that. What are you scared of the sweat for? I think you got a big confusion inside that you don't know what to do about. Seems to me you make it worse with what you're doing. Quit it, Tommy! Come home. We need smart young people. You're only seventeen. We don't need you dead."

I knew he didn't understand what I had talked about. I wasn't sure I even did, so I didn't say anymore. When he went down to the sweat, I got my gear and left. I felt right down. I could forget what he said, but not the look behind his eyes. I hiked out to Vancouver. Out there in the city it was like another world altogether. Johnny John was there; he was into dealing. I guess he had been for a while, that's how come he had a car and friends all over. He said I could stay with him, but that I had to do my share.

I did my share. I made pick-up and drop-off runs and scared up scores for him. It was exciting to stay in the city for awhile. Everything seemed to move so fast. There were always places to go where lots of Indians hung out. Lots of chicks. After a while though, it was all kind of empty. Everything was surface stuff, even friends that you thought were true. If you didn't have cash or a toke or something to offer, nobody wanted you. I learned that fast and it didn't feel good. Nobody seemed

to care too much about anything. I found out it was the same
with the meetings that I went to. Everybody could talk a real
streak, but when it came down to volunteering to do the
work, only a very small group of dedicated ones did the
work.

I didn't go to meetings very much, anyway, once I got there
and got into the dealing with Johnny John. It was the crowd
that I ran with that wasn't too keen on what the Red Power
people were doing. I drifted away from that scene. Sometimes,
though, when I walked down the streets and looked at the faces
of people scurrying by, I would get a feeling inside of fear.
When I looked at some of the Indians hanging around the
skids, I got a sick feeling because all the faces looked so
empty. Like they were dead people, walking fast to catch up
with something I couldn't see. I would feel like stopping
one of them and asking, "Why do you hang around here?"
Somehow I was sure I was only there temporarily, not like
them. I would flash on that play and think, "I'll never end up
like that."

Things seemed to go fast and I just cruised with the pace for
the next while. One night everything came crashing around
me. I had been in the process of a delivery near a place called
Turkey Tom's. Pretty rough joint. I saw the guy I was to
make the drop-off to, way across the smoke filled room
crowded with Indians from all over the U.S.A. and Canada.
Music pumped heavy and thick, vibrating off the walls and
sweating bodies. The usual girls with thick mascara, tight
jeans and cheap, flashy blouses, their black hair curled and
bleached in front, danced on the slippery floor. The talk was
loud like the growl of a wounded bear; the laughter reached a
pitch that sounded more like a screech.

The guy motioned me toward the john. I walked in there
to wait for him. That was dumb. I no sooner walked in the
door when two guys grabbed me and started jerking at my
pack. One of them had a knife that he was waving around. It
was either take the chance of giving them the stuff and hope

they wouldn't use the knife or try to fight my way out of it. The first choice seemed a bigger risk than the second.

I kicked the asshole that had the knife right in the stomach. By then the other guy had ploughed me on the side of the head and I reeled toward the can. Just by chance I hooked him with my foot and I went down as he fell backwards. That gave me the chance to make a grab for the knife. The guy was just a little quicker than me. He picked it up with a snarl and sliced at me with it. I felt it hit bone in my shoulder. The hot shock that ground upward from my stomach turned everything to a light orange-red.

I can't say for sure what happened then, except that I hurt and I moved fast. The pain was like a big fog wrapped around me. The rest of me seemed to act on its own. I fuzzily remember a few scenes. Me slamming one of the guys, and a scared look on his face as he fell out the door. I remember the knife glittering in my hand and slashing at what seemed like forty people frozen into different poses. What I noticed most was the way all their mouths stretched tight over their teeth. I remember cops and kicking one of them in the balls and then nothing.

I woke up in the hospital with this strange chick beside me. She said, "Hi, how's it going, Slash? My name is Mardi. I'm from the Friendship Center. We need to know your name and reservation enrollment number before these doctors kick you out. Christ, I never seen anybody put ten cops on their backs. You know you're good for some hard time now, but you're cut up pretty bad so you got to stay here for a while. In the meantime, we'll get somebody to try and sort out which charges we can get them to drop and stuff. Where are you from?"

I laid there feeling like somebody had taken the time to pinch every single part of me with a big pair of pliers. My shoulder throbbed and sent slow hot strings like worms inching along my arm. I looked at her and said, "Where am I? What the hell happened? Where is Johnny?"

"Johnny who?" she wanted to know. "What do you think happened? All I know is that you were at the Turkey Joint and someone thought to carve a few lines on your shoulder. I was there. All I saw was the john door busting open and these two guys stumbling out with big gashes in their shirts, and you slashing around and yelling, "I'll slash the nuts off anybody that tries that again!" Shit, man, the way you looked was enough to scare anybody that hangs around that joint. The cops came and they tried to stop you. It took a couple of billies to put you down after a few of them hit the floor. So here you are, Slash. Now, tell me what I need and I'll come back to see you later this evening."

I told her my name and the other things she needed to know and she left. Later on some cops talked with me. Seemed like I was being charged for assault and resisting arrest. I asked them about the other guys who started it, and they said they were also in trouble but that their charges wouldn't be heavy. I never asked them what happened to my pack or its contents. I suppose somebody got lucky and picked it up. Probably the drop-off who motioned me to the john for the set-up.

Mardi did come back. She was extra deluxe. Tough with hard eyes and long black hair that hung below her hips. I could tell she knew her way around. Nobody could take her for a ride. She came back lots of times, until I was well enough to face charges. She sat and talked about stuff going on. She made things sound exciting, like something was about to happen. She told me about the meetings going on among young Indians. A lot of it she called hard talk about how to change things. She asked where I was from, and she told me about some things that were happening up home. She brought me Indian news bulletins and things like that to read.

The hospital was the most boring place in the world to be. The nurses and doctors poked at me and talked to each other like I was deaf and mute. They didn't even seem like people. They must have had to study a long time to become as alien as those were. The smell in there was worse than any Indian bar.

So I had to do something to pass the time. I read a lot.

I read in one of them bulletins that the Government of Canada was proposing a new policy that would phase out Indian reserves in five to ten years. A lot of Indian people were pretty angry about that because they had been led to believe that consultations with them had been held to actually listen to their recommendations and do some good for Indians. The bulletin referred to this policy as the White Paper.

I talked to Mardi about it. I thought of old Pra-cwa and the things he had warned of. I felt lonely and I thought of my people at home. I knew there would be a lot of angry meetings and talk. I imagined the words and the concerned feelings in the air back there. One thing I felt was that maybe this was an issue that might bring the two sides of our people closer together. I hoped that's what would happen, even though I knew there were Indian people like that one big shot working for the government. I read about him in a Vancouver paper. It said he was "gratified by the federal announcement." Both me and Mardi snorted when we read that.

I told Mardi about Pra-cwa, my Dad and uncles and how they thought and lived. She asked, "Well, how come you're here?" I looked at her and said, "Why are you here yourself?".

She told me, "I was just a little kid when we moved to the city from the reservation. My Mom and Dad used to try to live there but things got really hard during the years after the war. My Dad was in the war, see. When he came out, he was changed. He was used to living with less poverty by then. He couldn't make any kind of living on the res. Every which way he turned there was nothing. Like he had property and good hayland, but the water licence was taken by ranchers next to the reserve. The only jobs he could get, that paid half decent, were in the cities or near there. So he went there, but he started drinking a lot. I really don't know why, except when I was a kid I remember him sometimes roaring drunk, talking to my Mom about that war. Once I heard him tell her that he killed people for a reason he didn't even know. I remember him sobbing and saying, "Shit, shit, shit!" over and over again, and us being scared and not knowing why. I remember him singing Indian songs when he was drunk too; beautiful songs, but when he was sober he wouldn't ever do things like that. The years while I grew up were awful. We moved from one place to another. Sometimes we went to school and sometimes we didn't. We never had enough to eat most of the time. I learned early how to hustle because by then my Mom was drinking heavy and near to dying. Her liver was shot and she died when I was thirteen."

"I guess my Dad tried to keep us together after that, but he was lost in a world of his own. I got an old man when I was fourteen and we lasted about three years. Long enough for me to have two kids that welfare got. I guess I'm to blame for that too, but my old man was mean. He drank all the time and beat me a lot. I turned to the streets and picked up a habit. After we broke up I really hit the gutter. In about a year I was nearly dead. The only thing that helped me was I ended up in a rehab center for Indians after going cold turkey or die."

"Well, that's the story of my life, Slash," said Mardi. "Now I work for the Friendship Center on their street program. I visit Indians in hospitals, in jail and in the Rehab Center. I occasionally pick them up off the street and send them home if they have one to go to. I do a lot of organizing too, for meetings that talk about what's really going on in the Indian world. Shoot, it's about time we start to do something about it. We can't just sit back and hope things are going to change. As long as more of our people end up like you and me we got to talk and organize and try to help out our brothers and sisters."

I sure liked Mardi. She cared a whole lot about the right things. She didn't care too much for people who were just interested in building up a good image for themselves. She came almost every free chance she got. She wanted mostly to listen about my home life, about Uncle Joe, and how it used to be on the farm. She said it must have been good to live like that.

I guess we got to feeling pretty strong about one another. I couldn't wait to hear her footsteps coming. I thought about her at night, too. Sweet secret thoughts. I wanted to take her home and show her my hills and teach her our language. I wanted to put my arms around her and hold her and never let anything ever hurt her again.

I was sure there wasn't anybody like her anywhere. God, I hoped then that things would work out. I didn't want to go to prison, I wanted to take her home. I wanted to help her to do the kind of work she was doing. Man, I just wanted her!

She got me a lawyer through the Friendship Center. He talked to me and said that he could maybe get me off with a light or suspended sentence, seeing as how I was not the instigator of the incident.

When I came out of the hospital I was put in Mardi's care. She had to see that I stayed put until a hearing was set. Those few weeks were the best I have ever spent, I guess, even though I was still weak and sick from my cuts, and even though I was facing a possible prison sentence.

I had a lot of chicks from the time I was fifteen upwards, but none made me feel so warm inside just by smiling. She took care of me those weeks. Sweet care. I fell terribly in love with her. I wanted to be near her every possible minute and breathe her soft scent. She smelled fresh like sage and cedar and her skin was even brown and smooth like those hills in the Okanagan.

I made all kinds of plans about going home. I wrote home and told my sister Josie that I was going home for good.

I said I was thinking of getting married, and where did she think would be a good spot to build a little log cabin. I knew she would tell Dad and them about it. I never mentioned about my hearing or my injuries.

One morning really early, we were sitting by the window in the basement apartment she lived in. It was early and there were all kinds of birds chirping outside. Green branches almost covered the whole window. The window was open, and the sunlight and a warm breeze poured through the leaves. The leaves whispered and seemed to tremble, just bursting with green life. A robin came and sat on a branch and just looked at us. Everything seemed to slow down. It seemed for a moment, I was suspended in a shimmering timelessness filled with bursting green life and bird song. I felt an almost roaring in my ears as the robin looked and looked at me with his round shiny eye. I wanted to reach out and enclose the whole thing with my hands. I wanted to keep it so I could open my hand and look at it once in a while. The robin opened its mouth and whistled, then it was gone.

The day I went to court, I guess Mardi did what she could, but the facts remained. I was an Indian, and I had resisted arrest and had defended myself with a deadly weapon, after which I had apparently embarrassed a few cops. Nobody seemed to care that I hadn't instigated the fight, that the knife belonged to the other guys, and that I was the only one who was seriously injured while defending myself.

My lawyer kept saying those things were irrelevant and that I should act as polite as possible to the judge and say, "Yes, Your Honour" as much as I could. He told me to plead guilty to the assault charges, and I tried to tell him that I wanted to plead not guilty to that, because it was self-defence, and only plead guilty to the resisting arrest charge. He said we couldn't do that. I was either guilty or not guilty, but not both, and besides, I would get a better deal if I just pleaded guilty. He had told me to get my hair cut short and wear a white shirt and a tie.

I really felt like a fool with my short hair and those honky clothes. I didn't like Mardi to see me like that, and I couldn't see what that had to do with getting a fair deal in court. It was all for nothing anyway. The judge listened to the charges and asked me if I was guilty. I said, "Guilty, Your Honour," the way the lawyer told me to. The lawyer then talked for a while about how I was a first time offender. I guess the judge was in a hurry, or maybe they all were, because that was it, sentence was passed. I got eighteen months.

I felt like somebody had knocked the wind out of me.
Everything seemed so blank. All I could think of was, "Mardi,
what about her? I can't live without her." I was eighteen that
year.

You could say a lot of things about prison, not many of
them good. One real thing is that you ain't free. You don't
make many decisions for yourself, even ones you usually take
for granted.

The time it really hits you is when you go through them
gates, when they shut behind you and you see all them armed
pigs up on the towers. It was the same with the guys who
were riding the bus in from the lock-up. Most of them you
could tell had been there before, by the way they talked. But
when it came to the gates, it was like they suddenly deflated.
You could see it in their eyes.

In there you had to learn fast. It's like everybody had to
kind of fit in somewhere. It's not a matter of wanting to. It's
that you had to. You were playing their game. You had to
form a new attitude. You had to, or you got swept away.

One thing I noticed was that there sure were a lot of Indians.
I couldn't believe it. Almost like more than half the people
there were Indian. Another thing that really struck me was
that discrimination was kinda like in reverse, as far as the pigs
were concerned. Us Indians were treated somewhat better
than the white prisoners. It was like they didn't expect any
more out of us than being in there, but their own kind, they
really despised when they saw them in there, so they were
treated pretty awful. In general though, everybody was treated
like dogs.

You just had to set your mind to live with it. I did that in a
way and in a way I didn't. You had take whatever was handed
out and protect whatever small freedoms you had. Somehow
little things became really important. I guess I functioned
alright, but, from the first month or so, I wasn't in a very good
state of mind. Inside of me the hurt, anger and shame was like

a pile of maggots gnawing away. Mostly, coming from shame over having to swallow all the shit dished out to humiliate you. I think they must have hired special people who train to do that kind of stuff because it broke you down, piece by piece until you're not really sure what's left is human. It made my days hard and the nights long.

Sometimes I felt like I had cellophane stretched tight over me, and all it would take is just one wrong little move, and the cellophane would split and the maggots would come spilling out all over the floor and on everybody around me.

Some of them pigs liked to call you dirty racist stuff and did stuff to make you mad. One of them did that to me first-off when I got there. It was during a line-up to go out in the yard. We had to pass through this screen gate, one at a time. This pig stood right beside it and roll called as we went through. When I came up, he stuck his foot out and would have tripped me but I was still strong enough to twist and catch my balance before his foot hooked me. His knee came up and caught me in the balls as he said, "Don't ever try and screw with me, Geronimo, or you'll understand what scalping means."

I sagged on the floor on my knees and swallowed vomit, and if I wasn't so weak, I guess I would have tried to fight, no matter what the consequences. He kicked me and said, "Get the hell up. It ain't Sunday and I ain't God," and he laughed and pushed me through the gate. Things like that filled you with such a shame because the helpless rage that's part of it can't come out, and the part of you that's a man needed it to come out.

It was especially bad after Mardi would visit. I didn't think I was going to make it because I was filling long night hours with pictures in my head about how I would look if I hung myself. I imagined my eyes bulging and my tongue all black and hanging out, like when we were butchering a cow and hung it up. I spent hours and hours trying to figure out how to do it without that happening. I had a lot of time to think when I couldn't sleep because maggots were trying to eat their way out of my belly.

I tried not to think of them things. I tried not to think at all
but too many things happen in that place and you couldn't
help it. I don't mean things just to you but to other prisoners
too. You noticed them things all right. Especially the gang
activities and the guys living up to the big criminal image.
You noticed stuff like the dope dealing and trade-offs that are
made in there for all kinds of stuff. You saw young, pretty
boys abused and used in ways that you don't even imagine
until you saw it. And they had to drift with it; they had no
choice. Some of them used it to their advantage too. Somehow
that was worse than anything else.

I had to fit into all that somehow. I couldn't separate myself
from it. It's them things and what happens to you that makes
you sick inside. You were forced to take a position and make
it work for you, so you can survive. That's where I learned
the most about people. You had to be able to read everybody.
You had to know their attitude, then you knew how to react
to them. You didn't make mistakes, because the pigs
worked with that system too. There was nobody to run to for
protection if you messed up. But it made you compromise too
many things that you were brought up to respect. It's what
made you hard inside. You couldn't care or else you found
maggots crawling all over inside and you felt like maybe the
maggots had more right than you to live.

For that reason, it was hard to see Mardi when she came.
When she did, I listened to her talk and it seemed like she
talked about a world that was far away in another place. A
shiny bright world with real people who cared about other
people. She talked a lot about things she was involved in.
Sometimes I just sat there and stared at her like she wasn't real.
I couldn't reach out to touch her. All I could do was look
at her.

Toward the end of that second month, I walked out to the
visiting area and saw her sitting there. So beautiful and so
free. I felt like a hard burning thing was wriggling around
trying to burst out of my chest. I walked over to her and said

harshly, "Get out of here! I don't want to see you again. Don't come back!" I turned and walked away but I could remember the stricken look in her eyes. Like she was saying, "What did I do?" I couldn't explain to her. If I even tried, I felt like I would crumble.

Going back to the cells that night after the long day, I flashed on how I could die quietly without looking grotesque. I knew it would be easy because I already felt a certain coldness creeping outward from inside my chest. I thought, "I'll just wait up until everybody is asleep."

It seemed like forever before we were all settled into our cells and I sat at my bunk waiting.

I looked up and faraway I could see the new snow on the tops of the mountain from the barred windows above me. The sun had set in a blaze making the snow look orange-pink with dark blue tinges. I could almost feel the soft cushioned brush of new snow against my shoes and feel the sharp wet bite of the fir and pine smells in the crisp air. Tracking deer in that snow would be easy. Tonight, I thought, I will go home to them mountains.

I knew it was near to Winter Dance time at home. Dad and my brother would be out tracking so there would be fresh meat for the feast. I could just smell the fresh fried deer steaks. Everybody would be talking and laughing while eating fried bread with lots of butter and all kinds of pies and cakes. I thought about that. I rested my mind on it, wanting to remember every detail. I had to do that so I could go through with the whole thing. I knew I was ready.

I closed my eyes as the last light dissolved and the early winter night drew her curtain over my window. In my mind I heard the songs and smelled the fire smoke in the big room where the dances were held.

I heard deer hoof rattles shaking louder and louder and there seemed to be a soft roaring sound in my ears almost as though lots of people danced around me with their feet stamping, their eyes closed and their bodies sweating. The song vibrated through every fibre of my body like a light touch of wings, and the hard ball inside my chest seemed to melt and spread like warm mist across my chest and moved outward throughout my body.

I felt tears, warm and real, wet my cheeks and I heard someone singing Uncle Joe's dance song. All at once I heard my cellmate ask softly, "You okay, Tom?" and I realized it was me singing that song.

I couldn't stop for a long time. I just sang until there were no more tears and the song became happy and light. Kind of like how Uncle Joe gets when the dance feeling is on him and everybody can feel it with him at the Winter Dance, and everybody dances hard and shouts to release that happy feeling.

I did that. I shouted and I knew that everybody in the cell block heard it and felt it. I knew, too, that they heard me singing Uncle Joe's song. I didn't care. I felt okay for the first time in about three or four years. Even the pigs heard it because one of them walked over and stood outside my cell and looked in. I knew they had been watching me close. I guess they know the signs when a man isn't making it.

Anyhow, this pig looked at me and I smiled real big at him. He said, "Tom, seems like tomorrow the sun is gonna shine real bright, so you better get some sleep now." He smiled too. It was the first time I saw one of them as human.

After that I was okay. The tightness in my chest seemed to have gone. I guess you could say I felt free, kind of, even though I was in prison. Feelings like that made me decide that I should make the best of my stay there. I inquired about finishing my education. I had a heck of a time to get someone to take me seriously about schooling. I was helped out by the Indian Education Club that was formed to help inmates.

One of the reasons it was formed, I was told, was that about a couple of years before that, Indians had been given a really bad time when they wanted to get into training of any kind. The prison people had a pretty bad attitude about Indians. They thought they were all dumb, so they put them in dumb-work like making shoes or mopping. Anyhow this Indian Education Club had a sit-in where they made some demands about that and other conditions. That was before I got there, so I did get to have courses in Grade 12 and college level and also I got into an art class. After that I concentrated real heavy on the work and the time seemed to go pretty fast. I did some pretty good art while I was there.

When things are drab and ugly around you it feels good to paint stuff that's bright colored and full of light. You can get lost in it for awhile and forget what's around you.

Mardi wrote almost once a week for the first six months. I think she kind of understood that I would rather not see her in person, but that her letters were more than welcome.

I was always hungry to hear the things going on in the Indian world. She told me that some Indians had claimed Alcatraz and were occupying it that winter. I thought that was pretty neat. I wished I was there after I read how they were offering the government twenty-four dollars worth of glass beads and red cloth to buy it legally.

She wrote me that she was involved pretty heavy in Vancouver in a thing called the Beothuck Patrol. She wrote,

"You should see it, Slash. There are all kinds of us from the Native Alliance for Red Power working on this. The Beothucks are a symbol to us. They were a tribe of Indians on the east coast that were wiped out so the land could be open for settlement. You see, there was a bounty placed on them by the government and they were hunted down to the last one. That's how we fit into this society. They just want us out of the way, no matter how. It's called genocide. It's what's happening to our people right now. We are dying off because we can't fit in. Help is offered only to the ones that are so-called progressive. The ones that are just brown white men. The ones that fit in. Soon there will be no more true red men, with their own beliefs and ways. There is nothing wrong with our ways. Just because our people hate to be grabby, just because they don't knock themselves out like robots at nine-to-

five jobs, and they don't get too excited about fancy stuff or
what I call luxuries, they are looked down on and treated as
outcasts and called lazy. Pretty soon, they believe it and they
think of themselves that way. That's when they give up and
drown in drink. Or else they get like us. They get angry inside
and fight back somehow. Usually they end up dead, in prison
or drunk. All of these lead to genocide of our people. You see
they only give us two choices. Assimilate or get lost. A lot of
us are lost. We need to make a third choice. That's what Red
Patrol is about.

We work in shifts on skid row. We pick up people from the
streets and help them out anyway we can. We keep the pigs
and others from harassing them. We help out even when there
is violence. And we talk to them and tell them to leave that
place. But most of all we set up an example of pride and power
in being Indian.

The pigs and city hall don't like us. They harass us a lot
because we cramp their style. But it seems like that's the
only way we can make a third choice for our people. We are
organizing meetings everywhere, too, to try to educate people
about their rights. Not only personal but Indian rights, too.
This is happening in the bigger cities in the rest of the country."

I thought about everything she wrote. It made some sense, I
thought, but still I thought about Pops and them. They were
neither assimilated nor lost. They were just Indian and they
didn't mind one bit. There were at least two or three families
like that on every reserve back home. What about them, I
thought. Then again, how come that wasn't good enough for
me. What was the reason I was here in jail?

I never really talked about it with Mardi, in my letters to
her. Somehow I knew she couldn't understand about Pops
and them and how they lived apart from everything and also
a part of everything at the same time.

She wrote that summer and told me that there was a big
fish-in demonstration happening in the Okanagan near my
home and that some people from their Red Patrol were going

up there to support it. I wished I were going, too. Her letter sounded excited. She wrote, "I guess it's starting to happen. There isn't any stopping now. Our people are awake now, from their long sleep."

The fish-in was good from her report to me. A lot of Chiefs and people attended and there was no violence. The cops laid charges against the leaders, not everybody. She wrote that she had met my Pops and even the Chiefs and Councillors of each Band. I was surprised that they were all there. It was hard to imagine after remembering the way things were when I left. It seemed like maybe there was a chance of our people getting together after all.

She also told me that she had heard that there was a conflict involving shooting over fishing rights at Puyallup near Tacoma in Washington State. She was going there with some of the Red Power people. I tried to get some reading up on that in prison, but everything we read was censored. I couldn't really believe that there was that kind of conflict happening, but I felt good that it might be so. Things just seemed to kind of drag after that, and I buried myself more in my studies and art.

It was a long time before I heard from her again. She wrote from Minneapolis, Minnesota. She wrote a brief letter saying that some guy that was involved had gotten shot up there on the Puyallup River. Things were pretty touchy there, ready to explode. She mentioned coming up to Chilliwack for the salmon fish-in staged by Indians on the Fraser River as a protest to fish regulations being imposed. She mentioned having realized that nothing much was happening up here in Canada, just a lot of talk, and that there were some things that were pretty important going on in cities like Minneapolis. She explained that they had a patrol going there and it was a lot better than the one up here. It was called the Bellecourt Patrol. She said a lot of things were happening besides the patrols, and that she would be involved in them so she probably wouldn't write so often because it might be dangerous.

I wondered what she was talking about. What could be

dangerous about writing about Indian meetings and stuff? I thought that maybe she had met up with somebody in Tacoma and that she had an old man from the Minneapolis area. It could be the reason she figured it was dangerous to write to me. I hated thinking that way, but what else could I have thought? She wasn't tied up like me. I knew she was free and she was so good looking it wouldn't take long for some fast talking guy to trap her.

I still thought of her all the time. Every time there was a mail call my heart would do a little skip. I thought of her smooth, brown skin and her husky laugh sometimes when I laid awake at night. The pain I felt at them times is more than I can even say in words. Nothing is worth that, I said to myself. I promised myself then, that the only way I would ever end up in jail again is dead. Of all the things that prison did, being without my woman was the one that turned me into a hating animal. Like I said, nothing is worth that.

During that time I worked real hard at my education. Most of the other prisoners kind of left me alone. Maybe it was the schooling or maybe it was the singing that night that made them all back off me. However, most of the Indians filled me in on stuff that happened outside with other Indians. I got the idea that there were all kinds of meetings and gatherings where Indians were making demands of all kinds in education, government, social services and even rights.

Inside the prison there was a rehabilitation program but it was mostly bullshit. We were treated like animals in lots of ways. To me it was that we were denied all kinds of things that were just basic to humans. It sure didn't have any bearing on rehabilitation. Most of us in the ward that I was in weren't big-time criminals, just small-timers, B & E's and fighting, stuff like that. There didn't seem to be any reason to treat everybody so bad if they were really trying to rehabilitate them toward a better attitude. Seemed to me, it just made you a worse person for having gone to prison than what you were when you first went in. Seemed to me if that were true, then what was the prison system accomplishing, other than producing more hateful people that would be out walking the streets in a couple of years? I thought to myself they might be farther ahead not to send petty criminals to prison, but find some other way where they could learn how to be better people.

I learned that lots of Indians were in prison with pretty stiff sentences for some pretty small-time stuff. I figured, for the most part, judges gave maximum to Indians whenever they could. I could have been wrong but I didn't think so. It could be too, that Indians didn't get lawyers and they just pleaded guilty. If they did get a lawyer, they were usually court-appointed and didn't give a shit, like mine, and just told you to plead guilty. Some of them things were what I noticed a lot while I was there and they made me feel more mad inside than before I went in.

At home, things must have been going on pretty rapidly. I found out after I wrote Josie and let her know where I was and I got some letters from her. She said that a lot of young people had become interested in what was going on with Indians all over. She said that they had started a club and were having war dance lessons and were talking about putting on a War Dance Pow-wow. She said that mostly everybody went to the practices and that everybody felt pretty good about it. She said lots of people who were ashamed to be Indians before then were now proud to put on head bands and chokers and try to learn the war dance songs.

She sent me a clipping, too, of a speech by some leader of the National Indian Brotherhood. He was from B.C. from a tribe near our own. He talked about possible Red Power violence if Indian grievances were not dealt with effectively.

She wrote, "Pops and them, they don't say too much, but they think something is going to happen as far as violence is concerned. Pops and them said it was a long time coming but they hoped nobody would get too crazy. They said violence was sometimes needed when nobody listens, but it is needed now mostly to help Indian people wake themselves up more than to wake up the whites. What do you think, Tommy?"

I wrote back that I didn't really know what to think. Mostly because things were too sketchy for me to get the feel of what was going on. I knew how I felt inside, because that's what got me there in the first place. As far as what I was ready to do about it, I couldn't say at that point.

Things went pretty smooth for the next long while, as my months rolled by. I got a card from Mardi, near to Christmas time. She said that she was over at the east coast and that she was there for the take-over of the Mayflower, where some Indians were making a point about the U.S. Thanksgiving. Her card seemed so distant, like it was from somebody I didn't even know.

I tried, that winter, to get out on parole but I was denied. I didn't even know why. I had my interview and I knew I never got in any trouble. I had done a lot of talking and helped with the Indian Education Club. Maybe that had something to do with it. We had made the prison people sweat, I guess, once in a while, when something really bad was done to an Indian. Anyhow, I had noticed that the parole system was kind of a farce for Indians. Nobody seemed to be able to do anything about that. While I was in there, about seventy-five Indians that applied for parole were denied. Only about ten got parole and of those about seven were for minimum parole. We tried to raise a stink but we only seemed to jeopardize our own chances by doing that. So I did all my time.

I got out that spring when the leaves just unfolded and the air was damp and sweet. I felt really lost. I had on prison shoes but they had issued me some normal clothes. It's just as scary coming out as it is going in. The first thing I did was I went to go to a restaurant to eat. I had wanted some meat, thick and juicy with baked potatoes and lots of butter. I had some money that I had made on different details while I was in there. I had saved most of it because I didn't have any habits to spend it on.

Anyhow, when I walked into this steak house, it seemed like everybody was looking at me everytime I turned around. I thought, "Maybe they can tell I've just come out by my haircut or something." Then I thought of my shoes. I hurried out of there and walked on down the street to another place. All that time I kept feeling like somebody was either following me or watching me to see if I would do something wrong. Pretty soon I was almost running down the street. Shoot, I just wanted to get somewhere safe. I found myself studying everybody's faces to get a clue where they stood.

I didn't know jail did that to you. I wish somebody had told me because everything slammed me right in the face that first week. I guess I would have ended up back in jail one way or another because I started drinking real lots just to keep my balance about me. I didn't head home right away because I didn't know how I could handle that. I spent all my money and sold my art work that I had brought out with me. I didn't remember one day from the next for awhile there.

I ended up at the Red Power Center one night. This guy called Lenny had hauled me there. He was from the Okanagan, north of us. He was on Red Patrol when he found me. He kept me in a room until I sobered up. They fed me and never asked me too much.

Later they did talk to me about the war they were fighting. A few of them sat around and took turns talking. They said that they were soldiers or warriors fighting to keep a race of people alive. They even wore red berets and cast-off army jackets and combat boots. They also wore their hair long and straight hanging over their shoulders. They called each other "Bro" and each of the women "Sister". They asked me if I wanted to stick around and help them out. Their faces were hard but their manner was soft. I had never met people like them. I had been impressed with the way they carried themselves and how self-responsible they seemed.

I told them my name was Slash. I told them about just coming out of jail and how I didn't want to go home until I was okay. I told them that I was looking to find out where a friend of mine named Mardi was. I said that they might know her since she had worked there over a year before that.

They exchanged looks that showed me they had known her and she had meant something to them. This guy asked me, "When did you last hear from her? How did you get to know her?" I tried to answer his questions, but I felt like they didn't really think that she would pay attention to somebody like me. But they wanted to know all they could about her.

I learned that there had been quite a lot of moving around by some of the guys from here to other cities in Canada and the U.S.A. There were always guys or chicks that just came in from Seattle, L.A., Minneapolis, Toronto, Winnipeg and other places where "the action was." They all kept us pretty well informed. A lot of the guys and chicks from Vancouver had gone to support some things that went on in those places.

I had been told by someone that had seen her in St. Paul that Mardi was in the Movement and was involved in some stuff in the U.S. as far as organizing and things were concerned. It seemed that anywhere there was any action concerning Indians, she could be found. A pretty solid group of them moved around almost continuously and protested this and that. Their actions got heavier and heavier.

I stuck around Vancouver with the Patrol for a couple of months. I liked it and most of the people working on it were pretty serious. We had meetings and talks almost continuously. Some of the members were sent to some meeting or another that was thought to have some potential, where our work could be done. Mostly I stayed put, kept quiet and kept out of things. I needed that. Not too many people noticed me anyway, I just kind of hung around in the background.

Once some people that came through talked about "Spiritual Unity Conferences" that they had been at. I didn't know what they talked about but it had sounded interesting. They described meetings where prophesies took place at those "Unity Conferences." They had seemed to be deep into Indian religion, sort of, but nobody there had seemed too interested and they had left quietly.

The Center had been like one big family. We had been at a place called Pandora House. It was a commune, kind of. A lot of different young Indians went through that place, but everybody had felt that they belonged. There always had been chicks around to help with making food and things. They had sure known how to make people feel comfortable. There had been always a lot of kidding around and laughter. Everybody helped with everything. Work details in shifts were sometimes followed. No kind of bullshit was tolerated from anybody for very long.

It felt good to be with just Indians, young ones, who were seriously attacking a problem only they seemed to understand. One which I understood better and better. I finally began to understand why I had deserved to be punished for working in the dope business. The Johnny Johns and people who helped them just helped our people into the gutter. For that, I was sorry.

I talked to Lenny one day, about possibly going home. I was kinda feeling like I wanted to find out if I could make it back there. He said, "You know, Slash, that's really a hard thing to do. You change when you leave home. Especially if you done time. Even living here with us, it changes your point of view. You don't quite see things the way they do at the reservation. I tried it. I seen too much that people seemed unaware of at home. I would get so frustrated when they wouldn't act on something or else they did something really stupid. I don't know if you know what I mean, but maybe you should go home and see. Anyway, there isn't much happening here in Van. By the way, you hear from Mardi yet? We got word that she went over to Alcatraz. They are doing some negotiating over ownership of that island. I don't think they are gonna get what they are after. We shall soon see. If they can lay claim to that island, that opens up a lot of possibilities, you see."

His words about Mardi were what made me decide. Like he had said, nothing much has been happening in Van. We sent a few guys up to Port Alberni to listen in on the talks over a federal park that the Indians there were claiming had been set up without consulting them. A committee working with some women's group was formed. This committee got involved in stuff like chewing out the chairman of the B.C. Centennial Committee for not including Indians in a commemorative book. We all thought it was kind of wishy-washy in comparison to things being done in other areas of North America. However, we added our two cents. I realized what Mardi had meant when she said not much was happening up there.

I hopped a bus home that weekend. It was May and the whole world looked pretty good. I finally felt alright about being alone. My jail paranoia was under control by then. I actually felt happy. I didn't realize how lonely I had been for my people.

The bus pulled into town late that night. The town looked exactly the same. It never seemed like I had been gone almost two years. I had to hitch up to my Pop's place. It was about three in the morning before I found myself standing at the gate looking toward the house. I remember thinking that it was funny that the lamps were all lit like everybody was up. I had this real tight scared feeling in the pit of my stomach thinking about what I would say to Mom.

Coolie, our dog, came running up to me. He started whimpering and licked my hands and I knelt down and he licked my face. It was then that I realized there were tears running down my face. Coolie seemed to be saying, "It's alright Tommy. We're all glad you're home now."

As I walked over to the house I saw Pops and Mom sitting at the table looking out. They didn't see me because it was dark, but it seemed like they looked right at me. Pops got up and walked to the door, opened it and looked out. I saw him framed against the lamp in the background. I said in Okanagan, "I've returned."

He walked out and put his arms around me and stroked my head for a long time. I felt all the things building up for a long time move up and seem to disappear into his gentle hands. I never talked and neither did he, but everything I wanted to say went through my head. I wanted to tell him how much I cared. And how much I hurt and how bad it had been in prison. Everything I felt seemed to seep into his hands and I knew I didn't need to say anything. He already knew.

Mom was waiting inside. She hugged me real hard then she said, "Tommy, how come you're so skinny? I cooked some deer brisket just the way you like it and some biscuits. We were waiting all evening for you. Uncle Joe told us you was coming. He had a dream. Eat now, Tommy. We'll catch you up on everything."

We stayed up all night and talked, that is, they talked. They told me all about the things the people had been doing.

Mom said, "You know, things is looking up. Ever since last year we been going to all them war dance practices and them fishing meetings. The trials are gonna start pretty quick. We might have a big pow-wow. Everybody is trying to raise money for it. We had a walkathon, or whatever its called, to raise some money for the pow-wow. Me and your Dad, we didn't walk, we took the old hay wagon and walked the horses ahead of everybody, so people could ride when they got tired. The radio man drove slow behind us all the way. He laughed when we told him about giving the walkers a ride now and then. He said it was the easiest walk he'd ever seen. It was more like a parade. Everybody wore Indian shawls and chokers and stuff and people clapped when we went by. People were glad to be Indian, same as at the fish-in."

The next whole month I relaxed at home and went hunting and fishing and worked in the fields with Pops. The kids, Jenny and Wayne, were almost grown up, so they worked some, too. I was surprised at them though. They were treated different than I was. Pops and Mom seemed to baby them more. They were allowed to do almost anything and got out of work a lot, too. They slept in lots of times.

I mentioned that to Mom once, when she was cooking and Jenny was getting herself ready to go down to a drum practice. I said, "Mom, how come you guys are so easy on Jenny? She should be cooking, not you. Same with Wayne. He doesn't help Dad very much. He just takes off to drum practice without doing his work."

Mom was quiet for awhile then she said, "I don't know, Tommy. But you and Josie and Danny seemed to have a hard time to just live because of the way we brought you up. We don't want them to suffer like you or Danny. Danny just drinks now since he's been trying to follow the rodeos. He's not interested in the ranch. Neither are you or you would have a wife and kids and a home here already. Josie split up with Clyde over him drinking and running off to rodeos, too."

"She lives on welfare, now, with her kids. She don't want to come home, even though we got everything they need here. My grandkids don't even know me hardly. They don't even talk Indian."

"We raised you kids right with hard work and discipline and tried to show you how to live good. Somehow it didn't stick. So now Jenny and Wayne are growing up a little different. Maybe things will be easier for them. Maybe they'll make out better."

I felt real funny about that. I wanted to tell her everything they taught us was important and how they brought us up wasn't the reason, at least for what happened to me. I wanted to explain that the reason had something to do with going to a white school where everybody was different and that was what made you confused and dissatisfied. I knew I couldn't convince her since she was right about none of us making it too good. I knew I didn't have any right to tell her otherwise. Heck, it must have been an awful thing for both of them to have known I was a jailbird, especially when I was kind of chosen by Uncle Joe and them to be the one to keep our ways.

I started to see what Lenny had meant about it being hard to go back home. I went to the Council meetings of the Chiefs concerning the fish-in and other things. It seemed that they were avoiding some really important things. They seemed to be more interested in out-doing one another at talking. Some conflict between some of them over wanting to fire the Indian agent in charge of all the Okanagan District seemed to be of great importance.

One whole meeting was spent in an argument over that. I sat in and listened. I wanted to ask why weren't they talking about the welfare problem and getting more people to the places where they could get ideas from other Indians. I knew those carefully dressed men would look at me like I was a worm though. They knew who I was. They knew I just got out. They hadn't seemed to consider that what was real was what I and Lenny and them talked about, not whether some D.I.A. man was responsible for making welfare or education dollars tight.

I wished I could have told them that I and lots of other young people were proof that the problems were deeper than funding levels or restrictions on spending from D.I.A. That most of it was like huge general things which affected all of us, but I knew they didn't want to hear that from somebody like me.

I went to meetings with the old people also. Again there didn't seem to be any understanding about what was happening to the young people. The old people were concerned about the loss of Indian rights and the encroachment on Indian lands and what that was doing to the deer, the fish and the roots and berries. They dwelled a lot on the injustice of the government in not living up to its promises. They were busy preparing for a visit by the Queen of England. They wanted to present her with a gift that had some significance as to the commitment the Crown had to the Indian people whose land her children lived on.

I listened as an old man talked and told what he wanted said about how the Creator gave us this land to live on and with it certain foods to eat and things to do. And how that wasn't being respected and how the people were suffering as a result.

I wondered how something like that was going to help the situation. I knew it was important to keep our reserves and our foods but a lot of Indians didn't even live that way, even on the reserve. It seemed to me that, like at the meeting of the young Chiefs and their Councils, there was a certain point being missed.

I went to the trial of one of the Chiefs for the fish-in. It wasn't very exciting, although a lot of people from the reserves and the Union of B.C. Indian Chiefs showed up. Some guys and chicks I knew from Van were there, but they were ignored and treated somewhat disdainfully by the others.

I visited with them and asked how things were moving in Van. They told me nothing was happening and filled me in on stuff from other areas. They had heard that Alcatraz was being evacuated. They also said that some of them were on their way up to Fort Nelson where there was a blockade. They said that a Chief and some workers up there had trapped a three car speeder and work train on a corner of the reserve and were holding it until talks with the Railway was straightened out. It sounded exciting.

The trial was slow and boring. Everything seemed like a show to the lawyers and some of the Councils. We finally left, because it was leading toward an appeal to a higher court. Most of the old people grumbled at how the witnesses were questioned and how the case was presented.

I sure felt like going up to Fort Nelson with the group that left that day. But I kind of felt that it was too soon. There were still some things I wanted to check out around home to see if I could make things move.

Nothing went on except the pow-wow. That was pretty great. The International War Dance Competitions attracted people from a lot of U.S. Tribes. I guess I hoped Mardi would show up.

Everybody from the reserves were there during the day for the salmon barbeque and the competitions. The whole club dressed up and lead the grand entry. It was good. I was proud to dance with them in the grand entry. I knew how they felt. Some of them really surprised me because they were ones who didn't like to be associated with being Indian.

Time went pretty fast after that, on into the fall. I worked with the harvest crews in the fields for my Uncles and Pops and helped round up cattle in the fall. Everybody in my family was glad to see me, but others on the reserve were distant. Even Jimmy, my friend from years back. He had sure changed as far as attitude was concerned or maybe it was me that had changed.

He was involved in an upgrading college prep program at the new Okanagan College. I guess he got tired of partying around or maybe he decided it was time to try to do the things he had always wanted. You know, get an education and get a high paying job and get lots of fancy stuff. New car, new clothes. An image. He lived the role, too. He stayed in town and lived on education allowance from the Band. He had sporty slacks and a short, neat haircut.

When he talked to me, all he talked about was how much money he had saved up to buy a really classy car. He said he was going in for accounting so he could get a good, clean job. He was going with this white girl, too. I had never seen her on the reserve with him. In town he hurried past any of us, especially me, since my hair was long and I still wore my khaki jacket from my Red Patrol days.

One day I went and sat with him in the bar and we talked. I asked him, "How's it going, Jimmy? You like what you're doing?" I had been trying to be friendly, you know, to strike up a conversation somehow. It had seemed like he was real hard to talk to, like he was a complete stranger or something.

He turned around and looked at me with a sneer on his face. "You damn right, I like what I'm doing. I'm going places, man. I'm gonna be somebody, not just a drunken Indian. I don't know why the hell you guys don't do the same. Look at you, Tom! What good did following tradition get you? We can't ever go backward. The sooner you accept that, the easier things will be. Shit, I can get you set up for college right now. In a year or two you'll be sitting pretty, you can marry any classy woman you want."

I didn't know what to say. I took a long sip of brew and then said, "I got to have time to look at everything, Jimmy. Some things just don't make sense about wanting what you want. I just can't get excited about it. I look around and I think, is that what it's all about? Is that all? Seems to me there is something more important I'm missing out on. I don't know what it is, maybe I'll never know. But right now I'm just going to drift with it until I at least have some idea of what I want."

I didn't tell him that I already had completed college prep and had a year of Arts and Sciences through the Prison Extension Services. I had been made aware that I could pursue almost any field of study without any problem.

I didn't try to talk with Jimmy any more after that. I got to be pretty much of a loner I guess. Most of the other reserve guys worked at the sawmill, which had expanded considerably during the time I was gone. Weekends saw most of them and their paychecks at the local Indian bar.

I stayed around all winter just thinking, doing a little bit of art work for a few bucks and helping Dad out. They seemed to be really glad I was home and tried to include me in all the discussions with some of the old timers. The talks were the same as always. I knew they were right about everything they said concerning government injustice and loss of rights, but I didn't see how doing something about that would change things on the reserves. I couldn't seem to connect these things with what I saw as the real problems on the reserve. I felt dissatisfied most of the time with things that others couldn't seem to see.

During that winter a man died, to the north of us. It

was said that the police had caused his death. There was an investigation and a lot of news coverage. I watched the news on T.V. at my cousin's place. A lot of people went up there during the investigation inquest. I recognized some of the people from Van.

I thought I might like to go up but it was just during the Indian dances that my Uncle Joe was having. I wanted to stay for that. I hadn't been to one for a couple of years. I had also been earning a few bucks on a project for the Band. We had been just cutting brush, cleaning up the res and stuff.

A couple of guys on the project worked on some carvings. They were really good. I wished I had gotten in on that work. They carved a totem with Okanagan legend animals on it. They really felt good about it I could tell, especially one guy named Randy.

He talked to me once about it. He said, "You know I might be good for something after all. I always thought I was just one of the usual reserve failures, but maybe I'm not."

That's the kind of stuff we needed, I thought. Who knows, maybe Randy might even quit drinking and change his life from doing something like this. I wondered what was so complicated that large conferences and long resolutions had to be passed to do something for Indians. Something as simple as to make a man feel good to be Indian didn't ever seem to be considered as an answer.

The investigation over that man's death up north caused a lot of angry reaction by Indians all over. It was like Indians were saying, through that investigation, that they were sick and tired of putting up with discrimination like that and that they wouldn't stand for it any more.

At home there wasn't much reaction by the leaders there. One guy, who was working on the administration, made a statement that there was "passive discrimination" against our kids in school. My Pops and them shook their heads over his other remarks that we didn't "wage war" with the whites like the Sioux or Blackfeet did, that instead, "we helped them when they moved into the valley."

I knew that what he said was true in a way. Like any other Indians, our people, I was told, didn't push anybody around except when they were threatened. Well, they had been threatened and it probably wasn't well known about some of the war plans that had been made. Some of them were actually carried out by some of our more practical ancestors when the reserves had been cut down very small at one time. The people hadn't been allowed to hunt or fish, and lots of them, Pra-cwa told us, starved to death at that time. It was true some of the Indians protected and helped the whites survive. They were well treated. But there were those that always resisted domination according to Pra-cwa and old Dominic.

After I explained the article to Dad in Indian he said, "It seems like there were two sides to our people from way back. There must have been less on our side or else things might have been different. I guess that's the way it still is and will be for a long time until something turns to change it so we don't have to be for or against. We can just be us."

I nodded and said, "Yeah. To me it sounds a lot like saying, We're good little Indians. Heck, I know that there was more than passive discrimination in the schools and everywhere else for that matter. The only time there is less is if you dress up like Jimmy does and change your voice to a higher pitch and use different English with big words mixed in, and even then there is some. In itself, to me, that is more than passive discrimination. It is an insult to a whole race of people thousands of generations old. It is the kind of discrimination that does more damage overall than any cops kicking the shit out of a drunken Indian. It's the main reason why that Indian was drunk. Why a lot of Indians are drunk. It makes me real mad inside that our people seem to be looked on as if we were less instead of just different."

My Dad sat there for a while and he said, "I guess I under-stand a little, Tommy. I am proud of what I am. I don't let it hurt me when I see that look behind some white people's eyes when I can't say the right English words, but I didn't go to school like you and many others. I think it's that what hurts you. You got mixed up inside. Not strong and steady like you need to be. Lots of you young people are like that. You got to find a way back, to be strong inside again. It's what you're looking for. Maybe that's what a lot of young people are looking for. That's why there is all them protests and angry demands. I guess you just got to fight for it. Nothing ever comes easy you know. I guess you'll be leaving as soon as it's spring. I can feel it. I want you to know that we're backing you. Only use your head."

In March of that year, there was some stuff in the paper about a protest somewhere in Nebraska. A group called the American Indian Movement was protesting the handling of a death. They were requesting a second autopsy because they said that an Indian man had been tortured and that the autopsy was whitewashed. I recognized a spokesman's name that I had read in connection with other things like the painting of Plymouth Rock red during the take-over of the the Mayflower. I knew that Mardi was kind of connected with those people. This group seemed to be getting involved in more serious stuff than before.

I didn't leave that spring because I still was trying to stick around and work on the Band Council to try to get them to join in some of the other things happening. I tried talking a few times with some of the guys to see how they would react to proposing some action rather than just talk. When the Old Crow Indians in the Yukon Territory made statements that they were prepared to fight the pipeline over their land to preserve it from destruction, I went to a couple of the leaders. I suggested that some guys go up there to listen in and learn and help out if they could. They just looked at me and one of them said, "The Union of B.C. Indian Chiefs sends observers to them things. It don't concern us. If the Union decided that we get involved they'll inform the leadership and then we'll decide if it's worth it to us."

It was like those guys had said to me, "Who are you, to try

to tell us anything. We have this all down pat. You're just nobody. Leave it to us who are your leaders. We are doing okay."

Around the middle of July, I read in the paper that a new inquest was being held for the Indian up north who had been killed. The Indians loudly protested that his death was a result of police brutality. I decided to go up there to listen in on the case. I thought that maybe a few guys from Van might be there.

Early one morning I told Dad that I was leaving. I told him that I was heading up north to that second inquiry into the death. It was being held in Kamloops. I told him to tell my Mom. I couldn't stand to see the worry in her eyes. I knew to her I would always be eleven years old.

When I pulled in there were a lot of people already there. They were all spread around outside the Kamloops courthouse in groups. Right away I noticed the guys from Vancouver. I saw Lenny out there talking to a bunch of guys.

Plans were made for a silent vigil outside the courthouse. A committee handled all the business in connection with the case. One of the main people, kind of heading the committee, that I really respected was there. He was the same guy who had done some pretty good organizing in prison.

I spent the next few days just visiting around and made some new friends between the sessions that I went to. Many other organizations' leaders were there. The Union of Chiefs people were there, as well as representation from the Non-Status group. Harold Cardinal got there, so did the leader of the Saskatchewan Metis Association. A lot of renegades were there, too, with a couple of guys from the States.

I got in on their discussion about things going on in the States. Like that torture death and others that weren't even mentioned in our papers at home. I latched on to what they had to say. Some pretty strong feelings floated around during the inquiry as witnesses for both sides were heard. A lot of talks, most pretty emotional, were carried on. In the end the police were absolved of blame. That really made a lot of Indians mad and seemed to fuel the feelings of anger and frustration.

I was right in there, too, feeling mad and frustrated. I decided to travel down to the States with some of the guys from Van to check out some of the things people down there were involved in.

We went from Kamloops over to Alberta for a few meetings. We had heard that a Chief over there who had moved his people into a wilderness area about three years before was being harrassed by federal and provincial officials trying to force them to move.

I got to meet some people who were a lot like my own back home. Strong, quiet people, simple in their ways but good of heart. We were welcomed. I sure was impressed with the old people there.

We ate some bannock, boiled meat and drank the soup with them from our plates the way our old folks did.

One of them sat and talked with us through an interpreter. He must have been close to a hundred the way he looked. He was small with long skinny grey braids and he wore a cowboy hat and boots. He told us how our young people were dying off from liquor and how we had to get back to our old ways before that would stop. He said, "You young people are doing right. Don't give up, no matter what. Us old ones, we will pray for you."

After about a week or so, we moved from there down across the line. We decided to visit different reservations and see what they were like.

The trip took us quite a while. We slept anywhere we could. If we ran into some people we knew at a pow-wow or a meeting we stayed a few days with them. We met a lot of good people that way.

A lot of other young people like us were on the move. We got together and talked about a lot of stuff. I was surprised a lot of them had good educations. I sure wished Jimmy could have heard some of the things they had said, he might have thought different. They made fun of guys like him, they called them "Uncle Tomahawks". I thought that was a pretty fair description.

We stopped in at the Crow Fair Pow-wow in Montana in a place called Crow Agency. There were so many Indians camped that it was like a town. I was overwhelmed. I just kept saying to this guy with us, called Mike, "Golly, there's so many skins. I never knew there were that many. I guess, I thought all the tribes were almost wiped out like us Okanagans." He said, "Naw, there's more skins than they can get rid of, though they'd have liked to." It made me feel good to see all those Indian people. Somehow it was comforting to know we were a long ways from total extinction.

Sometimes while we were travelling we ran out of food or gas. I found out then that some of the guys were experts at a lot of things.

Mike once said to me after I asked him where he had got the money to buy food, "Man, I got the food right from the supermarket. I just walked in and took what we needed. You see, Slash, we got rights to do that. It's food. We're fighting a war. The white people did the same thing to us. They just waltzed in and took everything. Our buffalo and our land are the same thing as a supermarket if you think about it carefully. Did they call that stealing? They called it "white man's burden." We don't call what we do stealing either. We call it surviving, only we ain't killing their people off. We're just trying to set things right. Besides, you ever hear of being honored to go right into enemy territory and steal them blind? Our people a hundred years ago were honored highly for that. What's the difference now? It's proof that I am a warrior."

I didn't know what to say to that.

The Indians on some of the large reserves we went through were really poor. I mean really poor. They lived in shacks and lived off commodities distributed by the government. No such thing as Social Assistance existed either, like up there where I came from. Band housing and things like that were available only through government regulated programs that were aimed at eventual control of the lands used as security. Agriculture was almost impossible because the water rights were owned by ranchers just next to the reserves so a lot of Indian land was leased dirt cheap to them. I heard that white ranchers could landbank the land then for ten times as much as the leases but Indians couldn't because Indian land wasn't allowed. Landbanking meant getting paid by the government not to grow anything. It sure didn't make sense to me.

I noticed that there was a difference on all of these reserves we had come across where there was little economic progress. The people were really hospitable to each other and other Indians. They felt insulted if you didn't eat when food was offered, liking to make visitors as comfortable as possible and treat them to the best of whatever they had. More traditional foods and traditional medicines were used by these people who were a lot like my family back home. Most of them had very little education and, because of that, they were strong in their ways. You could tell by the way they talked and how they carried themselves. Their pow-wows always had big free feasts or a daily hand-out of rations like bread, meat and coffee.

By the time we got to South Dakota where there were some good gatherings, it was nearly fall time. I guess I was looking for Mardi when we got there but I didn't see her. I asked around but nobody seemed to be able to tell me.

It was there that I heard some pretty hairy stories of stuff going on. I saw from the reserves we visited that conditions were really bad with open prejudice by the whites everywhere. It seemed that dead or beat-up Indians didn't raise any questions by the police. A lot of drinking and fighting went on everywhere.

While we were at a gathering in South Dakota, we heard talk of a meeting that was going to happen in Denver. This meeting was going to be set up for the end of September. All kinds of organization heads were going to get together, to talk about what to do, to get the government to make some changes.

We decided to head in that direction. We spent a week or so on the road after that.

About a week before the meeting, we heard about the death of one of the people who had helped organize the seizure of Alcatraz. Mike told me, "About a year ago, this guy got his head busted in, on his way to serve a large corporation president a citizen's arrest warrant. He was attacked and beaten with pool cues, causing permanent brain damage. Some medicine people fixed him up, and though he still had some vision loss and speech problems, he became active again. Now I guess they done shut him up."

We heard that he had been shot and that there was going to be a federal and state investigation requested and that many young people in the movement were angered over his death.

When we got to Denver, the meeting was already going on. We helped out where we could. Most of the time I just kept quiet and listened. Not that many people were there but there were all kinds of organization heads representing about eight major Indian organizations.

Even the president of the National Indian Brotherhood was there from Canada with a group. I was surprised to see him there and even more surprised at his speech. He said that Indians from Canada were no different and that there was really no border that was recognized by Indians. He said that we had the same objectives as U.S. Indians. I liked that. I was glad to see that some of our leaders were trying to get together with other to act on things.

Even though we didn't take part in the talking it was pretty good. I got a real good feeling. Like everybody there was on the same wave length.

Much of the talk was about how to get attention drawn on common problems that Indians had. One of the main problems identified was that the government was exercising control and manipulation through its Bureau of Indian Affairs. The B.I.A. in turn was using the administrative bureaucracy of Tribal Councils to achieve the things they wanted. An example of that was that access was given to corporations to exploit natural resources on reservations with the approval of puppet Tribal Councils. At the same time real problems of poverty and lack of education, poor health care and appalling living conditions weren't being addressed.

Out of that meeting in Denver, a people's caravan to Washington was planned to get the attention needed to meet with government officials to bring the questions to light. It was to be called the "Trail of Broken Treaties Caravan." I saw what they meant after having visited some of those reservations myself.

The Caravan was going to happen all across the U.S.A. with each section converging on Washington just a week prior to elections. The caravans were going to cross historic sites where large massacres of Indian people occurred. Each one would be led by spiritual leaders carrying the sacred pipes and the drums. Drugs and alcohol were to be banned.

It all sounded so big. The things those people were doing made me feel good inside. I wished that people back home could have been doing things like this. I wished that our Chief was here. In a call to a friend of mine from back home I learned that there was a new Chief on our reserve. I sure hoped that Chief was going to be strong and lead the people towards something like what was going on in the States.

CHAPTER THREE

Mixing It Up

We started from Oklahoma where we had gathered, with quite a lot of people. We were going to retrace the route called the "Trail of Tears". This was the route taken in 1838 when Tribes in the southeastern U.S.A. were uprooted to give place to white settlers. They were forced to march under military custody from Georgia to Oklahoma. Literally thousands had died on that route, from cold, hunger and fatigue.

I hadn't even heard of it, but then I guess that was the point of this whole trip: to educate.

I'll tell you it was something, that caravan. One night after we made camp and everybody was so tired they all wanted to sleep as soon as they could before facing the next long day, I sat and talked awhile with this girl named Elise. I told her I was from Canada and that I was Okanagan. I told her how things were at home. I said, "You know we weren't pushed out of our land into another part of the country that was totally alien like some of the people here were."

I had heard some of the things those old people there described in their stories. I thought it must have been terrifying

and horrible to be put in a place where you didn't even know
what plants to eat and medicines to use with the weather
making everybody so sick all the time and lots dying. No,
those things didn't happen to us, it didn't need to. By the time
the settlers started moving into the Okanagan Valley there
had been three waves of smallpox. According to the old people,
other sicknesses like flu, pneumonia, measles and stuff were
killers also. Such diseases were so hard on our people because
there was no immunity to them. A simple thing like chicken
pox could kill. In the first wave, two thirds of our people had
died. In the second wave, half again of that died. In the last
wave, about another half of those who remained, died. That
didn't leave very many.

I explained to her about that. I said, "Those left were so
weak and confused the colonizers were almost able to do just
as they pleased. Only a very small resistance group have
continued up to now to try to keep people's minds straight
about being Indian and free. That's why I'm here, I guess. To
learn and maybe somehow start something at home."

She looked down for a long time then she said, "Slash, it's
hard to be Indian. I guess it's harder in your people's case. The
diseases did a fine job for the white people in your area. For
us, what they did burns in our hearts and we cannot forget.
Some would like to forget and some try, but most of us don't
forget ever. Slash, the deaths from the diseases were not the
enemy, although that is terrible. It is that the colonizers used it
to their advantage and continue to use the disadvantaged
conditions as a means of control. It is oppression being exercised
on a people weakened and defenseless. That did happen. That
continues to happen. Sometimes in ways ordinary people are
not even aware of and would not agree with if they knew.
That's what this caravan is for, to bring those things to the
attention of the public. You see, it is the public that elects the
leadership for the things they stand for. If the public can be
moved to understand, then governments can be made to
change. We are going through these places where our people

were killed and massacred to remind ourselves that our people are still being killed through a psychological warfare in some places and real physical warfare in others."

She went on, "The conditions on the reservations are not of our own choosing. Some Tribal Councils down here are puppets of the B.I.A., high paid ones at that. They have the backing they need to continue their corrupt ways. In some places the corporations exploiting resources for themselves are causing sickness and death and creating a landless poverty situation for the poor on the reserves. So leave the reservations, the society says, join the twentieth century. So, okay, a lot of our people do go out to cities because they won't be used as B.I.A. puppets, but they aren't wanted there. No matter what anybody says, discrimination out there is very real. Jobs are only for those who fit a certain mold. A lot of us don't fit that mold easily. Most Indians work on programs for other Indians and they get disillusioned because all they can do is fight for more dollars, more programs, while nothing is being done to change the system that inflicts those conditions in the first place. I imagine things are no different where you come from."

I looked up at the stars that were scattered around overhead and I could feel them all looking downward toward us. Like they said something I couldn't quite hear. "How could we not succeed?" I thought, "We must."

I looked back at Elise and said, "I know, them are the same things some of my people back home know, only they don't know how to organize to do anything about it. Some think the answer is in fighting for better programs and more money and getting involved in the white community and teaching the young to be aggressively assimilated. They try to be white and they are against anybody they think stands in their way. They belittle and despise the "dumb" Indians for not doing that. To me it seems like it's clear that our people's thinking isn't the same as whites, and we can't change that without knowing it is wrong. It don't feel good to have to gain respect as a hog. Our people have always been respected for how much they gave away to each other. So you got people suffering because they won't change them values. Lots of those who are belittled and despised and aren't strong in their thinking about being Indian get hurting inside. Bad things happen to them: drinking, suicide, crime and all that. Yeah, I see that up in the reservation where I come from."

She was quiet for awhile then she said, "Slash, I like the way you think, but there are many things that aren't answered. I'm here to go to the length that's needed to state our case. I support the American Indian Movement for that reason. You are here to learn. I hope things come out like we want, but if it don't we can't quit. It's started and we got to go to the finish line, even with the confusion among the people. A lot of people don't even know what can be done with corrupt Tribal Councils, they just give in to them. One reason is Indian people who don't agree with mines and exploitation usually aren't educated and they don't like fighting their own people. B.I.A. knows that and uses it. Some right here in this caravan are confused. Some guys here are not really sure why they are here except that they got a hope something will be done. Many of them are just plain fed up feeling like the underdog all the time. Others are very clear why we are here doing this. One thing is certain, we are all together in our dream of the future."

So it was that we made that long journey across the country on the very ground that thousands of Indians had died, on their long walk to Oklahoma. On the way, the drums were used and the sacred pipes were used, and everyone prayed together at places where the deaths happened.

We stopped at one place where a monument had been erected in Minnesota where thirty-eight Sioux were hanged for trying to protect their people. The leader of the Caravan made a statement that the Indians were going to replace that monument with a replica of the scaffold that was used to hang those Sioux. He told the people Abraham Lincoln had authorized that execution, only one day after the Emancipation Proclamation for the blacks was made.

At another point, we were all banned in this one city from staging a drumming and singing rally. We saw across the street a workman had painted on a crane in big letters "Custer had it coming." That made everybody feel pretty good and we all cheered.

We had reports from the other caravans constantly. One came from Seattle, one from San Francisco and one started out from North Carolina. All kinds of press statements were made by the caravans wherever they stopped and a lot of national attention was drawn to them.

During the stop at St. Paul, where two caravans were converging, a meeting was held. At this meeting, a paper which outlined twenty demands was drawn up for presentation to government officials in Washington. While the organizers worked on that, there was word that all government support of the Caravan had been withdrawn in Washington. I knew the organizers of the caravans had made formal request for support, financial and otherwise, for the travelling caravans. Many church and private organizations had also offered their support. The organizers tried to find out if it was true about the support being withdrawn and why. They couldn't reach the man in charge of the B.I.A. in Washington. Nobody knew for sure if it were true and we moved on.

It was early in November when we pulled into D.C. It was morning, just pink and gray dawn and the city was quiet. I knew that a police escort had been requested because there was about four miles of caravan and everybody was sleepy and tired and didn't want to get lost downtown. I knew the plan had been to head directly to the church where we were going to be put up and rest a little, then carry out the schedule.

Well, as we pulled into that huge city which was spread out before us, just reeking of wealth and government power, everybody felt the ripple of feeling spread. We were here to speak for our people. Where were the escorts? Where were the welcomes? The leaders decided to greet the President and welcome the Caravan themselves. They headed out to the White House, horns blaring and people singing, all four miles of caravan. You can guess we got the police escorts, especially after stopping and singing a victory song at the White House.

We were in for a big surprise when we got to the church where the groups welcoming us had been cooking all the previous day. I will never believe the size of the rats in the basement where we were supposed to sleep. Man, it was freaky. Must have been that every rat in Washington smelled the food and had shown up. Everybody was scared that somebody, from the babies on up, would get bit and get some disease.

The organizers told everybody they were going to contact some of the other support groups to see if there was any place better. But they learned that the government had put pressure on everybody to withdraw any support that they had offered. So a lot of doors were closed that had been open before.

We found out that some of the people were going to Arlington National Cemetery to pray and make offerings for the War Hero, Ira Hayes, and also for John Rice, who was refused burial in a cemetery in Iowa because he was an Indian. John Rice finally had been buried at Arlington at the request of President Truman.

Our people were refused their request for the Indian religious ceremony because the army prohibited services "closely related" to partisan activities. That sure made some people mad because the Indian religious ceremonies were deeply respected by all, they weren't "used" as political tools. Besides, the way we saw it, the army itself was a "partisan activity."

The organizers decided that the best thing to do was for everybody to go up to the B.I.A. building to talk about the conditions of the accommodations. They would try to set something up with B.I.A., since they had endorsed the concept of the Trail of Broken Treaties Caravan when it was proposed. The BIA seemed to do everything they could to not co-operate with any of the planned meetings to present the twenty demands.

Everybody went to the B.I.A. building to make some points clear; that there were a lot of us; and that when we were coming we had been assured of places to stay and stuff; and that we had come in peace.

At first, everybody sat around in their cars outside, waiting for the organizers who had gone upstairs through a back door to look for the guy in charge. After awhile, everybody went inside and stood around. Finally, some guys got the drum and sang.

One B.I.A. official came down to report that he didn't know anything. Everybody just looked at him and each other and laughed. Talks still went on, and we were told they would probably continue until after supper hour. So we watched some films. By then more people arrived. There were about a couple of hundred of us hanging around. We watched the films and talked and sang. Some of the guys got pretty tired.

One guy said, "Shit, what the hell! When leaders from other countries come to Washington they get the red carpet. Us Indians, our leaders are no different, they are the spokesmen of our Nations, but we get the rat treatment and a bunch of people get pressured not to help out. And none of the meetings we asked for is set up. Man, what do they think we are anyway? They won't even greet us in a civilized way, how in hell they gonna listen?"

A few guys snoozed and others just sat around quietly, when this guard comes in and says we had to clear the building. Everybody said, "NO!" They told the guard that the organizers were still upstairs setting up some accommodations and food for the thousand or so others that were all over the city. I sat there along with everyone else not expecting anything, when this guard motioned to some others waiting outside.

Shit! Those guys that came in had helmets and armour and were armed to the teeth. They came in, clubs swinging madly through us. Everything went crazy for a while. People hollered and screamed. Just like a speeded-up movie, everything was a blur. When the air cleared the guards had been evicted by our guys and panic kind of spread through the whole building. Some guys with bloody heads ran upstairs and through the halls hollering for everybody to arm themselves for their own defense. Outside, we saw from the windows, riot police in full gear had started to gather around. They looked like a bunch of outer space people or insects the way they were geared up. Shoot, they didn't look like people at all. They looked like they would kill anything that got in their way. It was spooky.

In just minutes all the doors were barricaded shut, with desks, photocopiers and stuff. A couple of police got caught inside downstairs and there was a hard rush on the building as the others rescued their partners. There was kind of a scuffle but nobody got hurt real bad.

Staff people working in there climbed out windows to escape. Some of the guys went around checking rooms and broke into them and made the workers in them leave immediately. A lot of the workers looked really scared. Police then cordoned off the whole building.

It wasn't too long and the whole place was secure. There were some newsmen inside and they were told to stay. The organizers got everybody together then and talked about what had just happened. It was decided that we would stay until things were straightened out and some accommodations were arranged.

One guy told the newsmen that this stuff wouldn't have happened if we hadn't been put in that rat-infested cellar. He said, "There was no intent to occupy at all. We had come in peace, but you get pushed just so far and you've got to make a stand." He said, "Them riot police didn't need to bang people around and hit people on the heads for sitting around waiting for their organizers to set things up. Things that were supposed to have been taken care of by Washington co-ordinators for the visit. Our reservations are Sovereign Nations. Our leaders should be treated as distinguished visitors." He said that we would stay until proper arrangements were made, and after that we'd go back to things that we came for in the first place. So we stayed. More and more people pulled in from the other caravans as we waited.

I sat talking with Elise about what had happened when one new group came in from California. This one person with a Pendleton jacket faced away from me talking to someone. I felt a lurch in my throat. Her hair; the way she held her head; I knew before she even turned it was Mardi. I can't even remember what Elise said to me. I remember looking and my heart thumping bang, bang in my chest, then she turned and looked straight at me.

We stared at each other for a couple of minutes. Then I was on my feet going toward her and she toward me. She walked up and hugged me around the waist real hard and we didn't say anything. We just stood like that.

God, I felt so good, like the whole world was right there in my hands. It was strange, especially when we didn't know what the riot police would do to us. I had been remembering the Kent State incident when white students were shot down by riot police. Well, we weren't white or students, and it didn't seem like they would need much prompting to shoot us down. I felt like everything was just great.

We talked finally, both of us tripping over each other's words, telling each other where we had been and what we'd been doing. We started laughing. She said, "Slash, you look different. Your hair, it's long. You've changed some, but then I guess I did, too." She did look different. She had a pinched, hard look that I didn't see before. I said, "Yeah, you do look different. Are you?" She said, "No, I don't think so. It's just that I've seen a lot of suffering while I was around. People trying so hard and getting their asses kicked from all directions. How are things up in Canada? Still just as slow? I wish they'd get off their asses and start things moving. You know, like what's happening here. This is really gonna cause a stir. I'm glad I came. I was gonna stay in California to help out with the thing on that guy getting shot. Looks like it'll be white-washed, too. Yeah, this is where things are gonna be done.

She stayed by my side during the next ten hours, talking in snatches about a lot of stuff she was involved in. At one point

I noticed Elise, and I felt bad because we had had kind of a thing going. I went over and said, "I guess you can see how things are. What can I say?" She looked down and said, "Yeah, I can see. You don't need to say anything, I guess."

I was glad at finding Mardi again. I was happy she wasn't hitched up or anything like that because I had plans. I could imagine what it would be like back home if Mardi were there. She sure could talk. I watched her get right in there with the others who were organizers and help get some things done. I knew she would impress some of those old time bureaucrats back home.

Throughout the whole occupation she was constantly on the move. I didn't know how she could do it and stay looking so cool and in control. She seemed to thrive on it. Everybody just kind of gravitated around her all the time, because she always had ideas for everything. I was never too far from her either, and every once in a while she would flash me a look or a smile and I would feel warm all over.

We never got a chance to be together much because we were always standing at stations and getting ready for the pigs to crash in. If we weren't doing that we were sacked out in chairs or couches or on the floor to catch a few winks.

The whole occupation continued like that. Instead of the arrangements for proper accommodations being made, a federal court order was issued to evict the people by force if necessary. They said there would probably be another building made available if the Indians evacuated peacefully. Some guys went over to scout out the other building. It was locked. One of the organizers said, "No way, they just want to lock us out altogether. We're not going to get tricked." So we stayed put that day and the next, waiting to get evicted.

Meanwhile, we heard the next day that the courts had refused a request to overrule the army in their stand to refuse the Indian ceremonies at the cemetery. Everybody was angry. The negotiations over our requests, we heard, were not getting anywhere, either. We heard that a midnight deadline had been set to allow us to leave peacefully. After that federal marshalls had the green light to use force to evict us.

Everybody was edgy and getting themselves ready with all kinds of make-shift weapons: table legs, letter openers, broom handles; anything was prepared as a weapon. As the deadline got near, more stuff was piled up against doors. Everybody was sure there was going to be big trouble and they resolved to fight. They said things like "War is now declared on the U.S.A.! Seek your stations."

A lot of the old people and kids were evacuated and everybody waited expectantly until around four in the morning, with no attack happening. After that, people tried to get some rest in shifts. The next day, there was an announcement to the protestors that there would be no effort to evict at that time and talks were resumed.

All kinds of activists' groups during them days showed up to add their support. They formed people barricades outside the building when things got really heavy. Hundreds of them, blacks and whites, linked arms, putting themselves between the building and the federal forces, which were getting bigger and bigger every day. People inside were kept up on things happening outside in the courts and in the negotiations.

It got really bad at one point when they set another deadline. We were told by the organizers that the building was going to go with us if we were forced to leave without being listened to. I had heard talk that the building was rigged with explosives. I didn't know for sure if it was. All I knew is that smoking was restricted to the first floor.

Blacks from high up in the Panther movement came in and talked with the organizers and even Dr. Spock came in person, to offer his support. Almost constantly, there were new deadlines set. They came and went and new reprieves were issued to let us stay another so many hours. That kept happening.

It was weird, everybody would get all psyched up as each new deadline came and went. It was really tense. You didn't know if this one was going to be the big one and you'd get your head busted. The people outside were invited to stay to witness the brutality each time. Each time, prayers were said quietly, giving thanks to all Creation and the things that were given to us by the Creator. While, at the same time, strength was asked to help us to stand hard and our voices to be heard and our lives to be worth the giving, for all our children and the generations to come. During them times everybody thought together with one mind.

After days of this, everybody inside was getting tired and angrier all the time. More and more stuff was being broken and made into weapons and everybody was pulling out papers and stuff out of files and dumping them on the floors. Broken glass and stuff was scattered all over by then.

Flags and portraits were pulled down. Some guys draped flags around themselves upside down, as a distress signal. Outside, the B.I.A. negotiations were getting hotter and hotter and threats were getting heavier and heavier.

Finally, the White House intervened and negotiators were sent over to start talks. I heard that the organizers were received in the ambassador lounge and met with John Erlichman and others who worked directly under Nixon. They agreed to set up a task force to review the twenty demands. The task force would be composed of officers from all agencies dealing with Indians. The whole thing was termed a success after that. We were told we could go home. After that long week, things seemed to look pretty good. I didn't know if the task force was set up as promised or not.

I had expected Mardi to go back up to Canada with me. I had meant to talk to her about it but I had been really unsure of how she would react. So when everybody was packing up and heading out, I turned to her and said, "What's the plan?". I couldn't bear to ask her to come and have her say no. She stood with her back against the car we had been talking beside and looked at me straight in the eyes. She knew what I asked. Her eyes were soft like a deer's when she looked at me. Soft like those evenings we would steal a few precious moments to hold and caress each other when we were supposed to be resting. She said, "Slash, I can't go up right now. You must know, I can't let them people down in California. They need everybody to help organize for the inquiries for the brother that was shot. I was there, Slash. I knew him and what he stood for. I know its important up home and I want to be with you. I want what you are offering. I still think of them things you told me, about your old people and your hills and the coyote songs. Come with me down there for a while. Help me out. The guys I came with, they got room, they won't mind."

I felt real mixed up inside. I couldn't hitch on and follow her. I had to head up to Canada to help try to get things together there. I had already talked about it with the guys I was riding with. They all were excited and ready to "talk action" up there with others. It's a wierd time for a guy to suddenly get pride in the way, but for me it seemed necessary. I thought she would come to me when the time was right, maybe, but I couldn't let her think I had no mind to do what I knew I had to.

We stood there for a long while not talking. I knew she was really torn but she also knew that I expected her to do what was right for her. I hugged her real hard and she squeezed me so tight. She whispered, "We'll be together, Tommy, sometime when the blossoms come out and everything turns good for our people, but for now we'll do what we each have to." I couldn't talk, I just nodded and then she left.

Our crew decided to go up to Ontario to check things out around Toronto for awhile. One of the "Bro's" down at the sit-in was from up there. He said he was trying to get things organized up there.

I had never been in any of the eastern cities in Canada and I wanted to find out if there was any action going on. I had heard that wintertime is hard up there and that just surviving that in a city like Toronto was bad enough.

A lot of different things went on when we got there: meetings, communal houses and some partying. I was just as bad as anyone else out there. I was feeling badly shaken about Mardi and I can't say I paid a lot of attention to the talk about not drinking or toking. I looked for it and found it. I met a lot of people that way. I found out there were a lot of urban Indians from all over the country living in and around the city. Some of them had been there all their lives. I ran into some pretty different attitudes there about what was going on.

Some of the people there were involved in many of the same kinds of things the Vancouver people were involved in. Red Power kind of thinking with AIM overtones.

One thing that was kinda different was the belief that welfare and government grant money was owed to the Indians because of the great debt for the crooked treaties and the resulting loss of the Indian lifestyle.

Some people we ran into identified themselves with AIM. I wasn't really certain if there was a chapter there or not. People said there was, but what I found was some guys that had a big chip on their shoulders. They sure talked tough. Their attitude was somewhat different from the AIM people I saw at the B.I.A. occupation.

The people's attitude there seemed kind of off-key. Like something important was missing. They put a whole lot of emphasis on violence and very little on spirituality. At the same time they never seemed to get it together to do anything violent either.

Maybe I just didn't meet the right crowd, because I hung out a lot at the Silver Dollar and places like it. The music was loud there and the beer and talk flowed freely. I lost myself in it as often as I could.

I'll tell you one thing. We sure had it made as far as places to flop and eat. If we regulated things right, somebody always would be having "a meeting". We could always count on eating there and ending up with one of the chicks for company.

Yeah, it was alright, but not much was going on that I felt good about, so I just drifted with it for awhile.

We left toward the end of that winter, when the snow was piled in high dirty banks along the streets. We had heard though the moccasin telegraph that some things were going down, in South Dakota. We had heard that some of the Brothers were pretty upset about a guy that was stabbed to death down there. They were angered about the way the courts were treating it.

The details we got were sketchy, but we knew that the white guy who stabbed and killed the Indian wasn't being charged for murder, and that there was a riot at the court house and that some violence had broke out in Custer, South Dakota. A building was burned down or something. Sounded like real trouble was going to break out. We were told, too, that the National Guard had been called in. We heard that a lot of Indian support groups were headed that way. There was an appeal for others to go to Rapid City to help out. The struggle was centered around there at that time.

In D.C., I had met some of the people from Sioux country that were pretty bitter about the kind of corruption that was widespread down there. They had indicated that it had something to do with a puppet Tribal Council. I had read an article in "Akwesasne" about how AIM was denounced for the B.I.A. sit-in at D.C. Statements were made by some of those puppet Tribal officials that they would personally cut the braids off one of the leaders of that occupation if he were to show up on the reservation.

I thought that was crazy. How in hell could Indians back up the B.I.A. against their own people, I wondered? Especially when the demands that were being made at the sit-in was for making things better for all people on the reserve.

I saw I still had some things to learn. Anyway, I was tired of the scene in Toronto. I decided to try and find out what the score was down there. I knew that it had a kind of parallel in what was happening then back home, except that it was on a greater scale and in greater depth. I mean about the split between assimilationists and the traditionalists and the conflict that arose out of that. I knew I had to try to understand what it was about so that I could go home and try to do something about it.

I talked to some of the Brothers around the city about it. But they just looked kind of puzzled. One guy named Cheeze said, "Shit, man, those Sioux are warriors from way back; they got to live up to it, you know. Even if it's among one another. What do you want to get involved for? You're from B.C., it ain't got nothing to do with up there or up here."

I told him, "I don't think you know what them people are like for one thing. They ain't war mongers at all. They really believe strong in every person being created by the same One. But there are lots of things really wrong and they aim to change them things for the better. To make people understand them wrongs and change is all they set out to do, not make war. Its always the others that force the situation and make it violent. I know, I seen it. Them guys just don't back down until their point is made. I think I'm gonna go down that way and check it out. Anyway, there's nothing happening up here."

I asked around until there were a few of the other guys that were willing to go get some wheels together. This one guy Wiser said, "Yeah, man, I'll go. I know if we needed their help here they'd be right up here, long as we were serious."

I sure was glad to hear that and glad to know there were guys up there doing the right thinking. I later heard that there was a small group that had left earlier than us. I realized maybe I had been hanging out with the wrong bunch of guys in that city after all.

We packed some gear and headed out. We had to hustle some money for gas and some winter tires and stuff. It took a few days. Hustling for those things in winter was hard.

The weather was pretty bitter. Travelling was slow. We only stopped where we knew some skins would be friendly toward us; places we knew we could hustle food and gas and a place to crash. That was in bigger cities where there were Indian centers.

The going was tough, all right, but we got past Detroit and Chicago and was going to start to head to Minneapolis when we heard that there was a take-over at Wounded Knee. The press was really playing it up, saying it was a heavily armed stand-off and that the situation was "very grave."

I remember listening to the bulletin on the radio and everybody in the car visibly sucked in their breath. My heart started beating real fast and I felt that roaring in my ears. The bulletin said that AIM leaders were calling Indians from all over North America to converge on Wounded Knee. We knew that it was no publicity stunt. Nobody in the car said a word but you could almost cut through the silence. My mind raced. I was thinking, this is it, the big one, and I was afraid. Really afraid for all my people.

We turned west from Milwaukee to cut across through to Sioux Falls and then were going on over to Rapid City. It's not a good route at the best of times. Since it was winter you can imagine the ride we had. There was freezing wet snow piling up on the road and making the road slick as hell. I remember Wiser swearing and gunning the motor and fighting the wheel for control as we skidded around the curves in the black freezing night as we headed toward something that loomed dark and ugly ahead of us.

We ran into a police roadblock just past Sioux Falls. At first I thought it was just routine. Then I noticed that they were moving all white people through. We were pulled over and the cops jerked open the doors. Shit, they had rifles pointed at our heads. There must have been fifteen police. They tore the car apart. All our stuff was scattered all over the freezing wet snow and some stuff like knives were put into a pile. Everybody carried hunting knives in their packs. We use them for everything from mechanicking to eating.

We were asked where we were going and they checked I.D. It was a lucky thing we had no dope on us because you could see they were looking for any excuse to bust us. Our head man, Wiser, from the Toronto area, played dumb. He kept asking, "What's going on? We're just on our way back to B.C."

One cop kind of sneered at him. He asked "What's your business in the United States?" He had been really unfriendly, saying stuff like, "Shoulda done you all in at one time that first time," "Goddamn wagon burners, you think you're so damn tough now!"

After a lot of talk and hassle they let us move on. Wiser had told them that we would be talking to the immigration officials about our treatment as visiting Canadians. He was the head of some big organization for youth up there and he showed them his card for that. They kind of backed off after that. All our clothes and sleep rolls were soaked. Our grub was all messed up. I think they were disappointed we didn't have any guns and stuff. Shoot, we weren't expecting anything like what went down. It really shook us up and we realized that things were a lot more serious than the sit-ins and stuff previous to that occupation, and that there was going to be open season on Indians, any Indians.

We knew after that we would have trouble the closer we got to Pine Ridge. We all knew that we were open to anything they had to dish out.

We decided to go some back ways, in through the Badlands. One guy said he knew a way, so we drove along some dirt roads. Everybody was real quiet and I guess thinking about running into more cops. I think we were getting in pretty close when we were stopped by some skins. They appeared out of the dark and motioned us to stop. They had a set-up, kind of like security. We cut our lights while they asked us where we were from and what kinds of stuff we had and how we wanted to help out.

Wiser told them that we just came to do what we could. He told them about not being ready for armed occupation. We didn't have any guns or goods to help out with that. He said we could make some runs if that was needed. The only problem was that we would be easily spotted because of our foreign license plate.

We were told that we were lucky to run into them first and not some of the goons. They explained things to us. We learned that it was pretty dangerous to be caught by the goons hired by the Tribal Council. They were doing all they could to regain the B.I.A. buildings at Wounded Knee. There would be no questions asked by them or the Feds working with them if they caught anybody going through the lines with guns and stuff.

So we camped out at some people's place and ditched the car we were riding in. Over at that place there were a lot of other people like us who heard about the take-over and had come out to help.

We heard that there were about three hundred federal marshals, F.B.I. agents and police at the scene, with about seventeen armoured personnel carriers supposedly because some hostages were taken.

The whole issue seemed to have centered around the postponement of a meeting of the Council at which some of the members were to make a move for an impeachment. These things were explained to us because we needed to know exactly what we were getting into. We were told that this wasn't really a Tribal affair. We were told that the corruption stemmed from the B.I.A. control over the Council through the use of monies allocated by it. We were told it was a widespread problem involving almost every reservation anywhere, and that in aiding those people, we would make the chances better for the same things to happen on other reservations. We were told that the traditional people were strongly in support of AIM in their attempts to expose some of the wrongs. They wanted a new election with people who were concerned about the right things.

We were told that our part was to act as support in any way possible but that doing it was our choice. They told us that this wasn't a take-over at all. One of them speaking to us said, "This is our land. We have rights here. How can we take over? We're already here. We are just supporting the people who are opposed to the tyranny and corruption they have to live under. You tell me why the Council is so strongly opposing our attempts. You tell me why over sixty men were deputized by the Council. Why guns and mace were distributed and purchased with Tribal funds and a mini-course on riot control was held after that meeting was postponed due to 'weather conditions.' If we can be successful in our attempt here, then it can be done elsewhere."

I decided I would stay to help out as long as I was useful. I wanted to see just how things would work out. I knew I was facing some risks; the worst being prison again and the easiest being death. I believed in what they were doing. I saw great strength in what was being done. I understood it is easier fighting foreigners because racial prejudice is almost always an easy conscience soother, but protecting your people against your own is very difficult. Mostly, it's easier just to keep quiet and endure, and there had already been too much of that.

We spent a lot of time helping to organize food and other supplies to be brought to different stations. I never went any further than what was called "the perimeter." Beyond that, someone else more experienced was given those jobs. I believe that it was extremely dangerous. It was made clear that anybody spotted within that zone would be shot. Inside that zone, goons, F.B.I., federal marshals and B.I.A. police patrolled constantly, lighting the darkened areas with big sky flares at night, at almost constant intervals.

Barrages of shots went back and forth. It must have been hell to have to go through the zone with that going on, but I knew that people were constantly moving through. Even some reporters, which was very important because there was a news black-out imposed by the officials. The reports were supposed to be one-sided. Nobody was supposed to hear the Indians side, I guess, in case some truth came out. A lot of people knew, too, that an immediate bloody massacre was held off simply because some newsmen were "inside" and were ready to talk about it.

I knew a lot of people weren't as lucky as us to get through, even to nearby Rapid City, with food and supplies. A lot of people, white, black and Indian, from all over the country were busted just caravaning over with donated food and medical supplies, as those things dwindled inside to near zero. Some church organizations and other organizations involved with civil rights were harassed.

One church leader issued a statement saying that the cause of the occupation was justifiable. He said the whole thing should have been resolved, without it having to come to the kind of violence that the F.B.I., the B.I.A. and the federal marshals were inflicting because of an attitude of "putting them Indians back in their place."

We heard that some non-Indians were held on various charges, including treason. We were told that Indians were being routinely beaten, jailed and threatened if they were caught at various road blocks heading toward Pine Ridge.

I saw things them months that really told just how cheap the life of an Indian is to a white man who's status quo is threatened. There were vigilante groups organizing all around, expressly "to teach them damn Indians who is boss here." Armed ranchers roamed between roadblocks hoping to get an Indian trying to sneak in. They called it "rabbit-hunting" and joked about it, over their citizen's band radios, while we listened. A lot of people got their heads busted in that way. A lot of Indian women were raped and beaten and old people battered around. Many of them were not even connected with Wounded Knee, but they were Indian. They seemed to be too much to cope with. The hatred was ugly.

The sheer bullheaded ways of them officials that were supposed to negotiate to settle the thing was what kept things tied up for so long. They insisted on negotiating on terms of arrest for the members who were in occupation. They refused to discuss the demands being made and the prime reasons for occupying, which were an investigation of B.I.A. and Interior Department dealings on reservation land, the suspension of the Tribal government and constitution, the withdrawal of the hostile B.I.A. police force and an investigation of loss of sovereign rights as guaranteed in their treaties.

A couple of senators arrived to "talk" and they went in with that same attitude. However, they came out saying that the "hostages" didn't want to leave. One said that he had offered to take the hostages with him but they had refused. They had a list of the grievances and said that an investigation of the B.I.A. was in order and that every effort would be made to "get them a fair hearing on the matters they are concerned about." But they said that officials of the Department of the Interior refused to negotiate as long as "property or people" were being held. They suggested that efforts be made to get the Justice Department involved.

That sure put a crimp in the actions being contemplated by National Guard forces. The "hostages" were necessary to lay some charges against their "captors" to justify the massive military-like presence which was escalating rapidly towards a confrontation. What good were "hostages" if they wanted to stay and support the Indians?

The Indian people inside were firm in their stand. They said, "Either negotiate with us for meaningful results or you're going to have to kill us." The goons and B.I.A. police force stated publicly they were ready to move to "do the job right."

Things would get real tense and gunfire would start up. Then there would be a ceasefire called and talks would begin again. At one point, the Justice Department announced that the occupiers could leave without arrest and the U.S. forces withdrew their roadblocks. Then, suddenly, they were up again and threats were being made that they were simply going to move in by force.

We never really knew, from time to time, whether the people inside would be wiped out that day or later. Things began to drag on and on, both sides becoming angrier and angrier. Threats being made were more and more hostile and direct to the point. One official stated to the press that the Indians were going to be "starved out". He suggested that electricity and such things would be cut-off. He said that living conditions would be very severe without adequate food, fuel, electricity and water. He said, "We won't be responsible for those conditions and what happens as a result."

At the camp I was at, one of the guys listened disgustedly and said, "Is he talking about existing conditions on the reserve or what?" Another guy laughed and answered, "Naw, he thinks they are going to start them conditions new, like it ain't like that already." We were all worried constantly for those inside because we knew their food must be all gone and, more seriously, the fuel for heat. It was bitter cold. South Dakota weather is raw and killing in the winter.

During that time, news filtered through that many people headed towards South Dakota were caught in a nationwide sweep in which authorities all across the U.S. had been ordered to stop "all persons who are intent on crossing the state lines to participate in civil disorder." The news was filled with it.

In one unbelievable instance, some people from the Los Angeles area were arrested in Nevada and taken away in chains for carrying food, clothing and medicines. Some white doctors were part of that group.

I wondered if Mardi was with that group. I thought that it was very likely. I didn't like to think of her being put in jail. I knew it would just be a matter of time before I was busted myself. I didn't figure I could be of any help in jail so I stayed clear. I travelled around only at night when it was necessary to do the work I was assigned.

The months were dragging on toward April, after several "almost" agreements being scrapped and tensions building up again. Indian people all around there were still being severely harassed if they even looked like an AIMer or were known to be in support. I guess, to me, the most appalling thing was the

lengths that some Indian people went to back up a B.I.A.
system that wasn't set up to do any good for the people. They
wouldn't even listen enough to try to straighten things out.
I still couldn't understand the reasons for that attitude.

One night as I was heading out with a few others toward
another part of the reservation we were chased and shot at by
an unmarked car. Finally, our car flipped over beside the road
and some police jumped out and pointed rifles at us. They
beat the shit out of all of us.

I don't remember too much until waking up in a jail so
crowded that we were jammed together. I hurt like hell. After
days without being charged for anything, I was told that I had
to leave the U.S. immediately and that I would be dumped at
the state line. I was told that I could fend for myself from
there to the Canadian border. From some descriptions I got of
things that could happen to a lone Indian on a deserted stretch
of highway in those times, I knew it could be dangerous.

I don't know how the others made out after the pick-up,
but I didn't see Wiser after we were picked up from the accident
scene. Everybody said he was just "missing" like a few others.

I headed out on foot. It was damn cold but I was lucky. It
wasn't long before some skins from Manitoba with deportation
floaters picked me up. There wasn't a hell of a lot we could
do, so we went to Winnipeg.

It was pretty dreary up there with people not being able to
go across the U.S. border without being harassed.

We all felt pretty good when we heard of Brando's decision
to turn down his Oscar. Shoot, we all knew what it felt like to
sit in a movie and watch Indians being slaughtered over and
over again. Worse to watch the mock Indian raids they staged
where a whole group of "helpless" wagon trainers would be
burned and scalped.

I wondered why they didn't show things that really
happened. Why they didn't make movies about something
like the "Trail of Broken Treaties" trek. Why they didn't use
historicals based on those kinds of atrocities towards Indians as

a basis for at least some movies. I thought maybe the reason could have been that it was easier to go on stealing resources and land and oppressing people if you had an image of them from childhood that said "those savages deserve it." I guessed it was easier to say, "Why don't them damn stupid Indians be like us, fit in, assimilate?", if they refused to look at how despicable their kind of people really were.

I tried all the time to find out if Mardi was still in California or whether she had made it up to South Dakota. Nobody knew. She was one of the people that was "missing." By then I pretty well knew there was a list of people that could be eliminated easily. Most of the really high profile people couldn't be eliminated by "accident" I guess. I figured she was on the low profile list. I burned inside with an anger that was hard to handle sometimes. I seen too many things that were done to ever again be hopeful that justice could be done without confrontation. I guess them things made up my mind that I was going to do as much as I could to help things happen on this side of the border.

A lot of meetings were held and the excitement was pretty high during them times. I think everybody expected a massacre. I would say there was a feeling spreading that something would break out if the people in occupation were killed.

I listened with a different ear to the things that were going on down there while going with the bunch moving all across Canada. Holding meetings to inform other Indians of the situations was their main purpose. I saw things with a different eye than before.

I got to see a lot of the same kinds of things all across this country on the reservations that I seen in the States. There was severe poverty and all kinds of "social problems," especially heavy drinking everywhere, almost as if that were a normal way to be on the reservation.

However, on these reservations, there were a lot of Indian people that were afraid. They were afraid that meeting together and talking about them things was going to stir up such trouble that it could lead to killing and rioting like the Negroes did in the States. There were many of them, though, that admitted people were dying violently left and right anyways, from alcohol related deaths and suicides. Many were in prison. The people were tired of the conditions that caused those things. The same problems of D.I.A. rubber-stamped Band Councils was there, too.

We went across some really poor reserves where there didn't seem to be hope of any kind. A lot of young people on the move came from places like that. The realization that they didn't have anything to lose but maybe something to gain made most angry young people want to do something. They weren't interested in the Indian tradition aspects so much; they just needed to identify themselves as Indians and do something about it.

Many of the meetings and sessions didn't seem to have any real focus on what to do or how to begin to do it. Instead these sessions were a lot of what could be called "bitching" sessions, where everybody would denounce white governments, the D.I.A. and other things like prejudice in general. There were no solutions planned, just reactions to things.

I was as bad as everybody else. My anger came out in great gobs when I talked. I couldn't seem to help it when I would see how pitiful the people were in their timid ways, just taking everything dished out while they were rotting slowly from inside. I wanted to shout "DO SOMETHING!! Don't die begging and crawling!!! Die on your feet. Now is the time." I did say it sometimes when I would get so damn mad. You could always see the resignation in the eyes of the people but there was always that small spark that would start in their eyes. There was a small question there, like: *Is it possible? Might there be a way?*

Some of the guys talked about how important it was to remember that AIM is a spiritual movement. They said that, in order to achieve anything, we had to do it the Indian way.

We had to attempt to use every avenue available because violence is used only to defend. They said over and over that the advice of the Elders and the traditional people was necessary to keep the young people from going too wrong.

I knew them things were talked about, but it was hard to go by when everyone was talking anger. Like a lot of others, I wouldn't hear what was being said. I never gave myself that chance. I was hurting too much inside. It had a lot to do with Mardi.

Somehow I knew I would never see her again. I knew, too, that it would be a long time before things were good for our people anyway. Probably never. Even though I didn't have one shred of evidence that she was snuffed, I knew that was what had happened to her. I wasn't the only one that thought so. It wasn't like her to simply disappear. She needed to be right in the middle of things. What I thought most about was why she hadn't come with me or why I hadn't gone with her instead of having to "prove myself." I knew then that she would never see my home or meet my folks. She would never learn my people's gentle ways or walk with me in the soft dusk in those sage covered hills.

I couldn't think of home without thinking of her and hurting for both. It seemed like there was a huge gaping hole some-where in my chest. Like I had to keep doing stuff constantly to keep from falling down that hole. There was a darkness there that was scarier than any moonless night. It made me hate with a gut wrenching kind of hate that kept me feeling at least. I used that at them sessions whenever I could.

At the sessions there were a lot of young people who were really trying to re-learn the old ways. Some of them talked with old people wherever we went. They went to ceremonies and had sweats with the old people. Those young people were usually quiet and soft spoken.

Me, I couldn't face them old people too good. I couldn't go to sweats or ceremonies. I guess it was the hate in me. It was strong and big and ugly. Sometimes at night I felt it twisting inside my gut, making my stomach burn and turn sour. Them times I had to get up and find something to mellow out with. If it wasn't a chick then it was dope. I smoked a lot of dope and drank too, when there wasn't any dope or chicks.

Every time a meeting would come up, though, I would go straight and the anger would build. By the time everyone got to have their say, I would be ready. It would just come spewing out. I knew I was good with words. I knew how to say things to get everybody feeling what I was feeling. At them times, I felt like if I had a machine gun, I would have run out and started shooting at any white man passing. Afterwards, I would huddle somewhere and shake and be so tired I couldn't do more than get up to pee.

I met other guys who felt like me, but for other reasons I guess. We acknowledged each other. We hung out together. Yeah, we went to the rallies and gatherings with the others. We learned the drum songs and learned how to dress to look the part. We played the part too, I guess. A lot of chicks were impressed with it. Enough of them that we got pretty arrogant in the way we treated them. We were the bad guys nobody should mess with. We should be treated with respect because we were ready to die, God damn it, "for the people." That was my attitude them times.

The months went by that way, into spring and early summer. We heard, that an agreement had been reached at Wounded Knee, and it was evacuated. An investigation of the B.I.A. would be initiated and the old treaties would be looked at. Some arrests, too, of some of the leaders happened.

Somehow, to me, it didn't seem enough had happened. My head was pretty twisted. Maybe I was hoping for a massacre so it would touch off anger. I wanted it to happen. It was almost like a let down when it didn't. I was glad though, at the same time, that those guys in there did not die. I knew that there were two who had died right in that struggle and lots more on the outside that suffered and died because of it. I knew that was a big price to pay. The thing is a lot of the guys there would pay that price and not just say it.

Things started boiling all over in Canada that summer. We read that in B.C., the Union of Chiefs had made pretty strong statements about owning all of B.C. and that it was not for sale. In Alberta some people made headlines by demanding the return of sacred medicine bundles, held in museums, that belonged to Indian families. In the Northwest Territories, at the request of the North West Indian Brotherhood, the courts put a freeze on all land transactions where a pipeline was being considered for development. At James Bay, the Crees strongly resisted the hydro-electric project that would flood much of their ancestral lands.

We heard about all those things at the meetings that we went to. Most of those meetings were youth organization meetings. All I cared about was to keep moving, to keep doing things so I wouldn't have to stop and think.

The youth grew pretty strong and pretty vocal across the country. There was a rumor that a lot of them were "radicals" or AIM people. I'm not quite sure if both were meant to describe the same kinds of young people.

It was sometime near July, when we heard that the National Indian Brotherhood had issued a statement urging control over education programs by Indian people. They said that Canada's Indians have as high an illiteracy rate as most of the third world countries. It was made clear that Indians would do better if they controlled the education of their children.

For some reason, this hit the papers really hard. I couldn't see why. It seemed to me like there must be something at stake that somebody didn't want to lose control of. I was near enough to home, at that point, to call some people up and ask about it. What it boiled down to back home was a definite opposition, by our home school district, to relinquishing control of Indian education. I wondered why. There never seemed to be any real love for Indian students in the schools and I certainly couldn't see why there would be any concern over the education of Indians by an all white board of trustees.

It was at a conference in Edmonton that I learned the answer. I was shocked. There was an agreement made by the federal government and the provincial governments to transfer large amounts of money to the province to educate Indians in public schools. Each school district would get a portion of that money for every Indian kid enrolled in their schools besides money for busing and access to money from the D.I.A. to help build classrooms and schools. Indian Band Councils and leadership had no say in that matter whatsoever!

Man, the whole thing stank! I could see then why the opposition. It meant control over the money without the obligation to provide anything special to make sure that the problems of Indian kids in public schools were addressed. It was a good set up for them and they wanted to keep it that way.

The papers them days always had stuff in them about Indian land claims, Indian rights and Indian protests. The Commons was busy "furiously" debating Indian rights. The Indian Affairs Minister announced a new Indian Education policy which would allow Indian bands limited control over Indian education. This drew some reaction, however, as one of the youth leaders said, "seeming appeasements by the government in some areas are easier than in others."

Towards August, the days were so long and so hot that we travelled only at night. Heat waves shimmered off the blacktop and the cities were like hell holes all across the provinces.

In August, we attended another Youth Conference in Akwesasne, not too far from Ottawa. A lot of issues were brought up, most of the same ones that were brought up in other parts of the country.

One of the main issues was a Youth Liaison program that was being implemented. People at the Band said that this program hired a bunch of "radicals" to go into reserves and rouse other young people.

Some of the people in the national Native Youth Association

didn't agree. They said that it meant co-opting young people with bucks and thereby neutralizing the strength of the youth movement. They wanted the program to stop unless it was done through the National Youth Association.

Some of the talk was of the fact that certain questions were being asked about spending for the conference. The government or someone was accusing them of spending the money for other purposes than the Youth Conference. I tried to find out what "other" purposes, but I wasn't really anybody, so I never found out for sure. I was told only that some young people had taken training somewhere out of the country with the money.

At the conference, there was talk about what we, the young people, could do to have some of the Indian issues heard. Many angry young people talked about "doing something about it." That's how the talk turned toward demonstrating at the Department of Indian Affairs in Ottawa.

A lot of excitement was generated by that idea. We discussed how, maybe, we would really make an impact on some of the issues being discussed across Canada. The most prominent items were pretty general, like putting a stop to the Youth Liaison Program, halting government action on the James Bay Project, settling B.C. Indian land claims and implementing the Jay Treaty, an international agreement allowing Indians unrestricted passage across the border.

I can't say I attended all of the conference. I didn't, of course. I was busy partying around and finding people to do it with. In fact, I missed a whole lot of it and really just got sketchy reports of what went on. Delegates handled all the main talk and the plans. I was there just to be a part of the action. The decision was to go for it.

Once at the Department of Indian Affairs in Ottawa, things went down pretty much as planned. We just walked in and took over. Nobody really resisted. It wasn't like the occupation at the Bureau of Indian Affairs in Washington, D.C. at all. AIM security was in place and there was drumming and all kinds of stuff done, but the seriousness and deadly kind of panic wasn't there. I knew that files and stuff were broken into. I didn't pay too much attention. I just didn't feel too much for what went on. I wanted violence. I wanted things to break and people to get crazy, but we were constantly told that this was a peaceful occupation to emphasize certain points being made.

I guess it was okay. We just stayed one day and the guys at the head of the organization did all the talking. I'm not really sure if they got commitments on their points or not, but they did get some top secret files.

I learned about this the next day, when a press statement was issued by the Minister of Indian Affairs. I read, also, that he had called on the R.C.M.P. to "do their job" during the occupation but they refused to mount an armed attack on us for fear of heavy casualties on both sides.

All kinds of harassments happened after that because of the stolen documents. Police pulled over and searched any Indians all around the city and nearby. We read in the papers that even Flora McDonald's office was searched because the police thought she might have them. There sure was stink in the papers about that. I guess M.P.'s, even Conservatives, were supposed to have immunity from that kind of police investigation.

"Hell," my friend Mike said, "Why don't they realize? Nobody has immunity if the government is trying to hide something." Then he said, "They probably got plans on how to deal with Indians that they're trying to hide."

We were heading out to the prairies for some meetings in Winnipeg, when we heard on the news that there was an announcement by the Indian Affairs Minister that they recognized aboriginal claims, and the provinces were urged to join in "a fair settlement."

"Ah ha," said Mike who had come with us. "Those documents they were so hot to find must be plans on how to settle land claims. Their stand since way back was non-recognition of aboriginal claims. These plans were made because of all the demonstrations forcing the government to reluctantly admit that Indians do have rights. It might cost a lot of money to settle justly, however, so the easiest thing to do is refuse to recognize aboriginal rights for as long as they can. That way, they might not have to settle at all. Contingency plans to settle would then be needed. In that case, the cheapest kind of plan must be made which looks good, but really takes as much as it can for as little as it can. That's what's probably in them stolen papers. Now that we have them, the government is forced to announce recognition of aboriginal claims."

I thought that Mike sure was one smart guy. He was one of the youth organization people. He had a pretty good education and I figured he was using it for the right thing.

Later on that fall, we heard that the documents were returned but that copies of some of them had turned up at some major newspapers. Of course, Mike was right about land claims settlement. Hell, we heard there were specific papers on the Yukon, the Mackenzie Valley Pipeline, the James Bay Project and B.C. land claims, as well as a general settlement strategy with dollar figures. What seemed crazy to me was that somebody had known where the papers were and just what to take during the demonstration.

There was a parliamentary investigation of the whole thing but nothing too much was done. One guy's name, I think he was assistant to the Minister or something, kept cropping up in some of the discussions through the summer and even earlier.

All of a sudden I had a bright idea at one of the discussions. I said, "Hey, what if them documents were a set-up? What if that's what they wanted you to discover? Will they settle exactly that way now? Or will they listen to what Indians want? Maybe Indians don't know what their claims are worth and what their legal rights are as far as the rest of the world is concerned. Maybe we could hold out for a lot more legally. Maybe we need to find them things out from objective sources before we swallow any set-up plans by the government."

You would have thought I insulted everybody, the way I was heckled. Finally, one guy said, "Shit, man, them documents is secret. The government was just holding out." I answered, "Yeah, but who did know where to get them? And how did they know? They had to have been shown by someone working inside D.I.A. Shoot, that person is probably working for the government. Getting secret documents is probably impossible. You can probably get only what they want you to get. That way they already got their price named in such a way that the Indians fight for that."

The people there just laughed me down. So I shut up. Somehow it had just seemed too easy to me.

We all got kind of tired out around the beginning of November. Some of the guys headed out to B.C. to go to the B.C. Chiefs meeting in Port Alberni. I hitched along. I felt maybe from there, I could drop by home and see how the folks were doing.

At the meeting in Port Alberni there was a good turn out of people. Throughout, an almost tense atmosphere prevailed in the meetings, although the discussions were pretty dead. A lot of strategy and planning sessions on how to approach the issues that faced the Bands went on. Although the people discussed and debated those things, there seemed to be an undercurrent that the main topic was being deliberately suppressed. Like everybody was afraid to bring up whatever it was that was on their minds.

The most exciting things that happened were things that happened outside of the meetings. Entertainment things like traditional feasts and tribal dancing were, somehow, more serious than the meetings. Such an intensity flowed that you could almost feel the air crackling, when the songs for the dances started.

During one of those songs for a dance, a strong feeling of loneliness hit me. I stood there and listened as the song gathered force and the movements of the dancers became fluid, like part of the sound, and I felt like dancing with them. I stood there swaying, sweat running down my back and face, feeling like somebody was slowly squeezing the air out of my lungs. I felt like I should shout or run or something.

From behind me one of the guys said, "Hey, Slash, what's the matter? You interested in all this? Why don't we go check out some of those chicks we seen earlier?" I tried to turn and answer but I couldn't, then he came around and looked at my face. "Jesus, you look weird, what the hell! Are you O-deeing or what?" He grabbed me by the shoulders and I kind of fell against him. I felt the way something seemed to drain away through the top of my head. I felt so weak, I mumbled something to Bob to just let me be. He said, "Hell no, you're coming with me! I sure in hell don't want to see you kick the bucket if I coulda helped." He took me to where he was staying, and said, "I'm gonna go get my Grandpa, he might be able to help you. At least he can tell if you're gonna die."

His grandfather was just a little guy. He didn't look really old except for his face and eyes. He was dressed in baggy pants and plaid shirt under a Cowichan sweater that had seen better days. His hair under his toque was shortish and streaked with grey. He sat down and looked at me for at least ten minutes without saying a word then got up and said simply, "You better go home, young man. Your people knows how to take care of what's wrong with you." With that he walked out the door.

I knew what he talked about. I had been away from my people too long, and it was winter dance time back home. I needed to go there. I left the conference that next day with some people from my reserve that were there as delegates.

Sometimes, in late November, we get a powder dusting of soft snow at home. Then everything looks like its shining and feathery like the down on a goose's chest. Greys, soft blues and cool yellows, washed over the sides of hills as we pulled into the valley, late in the afternoon near sundown.

God, I felt good to be home. I mean in the Okanagan. Those prairies did something to me, I thought. Like I always felt vulnerable, without any protection around me. Maybe it was the mountains I missed. Port Alberni was okay but there was too much green covering the hills. To me the brown earth hills of the Okanagan are like a woman's skin: brown and rich, needing nothing more to be beautiful.

When I got home, I was surprised. The house had been changed while I was gone. It didn't look the same. It was painted and had a new roof with real shingles instead of the roofing paper it had before. Another thing that astounded me was that there was electricity. I could tell that from the way the lights were so bright instead of soft orange from the coal oil lamps. I went to the gate and stood there once again, not really feeling like I was home. It's funny but I had this mental picture of what home was I guess, and somehow it just didn't fit.

In the house things were changed, too, but the feeling there was still as I remembered. My Pop worked on covering a saddle tree in the living room. He sat there and looked up at me, his glasses way down on his nose, and I noticed that his hair had a lot more grey in it than I had ever seen before.

He got up and hugged me hard. Mom came and said, "Oh! Tommy! When did you get here? Gee, it's good you're back! You can help get some fresh meat for the first dance. You heard about all that stuff Indians been doing all over? Looks like there might be an Indian war or something real soon. Even here, everybody is getting mad. That new Chief and other new ones from close reserves are meeting and talking all the time now about some of the stuff you used to talk about. Where have you been, Tommy? I was scared when they were shooting out at Wounded Knee. I thought maybe you went over there. I'm glad you're back. Come on, I got some dumplings in dried meat soup. You don't look too good. You bin drinking again? That stuff's no good for you. You know Pop always tells you that. Your brother Danny, his liver's getting rotten. That's what the doctor said. He just gonna up and die sometime from that, if he don't wreck first. Eat now, I'm gonna go get ready for bingo. I go now once in a while with your sister Josie. She's gonna pick me up."

So some other things had changed while I was gone.

A whole month went by fast. I didn't even think about partying or anything during that time. I guess it was just the good feeling of being home that carried me through the times I felt lonely at night. Them times I got up and Uncle Joe, who had come up for Christmas and the dances, he would be in his bed smoking. It was like he was waiting for me to say something to him. I would get up and sit beside him and roll up a smoke, too. I didn't say anything though. I just sat until I felt better. I knew he wanted to talk with me about what was bothering me, but I couldn't seem to get the right words together. I wasn't really sure, anyway, what exactly I needed to talk about.

It was a good month, with Christmas and all. Gifts and big dinners and lots of people visiting. I never talked much to anybody, I guess I just wanted to hold that time to myself for awhile.

At dance time, I went out with Pops and my younger brother Wayne to get some fresh meat. Out there, time seemed to stop and the world of people seemed to go away. Fresh snow covered the hills and the green firs and pines were piled with thick layers of it. Pops rode Rollie, his old mule. I watched as he rode ahead and thick swirls of snow cascaded around him as he brushed branches in passing. Everything was fresh and clean and always so new out there.

I wanted it never to go away. I felt something close to pain, as I listened to the soft hum of the wind through the trees like a song. I thought, "Why can't we just be like this? Why is there all that shit around down there on the reservation and everywhere else? Why can't we just be free without having to shout and fight and drink and hate?"

I didn't have any answers. I knew how things were on this reservation and many others across Canada and the U.S.A. Man, I wished there was really a way without the stuff I seen happen in South Dakota. I thought about those things as I rode along behind my Pops, as the soft white snow dust drifted and settled around him. The only sound was the soft swish of hooves in the snow.

I tried to talk to Uncle Joe about that, when I got home that night. I told him how I felt about being in the mountains again after such a long time. I told him how, when you are away for awhile, those things just seemed to become unreal, like a dream or something. I told him how the people were feeling outside, that is, the people on the move and also some of the people on the reservations.

I told him that, yes, there was a lot of anger, but there was also something else that I couldn't quite describe, something like a strong feeling of pride that wasn't really there before. That feeling was getting stronger, especially at those demonstrations and meetings. I told him that I wasn't sure if everybody felt the same but there was a general feeling around that "something was going to get done and, by God, WE were going to do it ourselves without anybody's permission."

Uncle Joe puffed his cigarette and sent huge clouds of smoke into the air. He asked, "Do you think its going to do any good, Tommy? I guess you have seen some bad stuff in some of the places you been at. I guess you seen some of the angry young people and what they are really like. Do you know what they want? Do you know what you want? Can you tell me, Tommy, what you really want out of all of this? You know the people is ready to act, don't you. One thing has got to be clear and that's what things need to be done. You don't just raise hell and throw something out without having something better to put in its place."

I said, "I guess I was really kind of dumb when I left here. I mean about people and situations. I did learn a lot of things while I was gone, but I'm falling to pieces. I ain't as strong as I thought. It's like I'm mad inside all the time. I want blood to be spilled, for people to get hurt. I sometimes think that's the only thing that will unite people. I think that when a people have to fight, then pride returns and with it inner strength. It's like I'm being pushed to do something. I'm scared and the people seem ready. It seems like just a little push of support will get it rolling. Am I wrong or what?"

Uncle Joe sat for awhile looking out the window like he hadn't heard the things I said. Softly he said, "Tommy, you keep it up. You got the spirit in you, that's why them songs bother you so much. Don't deny them. We are Indians, Tommy. Them spirits are crying out to the people, the young people, because the land is in pitiful shape and with it, our people. Just don't let the drink and drugs and the hate win you over. You got to get yourself together. Its good you come home for now. You needed to. The dance will help you, it'll soften them hard lumps that hurt inside you." That's all he said.

To me, it didn't sound like an answer. I knew the spirits that he spoke about were the ones associated with our dance religion. I knew how good it felt to dance hard all night and holler and shout when the feeling was on you and you could just fly with the singer and, afterward, feel peaceful and good, hearing the prayers of the people for renewal and health and happiness. I was very glad to be there among my people. I knew the dance would be good for me and I thought maybe I would find my answers.

By January, I felt pretty much myself again.

I was ready when the first Band meeting was called. I went. I said I wouldn't say much, just mostly listen and throw in a few key questions. I was surprised at the turn out of people, not only from this reserve but also from some of the surrounding ones.

A couple of the men had got caught hunting off the reserve and it was closed season. A lot of discussion went on about what to do about it. Some suggested that we should plug up the courts with cases. Others said that we should use this case to set an aboriginal rights precedent.

I listened, with interest, as people voiced their opinions and became very emotional. These people didn't need any kind of urging. My people were ready for action. I wondered what the Chiefs had in the makings. I had figured that what they had in mind must be something to do with the cut-off lands.

A visiting Chief mentioned the cut-off lands. He was pretty vocal and said that we would resort to violence, if necessary, if our claims were not acknowledged.

He explained, "Cut-off lands are those pieces of land cut-off reserves without the permission of the Indian people. It's different from general land claims. General land claims is the claim to the whole territory which the tribe originally owned.

He explained, "Most reserves here in B.C. weren't set up under the Royal Proclamation of 1763, which says that treaties have to be made. So really the reserves are not legal." He continued, "But right now we're going after cut-off lands instead of general claims because it's easiest. The government was supposed to get permission from the Indians first to cut the reserves and they didn't. So it wasn't legal."

Nobody questioned what was being explained. It seemed it was pretty well understood. People just wanted to "get on with it," "do something," "act on it." Those were the words being used that night.

Only one Elder got up and spoke in Okanagan. He said, "All lands have been cut-off from us. Not just them little pieces off the reserve. There never was a good agreement on any of our lands. They lied to us. They never kept their promises. They make laws and they break them."

He continued, "We got to be clear on what we are doing. To argue for the little pieces that they cut-off from reserves that ain't legal anyway, would be like agreeing that those reserves are. Besides, we would spend all our time fighting for that little crumb. When we got it, we would get so busy fighting over who's to get what out of that, we would forget the biggest business of ours, and that's the general claims. We got to make a good agreement on all our lands, that will really help our people, forever. That is our right as a separate people.

That means we got to keep our land, and we got to keep our Indian rights. That is all I have to say."

You could have heard a pin drop in that hall. I knew some of the people were angered about what he said. They took it as a direct criticism to what the Chiefs were explaining. Some didn't. One guy stood up and said, "Well, isn't that what the Chiefs just explained?"

One woman who had gone away to Vancouver for awhile to work said, "Oh, this is modern times. We can't argue in courts about the supposed promises that the old Indians talk about. Heck, they couldn't even understand English. How do they know what was promised? I think it's about time we started moving ahead with the younger generation."

Another man stood up and said, "I agree with the old one who spoke first. We are deliberately missing the point. We are talking about still having our sovereignty. We haven't signed that away. We got rights. Original rights we want to keep."

He stopped for a while, like he was thinking, then he continued, "However, we need issues right now to get our people moving and to get the government's attention. If we can show our people that we can get these small claims, then we can be stronger when we go after the bigger issue. I agree, we have to keep after the general claims question on our aboriginal rights until we get what we want. But our people need a boost right now."

He looked slowly around the room, then said, "Lotsa Indians went to jail for just getting food for their families. Hunting and fishing. This meeting right now is over that. Over hunting rights. Over eating rights. Eating rights given to us by the Creator, not some government. I am glad we are going to court. Maybe for once they will hear our side of that story, but, as I said, lots of Indians are scared to hunt and practice that right. So we need some victories to give our people a boost. That's a good reason to do these small claims first. Heck, land claims been discussed for the past ninety years or so. The government won't budge on it now. We got to win a few to get our people thinking."

What he said sounded good to me but I knew something wasn't quite right. He made it sound like he agreed with the elder, but, really, he was disagreeing. I wondered if anyone else understood that.

It wasn't too long after that meeting that we were all notified that there was going to be an emergency meeting. It was at that meeting that it was announced there would be a peaceful demonstration at Okanagan Falls to protest the provincial government's non-action on settling cut-off claims.

Okanagan Falls was once a tribal-held land, registered to Inkameep Reserve before it was cut-off in 1913.

The demonstration was planned to inform the public through setting up a road-block and handing out leaflets of information and drawing the media's attention to the issue. We were told that signs would be carried and drum songs would be sung while we stopped or slowed down traffic and handed out information bulletins.

I went home that night and talked to Uncle Joe and Pops about it. I said, "You know, I think things might just start to happen here. I'm surprised to see the way people are really taking an interest in this whole thing. You should have seen the excitement when it was announced that there would be a demonstration. Are you going to come and help out? Somebody said some of the radicals from the States were going to be up. I wonder who that will be?"

Uncle Joe answered first. He said, "Well, I guess it ain't going to hurt any if we go. Your cousins from all the reserves will be there. It should be a good time to visit some old friends. Too bad old Pra-cwa is getting too old to even get around any more. He woulda liked to see what's going on. He woulda liked to be there with everybody else. Us old ones, we been waiting for this a long time. We'll be right with you all the way."

My Pops said, "Yeah, I agree, we'll be there. I agreed with that Elder that spoke at the meeting that we should be going after the big question on land claims first. But I guess what that other man at the meeting said about us needing to win a few, might be true. I hope that this will work that way."

It was cold and blustery that day when the demonstration was to begin.

As we were driving down to Okanagan Falls we were stopped by a road block of R.C.M.P. We were told that it was a routine check for licence and insurance. Well, for a routine check they were pretty thorough. They went through all our trunks and checked under the seats and looked at everybody's I.D. I was peeved at that, since the demonstration was announced as a peaceful one, and had been channelled through the news media, asking the support of the public.

I asked the cop nearest me, "What's the idea, are we being harassed or what? Everybody knows that this demonstration has been openly planned with the assistance of the R.C.M.P., and that the non-Indian public is being asked to support our information bulletin hand-outs." He looked hard at me then said, "You must be the Kelasket kid. Maybe what we should do is haul you in for questioning."

I shut up. I wanted to go to that demonstration. I knew that when you got a record you can be hauled in anytime for questioning for anything. I got the message, alright. They were saying, "We know your connections to AIM and this is just a warning, we can deal with you if we want to, so be a good boy now." I thought that was just shitty, but I wasn't going to get smarty or anything just to make a point to a cop who was obviously acting on orders from higher up.

The demonstration was carried out, with speeches to the people and conduct rules from the Chiefs. Almost all of them were there with all staff from all their administration offices. The mill crew and the vineyard crew all were there. A lot of young guys and girls from all the reserves were there and older people like Pops and Uncle Joe. Somebody had brought along a band-owned and operated video outfit to film the whole thing. Some pow-wow dancers and singers were there with a drum.

Surprisingly, there were people from other Tribal areas, and some of the Brothers and Sisters that I knew, who were on the move. I talked with them for awhile about other stuff going on in other areas.

When the drumming started, everybody formed a circle right in the middle of the highway and did a friendship dance. Cars were backed up for a long ways on both sides. We all joined hands and started the circle moving to the song. I knew how everybody felt. I felt it spreading all around the circle. I heard it in the voices of the people.

The drum vibrated and the sound coursed through every fibre of my body as I moved with my people in the dance of friendship. I felt so strong at that moment, so good, so clean. I cared for my people. This moment united all of us in a way that words couldn't. It was clear, there was a hope that we shared. Hope that we could make things better for all of us because despair could be banished from the hearts of our people that way. To me, that was worth anything we must sacrifice or do.

I don't know how much good media coverage we got or how much public support we got, but the whole thing was a success. The people who took part were glowing and smiling when it was over.

There had been a few tense moments when some red-necks almost ran down some girls. They cussed and made menacing gestures at the girls, who scrambled to get out of the way. They were lucky and only got sprayed with gravel and dirt.

Some motorists that were handed the leaflets thanked us politely and said they hoped we got what we were trying for because, "God knows Indians have had a real raw deal." Very few were openly hostile, from the survey done by the guy assigned to that, about seventy percent were supportive. That was good news. Of course there were some that just didn't care and some that couldn't understand what the issue was. I was proud of the way the Chiefs handled everything.

The rest of that winter and early spring was spent in a

flurry of meetings and talks with other Tribes and Bands. The Band meetings were always frequent, to inform the people of everything that was going on. I went to some of them.

I spent a lot of time talking to some of the guys all around from the different reservations, trying to help them to get a clear picture of what to expect when and if things were to get real heavy. It seemed to me that some of those young guys thought of it in real romantic terms. Like fantasy or something.

I talked with them about reality, if there was ever a showdown or something near to it. I told them what I knew could happen when there was a deadline to meet and you knew your only alternative was to either get out or face the consequences, whatever they may be. I tried to tell them how scary it was, when real showdown time came.

It was at one of those kind of talks that I noticed one of my older cousins sitting there looking at me with something like contempt in his eyes. This cousin of mine was from the reserve next to us. He was brought up in the same way I was, with a real heavy emphasis on Indian values. Somehow he made me feel really uncomfortable. I couldn't quite put my finger on it but there seemed to be something he did not approve of.

I talked to him afterwards.

He looked at me sarcastically and said, "You know, Tommy, there ain't that kind of thing going to happen here. You know why? Because everybody here just not been treated as bad as some of those people down there where you were talking about. If anything heavy starts happening, then you are going to see a lot of people copping out. Besides, there ain't nobody going to start that kind of thing here. There ain't nobody with the gumption that's dumb enough. Those that are smart enough to organize, know better."

Man, that made me bitter. I said to him, "How in hell are we going to do anything if there are people like you who tear our people down all the time? There are enough people doing that without our own people adding to it."

He looked at me straight in the eye and said, "I know how

easy it is to blame everything on Whitey. There are times when I get the anger boiling inside me and I do hate them. Them are the times I drink or go on a rampage of partying just to let it cool inside of me. At home though, I always have a steady reminder from my family what a shitty and weak way that is. I know that we have to use every measure of politics to achieve what we want but we must do it without violence for violence sake. I know that there are Indians in other places who have died defending their people from unwarranted attack and unwarranted violence in the name of law and order. You try to explain the difference between being forced to use violence to defend and beating people over the head just because you are angry. You try to explain that to a bunch of kids that figure it is in to be a Bro and to be that you had to want to kill every stinking white man around."

He lowered his voice a little and continued, "Just try to explain to them that respect for all races is the most important thing that some of the so-called militant Indian tribes go by. They demand respect for their own tribe and only give respect to those who respect them. Sometimes, in demanding respect, they're put down. But, it means they don't tolerate things like aggression because they truly believe one race is not superior over another. Everytime I try to talk about that, everybody looks at me like I was a bug or something. They think like you. They think I'm some kind of sissy pants or a chicken shit."

I listened with surprise until he finished. I hadn't known Chuck thought about them things. He was always very quiet, always listening. I knew he had a pretty good education. I thought maybe that had something to do with how he was talking. I kind of thought of him as brainwashed.

I answered, "What the hell! You talk almost like a sissy pants but I have heard others say the same thing. I guess, myself, I seen some things you people around here haven't. I don't think the white people have one ounce of respect for any Indian anywhere. If we don't push, we will get beads and blankets again. This is our big chance. You were brought up same as I was. Our people been resistance people from the first. We can't be afraid to act. You know we been fighting all these years for our people to come to this same understanding so we could stand together to do it. We aren't going to sit back and diddle anymore and wait for them to give it to us."

I didn't stop there, I continued, "As their population grows they need more and more. A lot of them things lie in our reserves or in lands not settled under treaty. They will find more and more devious ways to steal it from our people and humiliate them with their bullshit social programs in place of what they take. While more and more of our people die off from despair. That's the only kind of settlements they are willing to give us. That's the only kind of respect they are willing to give us."

A lot of the guys listening nodded their heads and waited for Chuck's reaction.

Chuck sat there with that look on his face again. He said, "You sound good, Tommy, I just don't think its a good idea to feed anger and hate. I think that if we are going to be strong and really do it, it must be done with a lot of planning and strategy and logic. Not a lot of high emotionalism. That can ruin us. That kind of energy demands outlet and sometimes the outlet is just not the right action to take. We may defeat our own purposes that way. We got to be able to act, yes, but what actions we take are critical. We have to be relentless, yes, but we can't allow our leaders to be neutralized through the petty courts system or though assimilationist press that is biased. Anger, when it is uncontrolled and directed towards anything and everything, is dangerous even to itself. You might see that in due time with this. I can't look forward to that happening. I hope there is enough good strong leaders to see that the actions are directed and controlled toward achieving a common goal. I wish you well, my brother." With that he turned and left.

I felt bitter about that for awhile but I never really thought
about it too much. I had other things to attend to, that
were more important. Meetings, rallies and talks, to name
a few.

The young Chiefs in our area continued to press for
demonstrations and roadblocks. They had gathered a large
force of people who followed them to meetings and talks.
They encouraged the young people to attend. They encouraged
anger in loud and long bitch sessions, where people of all
ages would get up and rant and rave.

I would feel the emotions soar anytime those meetings
were held. It was almost as if people were, for the first
time, able to express their anger. I knew that others felt
it, too. All kinds of issues were discussed, from the cut-
off land claims talks to petty local issues.

It was a busy spring and summer, with roadblocks in
the Merritt area being threatened and meetings being held
at the Indian Land Claims Center in Victoria. One of the
chiefs had said that, possibly, there would be Indian violence
unless the province agreed to settle land claims. The meetings
grew more and more emotional as the people talked more and
more anger.

Information was being spread around to the public to
try to educate them as to the real situation regarding Indian
grievances. Surprisingly, there were many non-Indians
who were sympathetic to what the leaders had tried to
get across. A big effort to get the support of church
organizations paid off. The United Church issued a statement supporting Indian land claims. I knew that counted
for something.

In June of that year, a large protest rally was held at the
Parliament Buildings in Victoria. Nobody seemed to be
really clear, at that point, whether it was the general land
claims or the cut-off land claims that was the issue. A
definite distinction was never made at the meetings.

The rally was good. It wasn't real heavy like those ones

in the States. It was more like a big parade or show. The
police stopped traffic and escorted the marchers. When we
had reached the parliament buildings there were crowds
of onlookers. Some people had cheered, most just gawked.

Almost all the demonstrators wore chokers, blue jeans
and headbands on their long hair. A drum group led the
singing and the circle dances. Feelings ran high as people
shouted and sang loud to gain the attention of the press.
CBC cameras, radio and newspaper people were everywhere.
Loud and demanding speeches were made by the U.B.C.I.C.
representatives.

Nothing seemed to have been achieved at that rally, as
far as committments by the government. For our people,
though, it was the biggest demonstration ever held in B.C.
More importantly, it definitely served as a unifying force.
It made everybody know what everyone else was feeling
like.

Somehow, though, things just didn't seem to have been
taken seriously, by some of the leaders. A few of the younger
radicals said that. I had felt the same way. I thought that
it was the right time to do something. It had seemed to
me that the people were ready. There didn't seem to be
any debating necessary or a bunch of resolutions and
motions passed. You could feel the concensus of the
people.

I had hoped that there would be some strong action
proposed by the Chiefs, after the rally. Nothing happened
though except more meetings in which loud and angry
speeches were made. It had seemed that it would take a
little longer for anything to start rolling.

I was frustrated and impatient, so, when I heard that
there was an armed takeover in Kenora, I headed that way.
The Indians there wanted a park, which had been taken
from them, returned. A ban on non-Indians was being
maintained in the armed roadblock. To me, now was the time
to go and find some action.

I got a few people together and we left the following day. We arrived in Ontario a few days later but we never got near to the park. We got stopped in a town just before Kenora.

I had been told that there was a real red-neck attitude about Indians in that area. It was true. We got hauled in the local jail and held without any real reasons. The damn cops were really ugly to us. Sure, I had a record, but I didn't think that gave them the right to hold us. However, I didn't want to end up in jail again for any reason, so I kept my cool and my mouth shut.

One of the guys, named George, raised hell about being there for no reason, everytime somebody came to talk to us.

They questioned us, gestapo-like, making accusations and wanting us to agree with them. We learned from their questions that they thought we knew something about an arms load to Kenora expected from B.C. An offer was made to George. He told us that they had suggested he tell them everything and they would go easy on him. I never was really sure why they kept picking on him.

It was insane, almost funny, though we knew these guys were serious. I didn't have a clue what they were referring to. They had obviously made some connection just because we were from B.C.

Finally, after we spent about two weeks in jail being questioned, they released all of us except George. He was kept because of contempt for the law. At least that was what they said. Contempt wasn't exactly the word I would have used for what we all felt.

They made it clear that we had best head back to B.C. instead of Kenora or we would join George. I didn't have to like it but I listened. I sure didn't want to join George. I wanted to get the hell out of there. I told the other guys I was going to let this one pass and head back. Some things were pointless to push.

I had a feeling something was about to happen at home. I knew that the action in Kenora would trigger something, because of the feelings of some of the younger people.

I headed back to Vancouver where I knew I could get caught up. Sure enough, things were buzzing when I got there. An armed camp had been thrown up in the interior. A chief was angry because of the suffering of his people, without adequate housing. A highway running through the reserve was being blocked and a toll was set up to collect money from motorists passing through. The people threatened to close the road permanently if no action was taken by Indian Affairs.

I caught a ride in one of the cars that was headed that way. On the way, there was talk about guns and ammunition supplies. Some plans were made about how to get food and other necessary stuff in.

I sat there and listened to all the talk and wondered who those guys thought they were fooling. I thought that if the going got rough, it wouldn't take much and most of those guys would find some excuse to head back to the city. I found myself thinking of my cousin Chuck's words. Some of those people you could be sure to see at all the demonstrations and rallies. I sure hoped they were more serious.

It was almost dark as we neared the blockade. We got stopped outside the reservation by some cops that were patrolling. They were pretty civilized to us. They knew which way we were headed but didn't seem too concerned or determined to stop us. Obviously, they thought about the same thing that I did.

When we got in, we were searched and questioned by some of the security on duty. We were told that everything had to be cleared with security without question. We were told that there were a lot of angry people that were trying to get through and that we weren't to let any white people past the blockade. All kinds of plans were made and there were lots of security meetings. I kept quiet and helped as much as I could.

The next few days were pretty heavy. Press people arrived and tried to get photographs and interviews. They seemed to get a real charge out of having a gun pointed at their cameras. Cars and trucks with rednecks came at all hours and harassed us any way they could.

Donations of all kinds came in. A lot of it food and needed sleeping gear. One thing bothered me as I helped maintain watch. I was not really sure what the actual goal was and whether or not anyone thought about it. I knew living conditions and poor housing and the lack of jobs, was the reason for the anger. I wondered what the blockade itself was going to force. I had heard the young chief from the local area talk. He was right to be angry. It had just seemed that action was happening out of sheer frustration without a clear plan as to what to demand.

I stayed only a few days. I kept on comparing the stuff that happened in other places with what went on with the blockade. I kept thinking that there should be a solid thing to hold out for. I didn't want to hang around and get into a hassle because of what I thought. However, people had turned out a lot more serious than I had thought, so I wanted to support the action somehow.

A deep feeling of anger and determination surged through the camp. The feeling seemed to be that violence of some kind would happen. I got to feeling pretty tense about internal things, so I left.

I knew a lot of public relations needed to be done on the road to tell the people something of what was going on. I chose to do that. I thought that if I was needed, I could be reached pretty quickly.

Support came from most Indian organizations. I had read in the paper that the U.B.C.I.C. was in support of the blockade. I wondered how they would show their support if things turned violent.

In travelling around the province, I found that some of the Indian people were against the blockade. In talking to them, I found out a lot of them were afraid of a back-lash against all Indians. They seemed to be afraid that things might get worse for us and not better. They said, all we would do is alienate people from our causes, and us from those who were sympathetic to us. Also a lot of people didn't like it too much because they found it really hard to criticize non-Indian people. They never seemed to stop and think that non-Indian people criticize us simply by their attitude. For that reason, it seemed to me, the more talk by us the better it was to tell people that it's okay to be an Indian. We had to tell them that it's okay to dress and talk different and especially that it's okay to practise caring for each other in our customs. Saying all of that was necessary.

We spent a lot of time saying those things over and over again. We said things to them like, "It's okay to sing and feel good dancing with the songs of our people. It's okay to be just what we are. This way some of the hurt that is killing our people and damaging them beyond any help will be overcome." It was hard, though, to talk about how that ties us to the land. It's hard to show just how much our pride, our culture and our lives all have their roots in the land. It's not easy to explain that to protect and attempt to regain control over it is really the way to protect our own lives as Indian people. It was not easily apparent that it is really the only means we have. I began to see that more and more clearly.

I think a lot of people never understood the significance of that concept. Many of the leaders simply saw a chance to add to the political power of Indian organizations. Many of them thought of it as a way, perhaps, to press the land claims issue so that compensation could lead to better economic conditions on the reserve. I felt what was more important was that the longer and harder the struggle was kept up, the better it would be for our people.

I talked to one guy that was pretty aware of some of the

issues. Sam said, "The government would never agree to negotiate freely, they would be agreeing to too much. It would cost them not only money but also they would lose a large measure of control."

I sat there and looked at Sam. Then I laughed. I said, "Shit, you know what I think about that? I think the worst thing the government could do at this point is to agree to negotiate. You know why? It would kill the whole thing. In the long run the government would be the winner. Because everybody would just go back to the same old routine, waiting for handouts and getting drunk. Nobody would care. Now they care because they are needed. They are a part of it. They are full of hope and feelings that the future can be changed. For that reason they feel pride in being Indian, because they are changing things. The struggle needs to be escalated and kept going until the people can develop to a point where they don't fall back again. If that doesn't happen then a lot of people will be turned off, never to make an attempt again."

I went on to say, "Whatever develops out of this would be good for everybody. Even the white people. Once our people pull themselves out of this mess, they could contribute much more to all of society. I really hope the leaders understand that. Sure, we need victories but we need to hold our ground and struggle longer. We need the healing it brings. Not too many realize the biggest victories won't be in politics and deals made, but in the putting back together of the shambles of our people in their thinking and attitudes."

Sam looked at me and said, "Slash, you sure got some funny ideas. If you said to the people out there at that roadblock, that agreeing to negotiate is the worst thing right now they would think you are nuts. So would the National Indian Brotherhood who just passed a resolution that Canada is still owned by all of the Indians. Certainly, the Union of B.C. Chiefs would tell you that simple negotiations on land claims in B.C. has been a priority for over fifty years with Indian organizations in B.C. They would tell you that's what this has all been leading up to, and if we get something out of that then we will be victorious. That's all everybody is pressing for. I can't really see how the social conditions of our people ties in with that. It's all a legal question, to be dealt with on paper. If we get some land back and we get some money in compensation, maybe things will get better on the reserve. That's what the Chiefs are saying. But everybody will have to take care of their own drinking problems. Maybe if there was more land and money that would help."

I said, "And maybe the problems would still be there, because its root isn't lack of money or opportunity. Maybe lots of money would just cause more people to die a lot faster. Things wouldn't change. You know why? The dissatisfaction would still be there. Deep down lots of people would still feel inferior and shitty just for being Indian. They would still feel like they didn't have any ability for anything. They would react in the same two ways that they do now. Some would burn themselves out trying to prove otherwise. At the same time, never really convincing themselves because they still stayed brown and they still saw the contempt in the eyes of simple clerks and it hurts. The rest would burn themselves out trying to forget, in copping out. Can't you see, Sam, we have a big chance to change that once and for all, maybe not for everybody but for more of our people. Even if one-quarter of the people come out stronger about being Indian, it would be worthwhile. The heck with what happens in politics. We would grow in numbers because we would pass it on to our kids, and someday there would be better days for our people in the new world."

Sam didn't say much after that but I knew at least he thought better about what I had said.

After some things happened on the inside at the blockade in which one person was wounded, a lot of people became pretty uptight about giving their support. I wasn't sure what had happened; I wasn't there. It was kind of a set-back because the powerful Union of B.C. Chiefs withdrew their support publicly. It was also publicly announced that the support of

AIM was being sought for the blockade. That seemed to set up a line of division where before none had existed. It set up a pro and con situation. From that point on, it appeared that there would be a division.

All that summer, while the blockade was kept up, there were more and more heated discussions at some of the political meetings of the Union. Some of the young people wanted the Chiefs to take a stronger stand. Sometimes they dominated the meetings with their questions and demands. You felt the frustrations of the Chiefs also. They wanted to make the right decisions for their people, but they had never had anything like this to face before.

I remember a meeting I went to in Kamloops. All the way up, I kept feeling like something was going to happen. The crew sang some 49's on the way up. Everybody felt pretty good when we got there. Cars were jammed all over the parking lot. When we walked into the gym where the assembly was being held there were young people like us all the way around on the bleachers. The Chiefs sat at rows of tables in the middle of the floor. There were little cards in front of each area. Only Chiefs were supposed to speak at those meetings, but they didn't stop the young people from going up to the mikes and demanding action. In fact, it seemed like they welcomed those that did go there. It was like they lent support to the Chiefs and pushed them to be stronger in their decisions.

Our Chiefs from the Okanagan took a stronger and stronger stand and were considered to be radical among other Chiefs. They said things like, "Our people are ready for action," and "Our people will not stand for anything less than some real changes." They knew they had the people behind them. There was support all the way, whatever the Chiefs decided should be done as "actions."

I thought that was great. I sure had to respect them, too, for sticking together in anything they decided. They never cut each other down during them times. They were a real strong unit. It was obvious at that meeting and the people picked up on that, all over the Okanagan. I realized that was something that our people up the hill had always wanted to see happen.

As summer turned into early fall, I heard that there was a move to caravan across Canada. The idea of it was to demonstrate all across the country, to educate Indian and non-Indian alike about the grievances of Indian people. Everywhere, stuff concerning Indians went on. Things were humming everywhere. It was a good time for the caravan. The people needed something like that right then.

My mind went back to the D.C. caravan. I thought of that caravan and wondered if there was going to be anything like it. I wanted to go, so I went to Vancouver where it was going to start out. I knew guys that I hung around with would be there. That whole bunch of people would be hot to do something. There was more determination.

When we headed out from Vancouver, spirits were pretty high. There was pretty good press coverage too. Everybody said dissatisfaction with situations on the reserve was the biggest reason for that caravan. Poor housing, poor education, high suicide and death rates and low economic opportunities, were all reasons to confront the government to make some decisions to acknowledge the land claims issue. The people from the blockade said that better housing programs were what they were after.

It was true many people on the reserve were homeless and had to share small and cramped houses. It was true there was almost no employment and little hope for anything better. To us, looking around, we could see the resources the governments were selling to corporations and the land they were taxing people for. It meant the government was taking too much and not giving anything back to the people who the land was taken from. It meant we had no homes, no jobs and often no food, and there was nothing else to do but get drunk or join the movement.

People were mad and frustrated, especially when there were all kinds of condescending articles in the papers about "that militant element" saying Indians would do better to "work through the channels." Hell, even the Chiefs, who were always known to be ultra-conservative, were coming out and making statements in the press about being "angered and embittered with just cause."

About fifty of us started out from Vancouver. More and more people joined the caravan at different points from there. Many were really young people from different reserves. A few of them looked like they were only about fifteen or so. Some were really young chicks. They kind of looked silly for the first few days until they got the hang of how to loosen their hair and wear jeans and old army jackets. All the guys wore reflective shades and red head bands with a hunting knife hanging at the side of their legs. Jeans, of course, were all anybody owned. Those shades really gave the guys a mean look. I guess that's what we wanted. A mean image.

On the first part of the route, the usual caravan stops were made. At Indian reserves and places in larger towns the press would come and take pictures and ask all kinds of questions. Some of those press statements that came out made you lose any belief of truth in newspapers. Some of the wildest statements were being printed about the caravan. Most of it was designed to sensationalize what was going on. It looked good next to all the other headlines from different parts of Canada and the U.S.A. about Indians uprising and protesting and demonstrating and taking over and blockading.

We read about one Tribe declaring war on the U.S. government because it had not signed a treaty with them before colonizing and settling it. That was in Bonners Ferry, Idaho. It was called a bloodless war.

So the caravan made good headlines alongside stuff like that, and the whole country hoped and waited in morbid fascination for something to happen. The press really built them up for it.

Internally, some things surfaced. A rumbling went on through different sections of the caravan about who should make press statements and how we should proceed. It was nothing too serious. A kind of a power struggle went on between at least three would-be leaders. It got worse and worse as we went along. Finally, when we reached Winnipeg where a larger group was ready to join up, things kind of reached a head. We spent a few days there.

The constant pressure and tension effected everybody. So did the fatigue of travelling with a large group and worrying about food and places to sleep and stuff. Some women argued as they aligned themselves with their champions. Jealousies ran rampant sometimes. You just couldn't avoid stuff like that with a lot of young people together. Most of the guys though, only went with one chick they called their "old lady."

Something about the women in that situation was really admirable. They worked harder than anybody realized. Things like no fresh laundry or places to bath and no beds to sleep in didn't phase them. The women worked with their heads in ways which guys didn't to make things run smooth when things got rough. We worked together though. Nobody worried too much about role hang-ups. People just did what they were best at.

The women, though, had some kind of pecking order among themselves that had to be strictly respected by all. If that pecking order gets messed up by the guys and their struggle for leadership then all hell breaks loose. It's really the women who keep things going smooth. All Indian men know that. We learned early from our mothers and grandmothers that it is women who are the strength of the people. We all know it was the women, too, who shake up any system if they get riled. Some of them got pretty riled by the time we reached Winnipeg.

A few of the guys got into dope and drinking along the way, too, which caused a big hassle from some of the guys that tried to be really strict about that. Some of the guys didn't go along with that. Others said hard slogan stuff like, "The only power there is, is down the barrel of a gun." By the time we reached Winnipeg, I was really in rough shape from holding my mouth shut.

I felt shitty as things got heavy, from the day we got there. It was easy to get partying even though I knew I couldn't handle it without getting going for a few days. I knew I was messing myself up again. I knew that I could only do something worthwhile when I was straight and sober, but sometimes I looked at what was going on and I got so down because it seemed like it was all futile. Like it was all just going to be another big mess-up and everybody would end up the worse for it instead of better.

I wanted to get it off my brain for a while. I just wanted to laugh and pretend that all that existed then was bright lights, music and some brew. All I wanted was to cruise with it for then, but waking up was hard, especially when there was a voice in your head that sounded like Uncle Joe and it asked, "What the hell are you doing?" When it said, "You so-called Warrior, you're just a weak chicken-shit good for nothing."

I did sober up, after about a week. I tried to find the rest of the guys I was travelling with. I found out that there had been kind of a split of sorts, with the main part of the caravan continuing on and another bunch with their followers going it separately, and some like me just copping out.

The press, of course, picked up on some of it, and tried to play it up big, but the only statements they got was that a separate focus was being put on the housing situation, and that demands to the government for money to build houses was being pursued. The press couldn't force statements of any kind about rumors of division, but they took their low shots whenever they could. The way things were decided to be worked out, without involving outside press, was good.

I caught a ride with another bunch and attempted to catch up. By the time we got into Ontario, the main part of the caravan had reached Sudbury, where they got some pretty heavy press coverage.

During one of the rallies which got more and more

emotional, a statement by one of the guys was blown all out of proportion. The papers headlined that Indians were going to go into Ottawa with bombs strapped to their bodies in a suicide mission, if their demands to be heard were not met. Counter statements accused the press of sensationalism and "blatant lies." The group of twelve who headed the caravan by then, issued a statement saying a peaceful demonstration was underway and no weapons or explosives of any kind were being carried. They said that the press had misrepresented them since Vancouver and were obviously working to discredit the caravan so that the power of their real intentions would be neutralized.

I bought that. It sure looked that way, from some of the stuff I had seen printed. Also, I knew Indians made good news when they were on "the warpath" and a lot of papers got sold that way. Seemed like everybody was cashing in on that one.

It was things like that which led to the kind of reception we got in Ottawa, the seat of government for the people. We had trouble all the way in. Searches and harrassments were continuous.

The day we marched on Parliament was opening night. We walked two miles through downtown Ottawa and gathered more and more people as we went along. The angry feeling that rippled through the air could be felt in almost all the speeches that were made. A new feeling of determination was also in the air. I knew the press picked up on that, as did others.

On the way towards Parliament Hill, there were some weird people who joined our march. Their signs said that they were communists. I didn't know if anyone knew who they were, or how they tied in with what we were after, or who set them on to us. They started shouting and putting up banners with Commie jargon, and all of a sudden they made the whole thing look like it was Communist spawned.

The people who had organized the demonstration tried to cool the whole thing with those people before they got the upper hand with the press. The press could really play havoc with that situation. The whole purpose of the demonstration could be lost in the shuffle. Somebody had been busy preparing a neutralizing element.

What happened after that was chaotic when we reached a barricade set up by the police and the honor guards. The mood of the whole thing turned ugly. People scuffled and jostled, with abuses being thrown back and forth. Those weird people seemed to be in the right places in the crowd starting stuff. They pushed just enough. Punches with the police were exchanged, then there was a big charge on the barricade to try to break through. Rocks, bricks, placards and bottles flew through the air. Guys rolled around on the ground and got kicked and clubbed. People screamed and kids cried.

Twice the barricade was pushed back as Indians knocked over the police while the honor guard stood behind them, shoulder to shoulder. The last time there was really a hard push, then the riot squads got there. It seemed that they were waiting for a chance to move in as soon as they could. They moved in and started clobbering people and throwing tear gas around. They dragged people away in wagons, some of them bleeding terribly. It was a nightmare. Nobody was ready for that kind of violence by the riot police. It almost was like they had been told to use as much violence as they wanted on the Indians. It seemed as though we had been set up in more ways than one.

I was right there in the thick of things. The police in their riot gear looked ugly up close. Like real aliens. One of them took a swing at me with his club. I grabbed it and twisted and at the same time brought my knee up into his crotch. Jesus, that must have hurt but he wouldn't go down alone and we fell to the ground rolling around. I tried to pull his mask off. I said to him between clenched teeth, "You son of a bitch, I want to see your eyes." For some reason, that really got him going. He wrenched free, grabbed his stick and whacked me across the back. He had meant to get my head, but I moved fast enough so that he got my back instead. Another guy jumped him from behind and they started fighting, then there was a whole crowd of people in a knot with people bumping and falling, getting trampled and bashed on the head.

One kid laid there with his head all bloody, sobbing. I tried to help him up, but we would just get knocked down again. He didn't seem able to hear me at all. Another guy and I dragged him to a bush and laid him under it. He just kept sobbing and groaning while blood ran down the side of his head. I don't know how he made out because then, these three ugly looking police started toward me and the other guy and we went at it. I didn't have anything in my hands to fight with and neither did the other guy, but they never made it to haul us in.

When it finally cooled down, there were a lot of injured people. Somebody said, about three loads of Indians were taken to the hospital, one girl with really serious head injuries. Smoke hung all over and a bush was burning. Broken bottles and bricks were lying around. A whole bunch of the group were thrown into jail, about thirty, I guess.

The press had a field day. They labeled it as "The most violent demonstration ever witnessed on Parliament Hill." Nobody was quite sure who was to blame.

One thing I noticed was, although I had seen thousands of pictures being taken of the aggression and violence being used by the riot police, none of them turned up in the papers. Only really tame versions of what went on were printed. It looked like somebody had told them not to make the police look bad or something.

Charges of police brutality were made by the organizers and the Civil Liberties people. An investigation was carried out, but it was all denied.

One thing never seemed to cross peoples' minds about the whole thing which angered me the most. We talked about it. One of the guys who was in the organizing end of things said, "You know, all our group wanted was an audience with somebody from government. All they wanted was to air their grievances and get some assurances something would be done. Their reasons were valid. If even one of those fat people in government would visit any of the reserves across Canada, something might be understood of what the group was trying to get across. It should be made a requirement for them to visit the poorest of the reserves as soon as they are appointed. Then they might have some insight. It doesn't even enter their minds, or anyone else's. The only Indians they see are the ones assimilated enough to wear ties and suits and speak passing English. Now the people like us, who are just plain, in jeans and long hair, we speak for those poor people on the reserves but they don't want to hear us. They don't even send anyone out to talk to us, like they do for the labour unions and others when they march on the government. Instead, they send out the riot squad to form a barricade to keep us away and beat us up. The group never expected that kind of treatment at all. It's a total shame the way they always treat Indians as if we were dogs or something. All the time knowing they have responsibilities to meet and wrongs to correct." I sure had to agree.

I know a few of the newspapers had tried to say that in a lame kind of way, but they had really focused most on the Communist element during the riot. They had said that Indians would do better not aligning with them. None of them would come right out and ask why the government did not meet with the organizers, even when all the big Indian organizations had thrown their weight behind the demonstrators in pressing for answers. They all had been angered by the whole thing.

All across Canada it added fuel and determination to the frustration and anger. It had been very successful from that point of view. It had acted as a binding force and had solidified in peoples minds where to focus their anger. Things in B.C. took off from that point on. A lot of the Indians from there had been really vocal.

Somehow, after that, we ended up staying at this old stone

mill building. I got there after quite a few of the brothers and sisters had taken it over. Nobody made a big fuss over that. A lot of people stayed there for the next few months. Nobody really bothered them, though the police always kept watch on who was coming and going. Donations of food and things kept coming in as plans were made about what to do next.

I don't know if the group ever got to meet with whomever it was they had wanted to meet with. I kind of hooked up with this lady from Ottawa. I spent a lot of time at her place. She was heavy into dope and partying and it didn't seem like I had anything better to do.

As fall turned into winter, I sometimes went up to the camp at the mill and checked things out. It was always the same. Everybody being Indian, doing artwork and beading or drumming, cooking or just living. Everybody pretty well kept up on stuff that happened around the country.

A report had come out from Statistics Canada that fall which revealed the "cause for Indian rise in militancy." In it were listed the very causes that the caravan people tried to tell the government about. In B.C., the Kelly Report recommended that the government enter into negotiations with the Indians on land claims questions. In South Dakota, the Sioux battled for the validity of an 1868 treaty guaranteeing their sovereignty. In Calgary, the D.I.A. offices were being occupied. I also heard from some guys coming in from B.C. that a large committee of bands in B.C. had formed to pursue cut-off land claims exclusively.

I spent the winter in that city. I hated it, but I couldn't seem to leave. Every day I said, "Tomorrow I'll head out to the Trans-Canada. Tomorrow I'll go home where I'm needed. I don't need this city. I don't need this depression that hangs around all the time, so it pushes me to find what I need to get it off my brain." But Cindy, the girl I hung out with, was always ready to find some action to feel good. She knew all the places and people and she was easy to get along with.

I knew that she was hung up on me. I knew that she thought

I was some kind of hero or something. I liked to flabbergast her with stories about the "Knee" and "D.C." and other stuff I had been involved in.

Sometimes, I talked long tirades to her and her friends about the shit in the world. It was funny, but them times it was like she expected me to solve the problems just because I could see them. She didn't understand that that was what made me feel so angry and helpless all the time. She couldn't see that I wished I knew the answers, but knowing that I didn't made things worse.

I always felt there was something missing, like there was something wrong about the way that things were approached. It seemed like anything we built on anger and hatred was just as bad as what was being done to us. Thinking them things didn't stop me from feeling the frustration though and the gut wrenching hate whenever I would start to talk about it.

For the next long while, I drifted more and more into a depression along with a lot of other people who were at the confrontation on Parliament Hill. I guess it had made a few people wary as well as angry. It became clear, brute force was used for that very reason. However, hurt pride made for a stewing kind of anger that laid low for awhile until the confidence was built up again in people like me.

It was spring before I headed out. I was in real rough shape when I did. I was really boozing pretty steady. It was something warm and sweet in the air that made me decide. By then, the Old Mill Camp had been abandoned by most of the people who had hung around all winter. I got a ride with some people from Vancouver Island. Most of that long trip across the country was just one big long headache. I was sick almost to the point of DT's from not eating and drinking cheap rot gut.

I got off in my home town, feeling like it was doomsday. I called up my sister Josie. She had a phone by then. She came to pick me up at the Indian bar.

Josie walked in and when she looked at me, there was

something that looked like sadness in her eyes. I got up and put my arm around her feeling scared. "How's my Sis?" I asked in a gruff voice. She put her head down and didn't say anything for a good while, then she said in a real low voice, "Tommy, I didn't want to be the one to tell you but it's better if I do instead of Pops and them. We couldn't find you to let you know. Danny died, Tommy. We buried him three weeks ago. He was drinking lots at the end there. One night he just walked out on the highway and got hit. Mom is really broken up and Pops went out and got blasted drunk a couple of times. I know they both fear for you, too. Hell, they didn't even know if you were dead or alive either. They had police bulletins out all over."

I felt like somebody had punched me in the stomach. I couldn't seem to be able to breathe. Things seemed to start slowly spinning and I heard Josie's voice asking, "Tommy? Tommy?" No tears came, just a hard quiet seemed to settle over my brain like a black fog. I couldn't speak. I couldn't think about it. I wanted to turn around and run away. Back to Ottawa, anywhere, anywhere back in time, back to when I could see Danny as a young man, so handsome and strong and quiet and gentle with the horses.

My mind turned around and around as I wondered how I was going to be able to go up to home. I wondered how I could bear what I knew Mom and Pops felt, when I couldn't even look at Josie.

She stood there, dead pan quiet. Finally she said, "I'm not going to leave from here until you come with me. I'm going to wait until you're ready and then I'll drive you up the hill."

It's that I never thought of people I was close to and death. I thought people close to me were somehow automatically going to live forever. I knew my brother had let his drinking get to him. I had known the last time I had come home, he was partying too hard to even come home to the winter dance. I guess partying really wasn't the word to use for what he had been doing. Or, for that matter, what I was doing then.

I wondered if Danny had known that I felt the same things he did. I wondered if he had known a whole lot of our people felt that way about life. Once I heard this girl sing a song that she had made up. I couldn't remember all of it, just little parts. One of the parts had asked, *"Why have you broken the circle, why have you taken my reason, my life?"* I wish I could have remembered the rest of that song. I wished I could find that girl. It could be she might have found the answer. I thought of that song and I thought Danny's death had asked the same question.

I sat there in that bar and thought about them things while Josie waited to take me up the hill to home. In my mind I knew that Danny had died a long while ago. Somehow there had been always the hope that something could change that.

It looked like all the same bullshit would happen or not happen as the case may be. It didn't look like the big stand would be made that could start the long road to recovery for our people. We needed to fight for it but we may have already been weakened to a point where we just couldn't muster it. I wished the damn white man had some understanding of what it was all about. That all their bullshit social programs didn't amount to one ounce of self-help. We had to do it ourselves, our way. I thought it might just show them some things with what was ailing people in their society, too.

I wondered why they couldn't understand that people needed to feel strong. That they need to be able to have choices to make. That it is the struggle for it that heals. I asked myself why all those big shot social scientists couldn't see that? Why our leaders couldn't see that? Why did we always have to be battered to our knees until we were lying flat and empty, then asked to be different, to accept the new world. I thought about how it was our world, too, but too many Dannys had happened. When we got up to fight, each time, it was harder, and fewer and fewer did, and that was frightening.

I thought of them things while I sat there and Danny's

smiling face as a boy burned in my brain. No tears came.

Josie sat there with me for about five hours. She never drank anything but coke. She never talked and neither did I. The bartender came and looked at us and sat a beer for me and walked away. He was used to Indians. He knew better than to try and make some easy conversation, but I felt he was bothered by our silence. I thought of how lots of white people were bothered by that. I never figured out why exactly. When there were no words that needed to be said and feeling was all that was needed, it seemed plain to me what silence was for.

Finally, I looked up at her and said, "Okay Josie." I felt more and more like I had to either go up right then or leave for a long time. I knew how Pops and them would take that. I knew that this was one time I had to think of somebody else's feelings before mine. I knew they would need to lean on me and that it would be hard for me to stay up, but I had to, or we would all go down together.

Josie knew that, too. She got up with me and said, "One thing, Tommy, you'll find things with Mom and Pops different. They can't seem to get themselves together so they get busy doing a whole bunch of stuff they never were into before. Mom plays bingo all the time and now even Pops is going. They are never home anymore. You'll see what I mean when you get there."

I went home and faced the people I most wanted not to, because of their grief. I went home and sobered up. I went home and fed the horses and cows and went out with my Pops. I sat long hours and talked with Mom.

All that time I thought about the things that made Danny into what he had been. I knew the same things were happening to me. I wondered what the answers were besides confrontation. Was there any other way that we hadn't thought about? I looked at my Pops and Mom. They were such good people. They had tried to give us the best background in raising us as they had. Somehow they felt they had failed.

They felt that way, too, about our beliefs. Mom told me they hadn't put on a dance that winter.

She said they had neglected to do it because "they just couldn't get around to it." She said, "You know, Tommy, even before Danny died it seemed like he was gone already. You were gone, too. Josie, she don't come around too much anymore. She's living with another man and he don't like our ways. Wayne decided to go to college and get to be learning business stuff so he can work in the Band office. Jenny, she's just running around all over. We hardly see her and when we do she don't look at us. I think she's using dope, stuff that they smoke. You know. Pops, he went on a couple of binges. I guess he just hurts too much inside, when he walks around here and tries to keep the ranch up and ain't nobody here to take over or help him. None of you care to live good on this land here. He gets lonesome for his boys. You should be working along side him, Tommy, you and Wayne. Long time ago the sons paid their folks back when they started getting old by taking over and giving them grandkids to be happy over. Now we just by ourselves in this old house. The dance, we put it up for you kids, you know, to make you strong. What good is it if none of you is there, so we let it go. I got nobody to cook for and get mad at and Pops got nobody to share his time with. I guess we just better off dead, too, Tommy."

I couldn't say anything to that. I knew that's how both of them felt. I didn't know what to do about it. I tried to explain to her as best as I could why I was doing what I was.

I told her, "I wish that the others would think about coming back and settling down. At least one of them to stay with you and maybe give you a couple of fat little grandkids to play with. It can't be me. I have no feeling inside of me. Once I thought that I could come home with one lady, but she got swept up and washed away when things started happening. I swore then that I would spend the rest of my life fighting for the things she got wasted for. I think about her sometimes now and I can't really quite remember how she looked. That's scary. It seems like I need to remember every detail about her. I need to keep it alive because it's my reason to burn myself out doing what I am doing. To me she is all that was taken from our people. Maybe someday we will be healed, if we could just keep it going."

She nodded as I went on, "People like me have to keep it going and people like you are the ones to get hurt. I seen a lot of people exactly like you in lots of reserves when I travel. They walk around with a sadness and a question in their eyes, wondering where their sons are and why they can't be home where they belong. Some of them know there is a war going on and their sons are fighting in it, but they really can't see how we will win without losing too many of our best. They can see that we are fighting without weapons. They know we have to do it or all our people might be soon gone, but they still wish us to come home. Every year more and more die from drugs, alcohol and suicide. Every year the prison and skidrows get fuller and fuller with Indian people, and the reservations get smaller and smaller as white developers get richer. What's the use of fooling myself or you? I can't live at home knowing these things and not try to keep moving with those who are giving up their home life to change those things."

I paused, then continued, "A lot of us don't have any answers. Sometimes things are too heavy and we get down and party for awhile. But when we are needed, anywhere at anytime, we're ready. It's ones like us that understand what we are fighting, because it's also a fight inside each one of us. We know we have to somehow continue to fight. The way all of us are doing it together makes it worth it to stand up again and again, everytime we fall flat on our faces. Maybe the others don't see it clear enough to talk about it but that's what I see."

Mom sat there and looked at me with something like pain in her eyes. She said, "Then why don't you quit your drinking and doping? I ain't dumb, I can see what you're doing to your body and head. Tommy, you and so many others just can't seem to see that the answers are right under your noses. You're running around all over the country raising hell along with those others like you, and all you get for it is hurts. You're just adding your number to those we lost, like your brother Danny. We don't want that. We want you to be able to help our people by using your smartness that was given to you for that. You ain't any good to anybody the way you are. You and young people like you are our hope. Us old ones, we already failed, we already weren't able to make any answers, but you, you believe strong in what's right. You ain't brainwashed and you got a good education. Now you acting the same as those who ain't got parents teaching them any better. That was the same with Danny. The rest now, too. How come? What did we do wrong? How you gonna change the world? How you gonna fight, as you say, for your people, if you do the very stuff that you are fighting against? Most of them think this is a land claims fight, you know. It is and yet it's more than that, that's what everybody overlooks. You can see it. I can tell from what you say but you can't seem to put it together somehow to come out right. Could it be that you are doing it for the wrong reason? Answer me that, Tommy."

I knew what she meant. I had thought about it sometimes. I had always came up with the same things. My answers were that we had to continue to push and raise hell and get the people worked up. We had to try to win some victories, and we had to try to get the government to listen to our demands. In land claims, in Band government, in overall policies in the D.I.A. We had to continue to show the wrongs and the injustices and try to correct some of them. In doing that we could win some victories for our people, and most importantly gather strength through the whole process.

Sometimes, though, the whole process seemed harder than imaginable, especially when things like the Parliament Hill clash happened. Especially when some of our people, who had the guts to take up really hard stands, were forced to compromise for things like freedom from going to jail. Things like that hurt those of us that tried to hang in there for as long as we had to. The stands that were made were for real injustice that should have been dealt with by the authority that was in place to do that. But no, it had seemed they were always so hung up on proving their superiority they didn't see the damage that they did overall to people, just by not listening. It went on and on, and more and more of our people suffered the consequences.

I stayed home that spring as the country around the Okanagan turned fresh and new. It was one of the most beautiful times of the year. All the trees sprouted little green leaves and flowers of all kinds bloomed between the sage and cactus. The hills were covered in a soft green that turned rich grey. Soft blue and powdery mauve covered the distant hills as the light would fade into deep velvet when the nights came. Meadow larks called in the early morning along with the "heap" "heap" of the blue grouse mating call.

I missed all those things when I was away. I missed them like the language of my people. I slept good at night when all I heard were owls and frogs and maybe sometimes a coyote laughing far away. Something about the richness of the nights, without lights and the sounds of the city, was healing. Like a warm blanket it wrapped around me and warmed me to the soul. The hard things inside me melted and I finally cried the tears for my brother whose death was the death of many. I cried the tears that were for them all. The warm, living earth breathed under my feet and the spring with its new life sent a song of promise. The pain of knowing that my brother would not walk those hills again was easier to bear.

Late in the spring, around the end of April, Mom and Pops started to feel a little better. They were beginning to visit around a bit. I kept after Josie to bring her kids to the house more and more. Her new old man didn't like them much anyway. Pops and Mom sure liked them around. They seemed to sparkle when the kids learned new Indian words and things. Mom was just like an old hen around them. There were three of them, Josie had from Clyde. Two girls and a boy.

The boy, Kelly, was the oldest. He was Pops' favourite, of course. I couldn't help it. I loved the little guy, too. I took Kelly up in the hills sometimes and told him some of the stuff that Uncle Joe had talked to me about. I showed him how to kill a grouse with a sling and how to snare a rabbit. I spent many days up there with him, feeling his excitement and seeing the wonder in his eyes. Pops was the same way. He sang the songs for Kelly while he showed him how to sweat and talked to him about all the important things.

I hated Josie when she came back to get them. Every time the kids had been gone for a while, they acted different when they came back. They talked about city stuff.

Mom and Pops moped around when they were gone. Mom went to the bingos every night. Pops went to go see some "friends". They ended up snapping at each other more and more. The house got neglected, and Pops put off stuff that needed to be done around the ranch. I got itchy feet. I wondered what had been happening around the country.

It was during one of them times that I heard that the meeting in Chilliwack was a real powerful one. A lot of young people there pushed and pushed, and finally, the emotions of all the people there joined, and a big decision was made. From what I heard, it was one of them times when the whole assembly feels the same thing at the same time. The people I talked to about it said, "You should have been there. You can't describe it, everybody just knew together because the feeling was so powerful."

The decision had been made to reject the Indian Act and all government funding until there was a settlement of land claims in B.C.

I thought about what that Elder at the Band meeting had tried to explain to the people, and I agreed with him more and more. The people had seemed ready to push for the larger question. They were ready to make a stronger stand in the face of the controlling tool that the government used, through their D.I.A. monies and programs. The people had rejected all of it, to settle the whole land claims question, not just little issues. I felt excited and pretty good about the whole thing. Hope built up again.

I hadn't gone to the meetings because of the way things were at home, but I had been kept up on everything by my cousins. Many of the young people from our reservations attended all the gatherings. They had been encouraged by the Chiefs to attend and back the Chiefs all the way. They did, too. I knew that my cousins had been excited about it because they referred to the signs they carried at the rallies, saying "B.C. IS INDIAN LAND" and "OUR LAND IS NOT FOR SALE." Those were the slogans they shouted at the rallies and demonstrations.

My cousins saw the rejection of government funds as a way to become independent, using our land and our resources. They saw it as a way for us to break out of the welfare cycle. It was a way they could say, "Screw you, D.I.A., we don't need you and we can prove it. We'll do things on our terms now, not yours."

To me, that had seemed to be the most important point of the whole thing. I thought it was that attitude that was going to make for rapid changes, if we held it together long enough for the people to gain the confidence they needed. I thought how desperately we needed to be able to do it. The one great hope that I saw looming out of the whole thing was that point. I realized that settling land claims might really happen, but only as a secondary achievement. The real achievement would be to raise our people up off their knees.

I talked with Mom and Pops constantly about it. I tried to let them see my life was not being wasted like Danny's if I could continue to help some of these things take hold in the younger ones' eyes. They began to agree more and more with the things I told them.

When the whole issue kind of exploded right on our home ground, we were ready. We got a notice that there was an occupation of the regional D.I.A. offices in Vancouver. I was thinking about heading down there, when one of my cousins came up the hill and told me that the offices in Vernon had been forcefully occupied for a short time. There was another occupation being planned for that next week. This occupation was to be a surprise. We would just walk in and take over.

I decided to go and help out any way I could. I told my Mom and Pops about it and asked them to round up some food and other things to bring once the occupation was in full swing.

I caught a ride up there with some guys from the res. Everybody was buzzing about the whole thing. The video guy for one of the Bands was there riding along. He was all rigged out. He sure was a funny guy. Everybody knew he had some kind of smarts with electronic equipment of all kinds. He did do magic with it. He was always at the scene of all the demonstrations and stuff, shooting and recording everything that happened.

I felt pretty good about that, because I thought that later someone might be able to look at those tapes and understand what really happened, even if they weren't there. Maybe even our kids.

The sun was shining and everything sparkled when we got to Vernon. It was a warm day. I knew things would be good. We had been told that nobody was to move in until the agreed time. At that time, a signal would be given and everybody would move in from all directions at once and proceed to the top floor of the building where the occupation would take place.

We saw cars beginning to to pull in and park on some of the side and back streets nearby. Finally, we saw some of the Chiefs go to the front and get together. It had been our signal to move in. Everyone moved in at once from all directions. People were there that I hadn't even seen. They seemed to come out of nowhere. By the time the Chiefs were inside where the offices were located on the top floor, all the rest of the people filed in up the stairs and filled the hallway.

The staff seemed surprised to see so many people at once. One of them said, "What's going on? Is this an occupation again?"

One of the Chiefs answered by reading a statement, "The Bands of this district are now assuming control over these offices. All personnel are requested to either leave immediately, if they do not wish to participate in this takeover, or indicate their willingness to support our occupation. We request a meeting immediately with the superior official in this office. You will be informed when and if you are to return to work. The security heads assigned to their tasks will see to an orderly dismissal of all staff and set up and maintain a barricade at the entrance to this building. No press statements are to be made by anyone in this occupation under any circumstances, unless they have been approved by the Chiefs' Council. Those of you participating in this occupation will be informed by security of areas designated for certain things. Please follow their orders without question or you will be removed from the premises immediately. There will be no violence or destruction of property or abuse of the telephones. Only authorized calls are allowed. Should there be danger or threats on lives, there will be an immediate security enforcement of how the situation must be handled."

With those words, the occupation began. People arrived all day. Meetings and meetings went on all day. The head official, as well as R.C.M.P., came in at different times to meet with the Chiefs. All the different work details and watch shifts were worked out. Food kept coming in, and people from all the reserves around came in and went to the meetings and offered encouragement.

The drum group brought out the drum and started singing the D.I.A. song. It was a pretty popular song. It was originally made by a guy in the States. The song said, "D.I.A. don't you change me, don't you try. We don't want your white man ways no more, Custer died for your sins. We put an arrow in his back and we got one for you." Some of the guys would say, "We stuck an arrow in his ass and we got one for you," and everybody would laugh. Those D.I.A. people that were listening sure didn't like that song.

Old people, kids, women and all the tough AIMer's sat together all over the place just talking. Some carved and did art work and other things as the days passed. We were told that we would stay in occupation until we had assurance that this district office would be closed for good.

The Chiefs said that this office was no longer necessary. They said that the staff in each Band office could carry out the jobs that were done by the D.I.A. staff. Only they could do it better because of being Indian. Because they were a part of the reserve they would have a better insight into most of the problems and be able to deal with things better than any non-Indian. The Chiefs said that a large percent of the dollars allocated by Treasury Board for services to the Indians under the Indian Act was used up by the D.I.A. staff, who knew little or nothing about the real situations on the reserves.

They said that our Band offices were terribly underfunded to carry out the tasks for the members. Such things as shortages of funds for education and housing had been identified as common problems on all the reserves.

Some of us got together and counted up the numbers of people employed to service us, and counted the number of staff cars they had and their salary range as civil servants, and the figure had been appalling.

The people knew that many of the problems of shortages could have been eliminated if Bands had been able to use that money. Also regulations and restrictions to its use was talked about. The problem pointed out was that there never seemed to be any money to do any worthwhile things our way while there was always lots of welfare money which kept the people dependent. The people said they didn't want any more welfare, that what they really wanted was more control over their futures. They said that we didn't need white men running our affairs, that we were quite capable of making the same mistakes they had made, maybe fewer because we knew what our needs were. All these things were discussed over and over.

While telexes went back and forth, to and from Ottawa, and endless meetings and talks were held, the occupation continued. A number of occupations all over B.C. went on at that same time. The one at regional office in Vancouver continued. People came through to ours, at all times, from the other occupations, to bring information and to strategize and to find out what the feelings of the people were.

We watched some of the things being said on T.V. The news was filled with it every day as the talks got more and more heated. A number of threats were coming in daily from the lunatic fringe of the rednecks. A bomb threat came in almost daily by some guys who claimed they were KKK.

Sometimes, it was a little tense, but most of the time things were really good. A deep feeling of being free to do what we pleased together with a kind of quiet excitement rippled under the surface of everything that was done. People were drawn close to each other like they were brothers and sisters. It was a feeling that was there all the way through. Everyone was made to feel equal in the decisions being made.

One of the most exciting things that happened was the learning by the young people from the old people. That went on constantly. The old people never seemed to get tired of talking and teaching about anything they knew about. I knew that a lot of young people changed their minds during them times, about what being Indian was all about. Of course, there were some of the young ones that just took it as a big thrill and a place to snag on to some new girl or guy.

The one thing that everybody felt was good. Everybody smiled a lot and treated each other good whether they were old, young, good looking or ugly. It was what I remember best about the whole thing. I can still feel the great way I felt them times, when I picture it.

The occupation lasted nine days. I stayed throughout the whole thing. It was finally over when the telex came that said that the district office would be closed for good. Everybody was called together for the news and were told that we could now go home. The Chiefs talked with the people about what they had accomplished and assured them that now things would begin to change for our people. Everyone cheered.

One guy from Vernon asked a question I had been thinking about but hadn't known how to ask. He said, "Now that this office has been closed and they have agreed, does that mean the money that was used for these staff and the office and cars will be turned over to the Bands? Seems to me, that we own all this here and this is the reason we occupied. Do we have their assurance on that? That is more important than this office shutting down. You know they can set up a new office anywhere they want. Just getting them to agree to shut this one down isn't enough, I don't think. We have come this far, we can't give in at the first until we get all we came for."

One of the leaders looked at him like he was joking. Another said, "Closing this office is symbolic. Now its up to us to maintain the power and use it to build strength in our own offices to better our people. That's what we came for and that's what we got. We made our point. Now we can go home and get to work to change things."

Everyone got quiet for awhile, then another older man spoke up and said, "To me it's not just symbolic. To me all this equipment and all the files and records in here belong to us just as much as the money that is being used to keep this stuff. Do you know there are secret files they keep here? Why are there secret files? I know why, we went through some of them. They have stuff on Indian people who work best with D.I.A. They call these people 'good D.I.A. men.' They also have stuff on people who are labelled trouble makers. Do you know that an eighty-six year old blind man is called 'a dangerous radical, capable of violence.' This is an old man that is one of the gentlest people I know. This old man has always acted as an advisor to the people in matters that affect us all. Old Pra-cwa is that 'dangerous radical, capable of violence.' I think this kind of stuff should be stopped. It's wrong. If we close this office we got to not only make sure all the dollars are put into the hands of our own people, but we got to have all the information, so we can go after land claims without being stopped. Settling that one question is why I am here. My rights is my stand."

He got the same kind of look I got a long while ago when I got out of jail. The leaders who were there, looked at each other, almost like they were saying, "Let's humour this guy, I mean gung-ho is fine but there are limits."

One of the councillors from one of the reserves spoke up. He said, "You know something? We took this office over to do away with D.I.A. What do we want the files for? We are starting out new. As for the money part of it, well it is the intention of the leaders here to look very closely at the whole thing. We have to get out of this frame of mind that D.I.A. is the culprit for all our problems. We have to start new and that means us doing the work to rebuild our systems. We have to throw away the old ways of doing things. Especially important will be for us to re-define how our systems work, not just using the same old D.I.A. model. I know it is fashionable with certain people to denounce government and D.I.A., but remember it isn't D.I.A. we are against here. It's the way they do things. That's what we want to change. As for land claims, well that's for the courts to settle, not us."

One of the guys from the movement group sat there shaking his head. He said, "I never thought for even a second we weren't all together in why we were here. It's clear to me as well as those people who travelled all across this country talking about this. The government has a big bureaucracy in place that employs thousands of people to take care of "the Indian problem." Of all the money being spent to keep that system going, very little of it actually goes to solve the problems. The problems are still there and are getting worse. That's why there is all the frustration that led up to this. We have to go all the way now. We have a right to control our own destiny. Right now we are controlled by some honkies who live in eighty thousand dollar houses and drive Lincolns and make 'hard decisions for OUR Indians.' Yeah, I guess we do belong to them, like cattle. Enough of them live pretty comfortable off our problems. They want to keep the problems so they can keep making their living at solving them. I say we got to get control over all our lives. It means settling land claims. Only after that can we make some changes. We can really start solving those problems. You people all heard that song, 'D.I.A., we're not your Indian anymore.'

He looked around at everyone and continued, "Why the hell are we scared of them? If that's how it is, then we just spent nine days for nothing. What did we prove? We proved to them we could make them shut this office down, but what's to stop them from setting up another office? Just for the interim, to regulate affairs until your Chiefs decide what to do, just as that head honcho said this afternoon. What he meant is 'until we can figure out a way to get you to do what we want.' They will find a way, if we give them time. That's been the trouble from a long way back. I think we should stick this thing out until we get a statement from the Minister that total control will be given to the Indian people for their affairs, with a commitment to settle the land claims. If we stop short of that, we will just be fighting for this same thing in another five years or so."

One of the leaders responded. He, a councillor for a southern Band, said, "We have to remember we are not the only people in the province who are in occupation. We must make decisions that are consistent with the wishes of the other Bands in the Union of B.C. Indian Chiefs. Now please let the floor stand clear for the leaders to speak."

I sure didn't have a good feeling about the direction the whole thing took. It left me, and quite a few people, feeling dissatisfied and confused. Most of us weren't really sure what was wrong. It seemed there was a reluctance by some of the leaders to move any further. I supposed they had their reasons. The people were willing to follow the advice of the leaders to the letter, so they went home, but they had been just waiting for action and would have acted immediately if the leaders had directed them. I saw, though, that there would not be any directive telling the people to remain in occupation until there was a stronger commitment. Many of the people left feeling bewildered, frustrated and let down, even though they had been assured that we had won a victory.

I talked with my folks about it when they came up that day. Both were feeling pretty excited about the whole thing. They had brought cow's milk and eggs and some deer meat for the people in occupation. They said it was about time Indian people made up their minds to do something about what D.I.A. had been practicing on us for years.

Pops said, "Now our people are beginning to stand on their feet. We got to help in every way to keep this thing going. It is good. Lots of the old people are really happy about it. Nobody is scared of the agents, the way they used to be. The only thing that bothers us old people is that they think some of the young leaders don't really know what they are doing. They haven't talked about the things that should be done after the shutting down of this office. After the kicking out of D.I.A., there needs to be a plan that can be followed. They need to sit down and plan how the land claims question enters into the whole picture. Once that is settled, then we don't have to be beggars anymore. We still own the rights to all them trees and minerals and all the range and water. The government is busy selling them things to Japan and U.S.A., yet they aren't willing to settle with us about it. What it amounts to is they owe us a lot of back rent because when we say 'settle' we don't mean 'sell out.' We want our back rent for what they used. Even if we have to go to some big court in the world to do it. We are right, that's our biggest defence. We can't give in with the first promise that D.I.A. monies will be given to us to handle. We can't give in with the promise that there will be more D.I.A. money for us to spend. Don't you see, Tommy? That's selling out. We got to stand on our own feet. That's the only way our people are going to be able to come out of the mess they're in, because we will be the ones doing it. We aren't children the way the government wants us to be."

I didn't know what to say to him. I agreed with him. A few of us tried to say it, but some of the leaders talked too fast and didn't want to listen. I told my Pops, "You know that's what's hardest about this whole thing. Everybody wants action. Everybody is emotional and willing to back the Chiefs and leaders up. There has to be some clear directions given to them. Nobody is doing that. Some of the leaders seem to want something different than what we are talking about. Some of them seem to be pushing for more D.I.A. money and programs, and stopping there. Some of them seem to want only a little more control. Some of them seem to be using the land claims question as a way to reach those things, rather than actually wanting to settle that issue."

"Pops," I said, "I'm scared things aren't going to work out so good. I think there's going to be a split over this whole thing. I hope not, because of what it means to all the people. I don't see how we'll get around the question unless we really do get together."

He nodded and said, "I know. One thing makes it all worthwhile, though. Now there are more and more people starting to think the way we do. Even if a lot of the young ones don't know all the stuff the old people talk about, they are starting to feel strong inside, and they have some sense of knowing what is right. It has started and it will not end, no matter what comes out of the stand right now and no matter what actions the government or others take. In the long run our people are gaining ground. Just you stick with everybody in everything they're doing and keep pushing them to go all the way and not stop just at the first candy stick handed out. Never give up even if there's only a handful of you."

We headed home after that. A lot of the people were tired and needed time to rest.

At home things picked up a lot. Pops and Mom felt good. They held a big dinner feast. All the relatives from nearby went to it. Many of the old people visited during that time. It was great. For the first time in quite a few years, I saw all my family together. My big surprise was all of the young ones. There were more than I could count. All the ones who were just kids when I started moving around had kids of their own.

It was strange, the feeling I got. I felt lonely and left out as I sat there watching my cousins, and even my younger brother Wayne, with their wives and kids. I saw little Kelly and I felt my chest get warm. I realized that's how it must feel to be a father, only a lot stronger. I had this feeling that my whole life was slipping by like a film without sound, like I had never really lived. It was as if I had been just an actor, acting without being really part of the scene. I had never felt anything real except other peoples' lives and concerns. I felt like I wasn't real, like I could just fade away into nothing.

I had to get up and walk out to the hills for awhile. I went up and sat on a hill overlooking Pop's place from where I could see for miles around. I saw the town and the roads, and I saw the house with all the people down there, all busy visiting and enjoying their families. They were living. I sat there and looked and thought for a long time about my own life.

I asked myself some questions then that I hadn't wanted to think about before. I asked myself what I was and what I was going to be from then on. I didn't like the answer I got for the first question. The second question was one that I hadn't even thought about.

The thing I realized then was that I would have to spend some time searching for what I really was, as an Indian. I didn't know anything when it came down to that. I didn't know a lot about really Indian things. Before that, when I came near to looking at it, I got very uncomfortable and tried not to think much about it. I had spent a lot of time convincing myself that we were the same as non-Indians in every way, except that we were oppressed and were angry. Sometimes there were things, though, that would be said or that would happen that were not quite explainable.

Some of those things bothered me a lot, but I could never put my finger on why. Some of those things had to do with medicine ways, like the Winter dances, and other things that were practiced by our people. Even though I had grown up close to those things, and I felt something happen inside me when I heard the songs and stuff, I had never really tried to find out anything about it. It seemed to me a big part of what was missing from inside of me and the reason I couldn't feel anything except bitterness and a compulsion to go with the action was tied up with understanding that. Without finding what was missing, I felt I could easily slip into oblivion like my brother Danny.

I thought about those things, sitting there watching my family talk and be happy together. I thought about those things during the rest of the summer, as things exploded around the province.

So many things were going on all at once even the newspapers and television couldn't seem to keep up. Roadblocks were being thrown up sporadically everywhere in the province over the cut-off land issue. Occupations of D.I.A. district offices in different parts of the province were in progress. Sit-ins and demonstrations in government offices and on Parliament Hill were continuous. Rallies at almost every Band in the province went on to keep the people informed on all the stuff that was happening.

Most Bands had rejected all government funding and had

closed down their Band offices. No monies were being spent for any programs like welfare, education and economic development. Money was scarce, except for the donations that were being collected at all the rallies and at all the gatherings. People were urged to harvest all Indian foods and exercise their aboriginal rights in their traditional territories to do that. They were encouraged to plant gardens and begin trade patterns with other Bands and tribes to spread the food around to insure nobody went hungry.

Everywhere, on every reserve, there was a feeling of high activity and energy. If people weren't occupying or attending rallies they were busy hunting, fishing, berry-picking and planting gardens. Wherever there was a gathering people brought out the drums and sang the protest songs and the friendship songs. Almost all the people grew their hair, and wore chokers and beads and blue jeans.

A strong feeling of unity persisted among the people. Nobody questioned which Band or which Tribe a person belonged to; everybody was Indian and that was good enough.

It seemed for a while we were going to make it. It must have seemed that way for a while to the government as well. We heard some reports that a statement had been issued to the R.C.M.P. which said that Indian people were the biggest threat to national security since the F.L.Q. thing in Quebec.

Attempting to break out of the government's economic grip must have sent them into a virtual panic. Some of the measures they took were ridiculous. Much of it was clearly over-reaction.

In other parts of the country and in the U.S.A., all kinds of things were happening to indicate a backlash. The news was filled with it. Some of the articles that I came across were definitely propaganda, deliberately set out to make Indians look bad. Most of it was designed to make them look militant and a threat to the safety of ordinary people.

Throughout all of that happening I simply went through the motions of participating along with everybody else.

I was looking for some answers to my own questions. What was the whole thing about? What was being Indian about? Somewhere way down inside there were some things that I couldn't speak to anyone about. I knew there were some things that science and technology could not answer adequately for me as an Indian. I realized I had feelings that arose from somewhere, that seemed to be a really old part of me that I couldn't explain away as teachings from my Elders. I recognized the same thing in some of my friends who were asking the old people for guidance and knowledge.

Throughout that summer, I had felt a need to stand for more than being just a mad Indian, ready to do damage. I began to feel a deep pride whenever the songs were sung and whenever the prayers were being held. Whenever some of the young people got together and suggested to each other to have sweat baths so that we could be clean and ask for help in the things that were being done, I felt good. At times, I saw some young people hang around, acting militant and tough while drinking or toking, and I felt like telling them, "Don't do that. We got to be strong and different now. We got to really change. It's our responsibility." At the same time, I felt helpless and ignorant. I didn't know what to do about it.

All the way through to July, I went to blockades and demonstrations. I even helped set up a militant camp on one of the reserves in the Okanagan. Many people who claimed to be AIM stayed at that camp. I had heard all kinds of talk about guns and weapons, or where the action was going to be next, and how to organize to keep things rolling all around the province.

Only a few key people seemed to head the actions and decisions. I watched those people and hoped that more of the things I had started to like would happen. Things like the practice of the old ways of the tribe, and the way it made people feel.

I didn't find much of it though. What I saw were many young people, much like myself a few years ago down at D.C., all gung-ho to act. An Indian power through confrontation kind of attitude. I knew it was necessary for them, in the same way it had been necessary for me, to develop a certain kind of awareness and self-confidence. I was past that. I knew I had to develop further, towards something that would carry me beyond the point of sheer anger and frustration. I couldn't see clear what it was so I didn't do anything. I just waited and watched.

One time I went up to the camp up on the reservation and listened to the talk going on up there. It was an old logging camp that had been abandoned some years earlier. On the old buildings there were slogans painted in red. Some said, "WE WOULD RATHER DIE ON OUR FEET THAN ON OUR KNEES," and "THE ONLY POWER THERE IS, IS DOWN THE BARREL OF A GUN," and "INDIAN POWER—THAT'S US."

In the camp, teepees and tents had been set up. There was a cook shack stacked with food. People were doing all kinds of things; some of it you could call training physically, some of it you could call just passing time. Mostly there was a lot of drumming and singing and talking as people came and went from one rally to another. Quite a few of the people were really young. Everybody there was young, under twenty-five. Many were just teens. No old people were there except when they were brought from the reserve to talk.

I sat there one night, and listened to the talk. I thought of how all of it seemed to be without any kind of realness attached to it, like a dream that we were all living at once. A common dream that we would somehow overtake and defeat the white man and be our own bosses. We would change things for all people for the better. We would no longer have to feel inferior to anybody. Our world would be different. How that was going to be accomplished wasn't talked about, except in terms of "brutalizing" the system and "bringing them to their knees."

I knew there were some specific plans that were laid for certain militant actions, but these were not discussed with anyone who didn't belong to the "in-circle." I didn't.

The in-circle had mainly consisted of radical Chiefs and ex-Chiefs and some people who had been involved with the Red Power and the AIM supporters in Canada. I hadn't been really trusted or liked by some of those people even though I had been a strong supporter of AIM stands in the U.S. I was disliked for daring to question things that were suggested. Sometimes I knew those people were never really sure of whose side I was on. I knew they sometimes felt like I was against what they were doing.

I sat there that night and listened to the talks and then later to the songs. As evening settled over the hills and the night birds called to each other over the voices of the people, I felt a terrible pity for us all. I thought of how we were a bunch of young kids, trying desperately to be Indian in the only ways we knew how. We wore beads and an eagle feather and sang drum songs, and shared our food and our common dream of being the warriors to free the people from the hurts of two hundred years. We wanted to fight somebody to right the wrongs. We wanted to be worthwhile. We needed to be, though this way the consequences would be terrible with defeat inevitable. None of us really understood what we were fighting for or against. AIM came closest to defining it, when one of them said somewhere in something I had read, "We fight for survival, we fight to stop genocide. Our war is real but our enemies are like shadows."

Up in the hills I had heard the coyotes' shrill cries, soft and floating through the air like part of the songs. Shadows had danced as fires lit up rich brown faces and black long hair.

I knew that I would never forget those nights, and I would never be able to listen to the AIM song without feeling the way I had that night.

A burning tightness had filled my throat, and I had felt the sadness move up from my chest and spread outward to my fingertips in waves of hurt as tears came.

I had lived that dream with my people. I had wanted to stand and be proud to be Indian, and have everybody else know that being Indian was special, not something to be forever ashamed of for some unknown reason. I had wanted that more than anything. The success of the movement depended on that, but something had been missing. I had known I had to somehow find what it was that was missing.

CHAPTER FOUR

We Are A People

Late that summer we heard that some F.B.I. agents were slain in South Dakota. We learned that some AIM people being blamed were on the run. I left on the long trail again after that. Somehow it had all seemed to tie in with other things that were beginning to go wrong.

Sometime during that summer, things slowed down as people felt the impact of no funds. With no easy ways to get money on the reserves except through the funds, payments that had to be made weren't made. People's cars and other stuff were repossessed. It was hard on the people that there simply was not any funds for jobs at the offices.

People found many reasons why the funds should be re-accepted. There seemed to be a big split where there was none before in the thinking of the leaders about the rejection of funds and the mandate of the Chiefs.

Around August, most of the blockades had been abandoned, and most of the sit-ins were over. Many Bands took their funds back because of a growing number of people who had expressed concern over "those on social assistance."

Some Bands were outright in their statements that they would gladly take the share of those Bands who still refused their funds. It was a time of deep depression and a growing chaos. Everyone was suspicious of everyone else.

The leaders were busy blaming one another over everything that went wrong. Many people accused the Movement renegades of acting without direction from duly elected Chiefs and Councils.

D.I.A. had a grand time making deals with whomever would listen, wherever there was a chance to breed further division and suspicion. An interim office to service the Central District Bands was set up in Vancouver at regional Indian Affairs office.

Things turned sour all over the place. Nobody seemed to be feeling strong and confident like they had earlier that year. I had thought a lot of it was because of the inaction, but then I realized it had been more than that. People had wanted something to happen. At the same time, all decisions made had been against violence. People, including the press and the public, had been waiting for something violent to happen. When nothing had, it was a real letdown.

One of the main reasons had been that the Bands which had organized the most well attended demonstrations had signed an agreement with the provincial government. The agreement was not to hold any further demonstrations while negotiations over the cut-off lands were held.

Most of the Bands in the Okanagan had been involved with those negotiations, so they had to stop demonstrations. When that had happened, the other Bands which were holding out for settlement of the overall land claims question didn't get the same support for their actions. The actions stopped and there seemed to be nothing to do. A lot of young people were pretty dissatisfied and didn't understand what had happened.

With the reason for the demonstrations gone in the Okanagan, there was no reason to continue the rejection of funds stand, especially since some of the Bands had already talked with D.I.A. about taking funds back.

All kinds of internal upheaval happened with the leadership in the Union of Chiefs during that time, as well, over the whole issue surrounding the rejection of funds. It was pretty clear who had won the round by the time August rolled around. It sure wasn't the Indians.

About that time all the militant youth drifted away from the camp. Somehow they knew that they were no longer needed or even wanted by those leaders who, just months earlier, had driven them around and treated them like celebrities.

Somehow that had bugged me the most. To me it had been like using people and then discarding them when they weren't needed anymore. When tough-looking Indians with the militant image that could sing the drum songs and put the scare on the honkies had been needed it had been fine to have them around. When the confrontation was over, and the agreements had been signed that had spelled out a lot of money, then suddenly the question had been "What are those people hanging around here for? Welfare checks?" Some of those same leaders, who had taken to wearing long hair, blue jeans, army cast-off jackets and red bandanas, had cut their hair and bought three-piecers in order to "look presentable" to government negotiators.

I figured it was a good time to leave. My Mom and Pops had been doing good again since Josie had decided to leave the kids permanently with them. I felt like staying and being with little Kelly, but I felt that I didn't have anything to teach him, while there were some things I had to learn myself.

I didn't know how or where to start, so I left with a couple of guys and a girl from Alberta. They were headed there for a conference on Indian religion. It sounded pretty interesting and I decided to go. I thought maybe I would hear from some of the people from down in South Dakota, where there was that shoot-out in which two F.B.I. agents were killed.

We had been all glad to be on the road again, camping and hustling wherever we stopped. Nobody was into drinking or drugs that I travelled with and that had been good.

During that summer, there had been a growing number of those that insisted that it wasn't Indian to be doing that stuff. At the rallies and blockades those young people had stuck together and demanded that there be no drinking and no drugs at those things. They had asked they be respected for their fight against those things.

I had grown to know quite a few of them and I had a lot of respect for them. I hated it when some of the political leaders overruled those wishes and brought in booze and drugs to some of those gatherings. However, there was a strong and quiet determination by those young people that pitied and despised those leaders for them things.

I lost a lot of respect for some of them leaders during that time, and gained some for others who I felt were the real leaders but were never recognized because they spoke with actions and not words. The group I travelled with was like that.

At the conference, we were given a teepee to camp in and told there would be food served twice a day. I was surprised, there were hundreds of people there. Some were very old and some were young and obviously on the move like ourselves. Many things were new to me.

An arbor was set up where a fire was kept burning continuously by some medicine men. Sweat lodges were going on almost continuously for people to cleanse their bodies and minds. Ceremonies of all different kinds from different areas were going on at night. Most interesting were the talks during the day in the arbor.

Medicine men talked to the youth continuously about returning to the medicine ways of their people. It was said that it was important if they were to conquer the disease that was eating away at the foundations of our reserves. The young people were urged to continue their struggle in finding their true identity.

One old man made a lot of sense to me. It was almost as if he were speaking to me. He said, "Many of you are talking about losing out to the white man. You talk about losing your culture. I will tell you something about that. It is not the culture that is lost. It is you. The culture that belongs to us is handed down to us in the sacred medicine ways of our people. Our strength lies there because it is our medicine ways that feeds the spirit of our people so that they will be healthy. That is not lost. It is here all around us in the mountains and in the wild places. It is in the sound of the drum and the sound of the singing of the birds. We got to go back to them things to feed our spirit. We are the ones who are lost, in alcohol and drugs and in cities in the rat-race. We will soon be as extinct as the buffalo if we don't get back to them things. Our spirits will starve and the only thing to fill the empty hole inside will be alcohol, drugs or greed for money. That's what happened to our people and what is happening right now."

I listened and heard some of the same things that my Uncle Joe had tried to talk to me about some years ago. It seemed to make better sense than before.

I wanted, from that point on, to try to find out as much as I could about the things the Old Man talked about. I travelled again but with a new head space. Throughout the rest of that summer and fall, I followed a group of young people who gathered for the same reasons.

As far as politics were concerned, there was a growing depression everywhere, as agreements were reached with confrontation groups and others were battled out in courts and lost. Still others were brutally squashed with military-like violence. It was clear that the government had been busy rallying it's bureaucratic support because there was always some prominent Indian businessman, or other "white success" story, making some statements about "those few radicals" not really representing anybody.

By the time winter had come around things had degenerated to mostly internal bickering. Everybody I talked to seemed deeply disillusioned. It seemed like the worst had happened. I had hoped for a resurgence of the strong feelings of the year before.

I waited for it, thinking that a new internal strength would be a part of it. With that in mind, I went home that winter to take part in the Indian dance put on by my family, but things back there were appalling. Most of the reserves were embroiled in internal upheaval as Chiefs and Councils were challenged by younger members who were unhappy and disillusioned with the seeming lack of action through the summer.

A certain idealism had still been apparent in the peoples' actions. The attitude seemed to be that since we had control over our own affairs, we had to shape things up.

People had different ideas about how that should be done. All kinds of committees were busy meeting and making recommendations about everything under the sun. Education and a lot of new approaches to social services were on the top of the list. A lot of controversy developed over proposed development schemes. Young people were agreeing with some of the old people that it wasn't good to have developments that didn't fit with our idea of fitting people resources together with the economy. They felt that we could just compound the social problems that were there already.

People seemed to have a renewed sense of community awareness, but there was an obsessive quality to the whole thing. In that way, it seemed like a few good things had come out of the last couple of years. Not some of the things people had aimed at, of course, but some hidden things. A stronger sense of community and the vigor with which everything was attacked and criticized was good. The process was painful, however, because of the internal conflicts that arose.

It was a time of building in the community those things that could be done only by the people. Indian control was what it was about. No D.I.A. people were allowed on the reserves them times without being invited. Very few were invited no matter how hot the internal fighting got. It was a healthy sign, whether people understood what it meant or not. I sure didn't want to stick around and get involved with that stuff, however, no matter how necessary it was. I knew I couldn't handle it.

With the first signs of spring, I headed out. This time it was down into the States again. I figured that if I travelled down there I might run into what I was looking for.

When I hit Seattle, it was like something from out of my past reached out and took hold of me. I don't know how it happened.

I had gone to the AIM house to crash and visit and get caught up on the news. The guys there were many of the same people I had known from the caravan and from other places. I slipped easily into their casual talk about waiting for something to happen.

Things were pretty tense because one of the people wanted in the F.B.I. killings had moved through the area and had been arrested in Canada. A defense committee had been drawn up to try to fight his extradition back to the States.

As I listened to the stories of what had happened, I wondered how in hell the courts would handle it. There were a lot of different stories of what went down during that F.B.I. attack on those AIM people, when the killings happened there at the house on Pine Ridge. Most of the stories in the papers were so out of whack, they didn't even make sense. One thing I saw was that there had been definitely some kind of move to get as many AIM people as possible. I saw that, from the way things had been done whenever something went on.

I wondered how they were going to determine who shot who, when I heard there had been lots of guns inside and outside that had been blazing. Anyway, people there said that one guy had been set up as a scapegoat. I believed that.

I listened to the talk and felt the frustration and the weariness in the voices of the people who were organizing the defense. I felt the hatred start to stir inside of me again. It seemed to me like, all of a sudden, all of the stuff about taking things cool and non-violent just didn't work. It seemed Indians were being pushed so far down that they couldn't do anything about it. Things seemed so hopeless. The whole past year of participating in a quiet way, without a lot of violence, had just piled up the frustration more and more inside of me.

I went out and got loaded with the Bro's who were into that while we discussed everything going on. I fell flat on my face with it.

After that, I drifted around that city for a long while that way. I didn't care anymore. You don't seem to know how fast time goes, when one day and one week just meshes into one another.

I kept saying that I was going to head out next week, but I just didn't make it. The city is like that when you're drifting. It draws you to its lights and music and you lose yourself in it.

Sometimes I went up to the AIM house to get word on stuff that was happening. A lot of people had just drifted out of the scene right after the courts up there had decided the guy up in Canada held for those F.B.I. deaths was going to be extradited. He had to face new charges in the U.S.A. Everything was depressing. There didn't seem to be anything to sober up for.

Summer was deathly hot and muggy in that city. I had heard stuff about a woman who had been found earlier in the year, supposedly dead of exposure, in the States somewhere. The woman was from Canada and she had been a pretty well known activist. People said that the F.B.I. were probably responsible for her death and that her people had asked for a second autopsy. From what I heard there had been a lot of really brutal things like that which were carried out to neutralize the AIM.

Later I heard that there was a second autopsy held and that the body of that woman had been found with a bullet hole in it. Somebody said that Trudeau had promised to "look into the matter."

I also heard that a really good friend of mine up there in Canada had been found dead. He had also been a known activist. The report made, we heard, was that he had committed suicide and had left a note demanding an investigation of the D.I.A. and the removal of the head Indian Agent in Ottawa. Trudeau had mentioned his intention to look into that matter, too.

Man, that had just blown me away! It had hit me over the head so hard that I couldn't think clear. It just hadn't made sense to me. I didn't believe it. Somehow it had hurt me, way inside, the way Mardi's disappearance had. I never went up for the burial but I saw reports of it that were broadcast and it reminded me of that famous painting called "END OF THE TRAIL." Somehow his death had given me the same feeling inside.

I had a kind of defeatest attitude about everything I felt after that. The way I heard, it was the same way almost everywhere with everybody. I could imagine what it was like back home. Same old ham and eggs, as I had heard somebody up there say. Same old conferences, same old bitch sessions, same old resolutions, same old speeches. Same old problems growing worse and worse added with a definite backlash toward all activists, even by some Indians themselves.

I knew a few groups and some people would be hanging in there with the old idealism burning. They would continue at all odds to try to set some things right and keep things moving, but things would just happen to stomp those people out or negotiate them out or buy them out.

Sometimes I picked up the Indian papers to see how right I was. I wasn't far off target at anytime. Them times, I never really cared too much about anything when I woke up and straightened up for awhile. Those intervals grew shorter and shorter. Sometimes in those intervals I called home or picked up a letter from my little sister Jenny, who thought I was some kind of hero because I knew some big name AIMers. She filled me in on the stuff going on politically at home. For one awful year and a half things were the same at home as with me. Things just kind of drifted and deteriorated.

Something about the city was just like a slow rot inside my brain. I guess what I felt was close to total defeat, almost suicidal. Like there was nothing left to try for anymore. I felt like the only chance we had going for us had slipped away like a fog. One day it was there and real and the next it was just gone.

I sank farther and farther into that shadow world of drink and drugs; a world where things can be made to vanish like magic; a world where there is little feeling and less caring.

Sometimes I surfaced for awhile and then I would begin to think about the total hopelessness of everything. I looked around me and saw the stink and the filth of the others around me. Many were Indians like me. I looked at the city and what it stood for. Sometimes I shook my fist at it and shouted, "Screw you, you can't suck me in. I'm free. I always will be. I'm like the buffalo, man. You'll never own me because I resist. I won't join the stink that you are. I'm a dirty, drunken Indian, probably full of lice and that's how I resist. That's the only thing that makes you look at it and see that I will not be what you are. I refuse. I'll die a dirty, drunken Indian before I become a stinking, fat hog."

Sometimes, I thought of going home and tried to get myself together. I thought of the food sometimes, when all I had eaten for days was some bologna and bread at somebody's dump. I thought of the sweet fat on smoked deer meat and thick pieces of fry bread dripping with butter. Sometimes my stomach would hurt like somebody was drilling a hole from the inside. But I couldn't think about going home seriously. I felt like a stranger whenever I thought of Mom and Pops and my people.

One time, I was sitting at this bar, drinking cheap wine, when I saw the face of a guy sitting directly in front of me. Somehow, the guy's face looked familiar but his eyes, that stared straight at me, were like those of a gorilla I had once seen at a zoo. The eyes were hard, bitter and alien, but deep behind them was a pain and a question that asked, "Why?"

I had looked at the guy for a long time before I realized I was looking into a mirror.

I drank anything and everything. I scraped pennies together with the other winos to buy bay rum and shaving lotion. I ended up in the drunk tanks and detox centers and ate whenever I thought of it at the Salvation Army. I don't remember too much, but sometimes, when I woke up in jail or in the D, I got flashes of things that I had done. Sometimes I didn't remember a thing for weeks. That was frightening but somehow comforting, too. Frightening because of what I might have done and didn't know about, and comforting that I didn't have to bear those days. They were just gone, forever.

Summer, fall and winter passed like flashes across a screen. Each only meaning that I had to find a different place to hang out.

The end of that road stands out clear though. It was spring again and I was sick as a dog. I woke up down by the wharves. I had been lying there listening to the water crashing and I felt the sun, warm on my face. I looked up when I heard a friend of mine from back home say, "Here, have a drink." I sat up and reached for it. I looked around and nobody was there, but I heard laughter echo and echo in my ears. There were some driftwood piles and big boulders scattered around. All of them looked black and ugly with slime. I looked again and some guys were sitting there. They all dripped slime, oozing and grey. They were the guys that had been talking to me. There was a stench all over everything that smelled like dead bodies. The waves were oily looking and seemed to do things water doesn't do. It formed into shapes that dripped slime and oozed with green and black sludge.

Those guys sat there and kept talking to me. I couldn't hear what they said, but they laughed with gaping toothless grins at me. I started answering them in a conversational way and the next minute they were gone. I was shaking and felt hot all over like my skin was on fire. I looked down. There was slime stuck all over me, too. It seemed like it ate into my skin right down into my bones and my flesh rotted away in gobs. That's what I smelled. I jumped up and ran, screaming. The other guys ran after me, laughing and shouting and offering me a drink. Every few steps I took, my feet and legs gave way and I looked down and thought they were rotting away. I saw I was leaving big wet marks in the sand from the slime that slid down my legs. I remember falling and feeling the stuff slowly spreading over me. I fought it, but it was like quicksand sucking me farther and farther down. I screamed and screamed for what seemed like days. I really don't know how long it was. I'll never forget the pain all over my body and the horror. It was real, more real than anything I had felt for a long time.

I got over it though. I woke up in another detox and wished I had died. I looked out at the grey sky and the grey room and the grey food, and wished I had another drink.

After staying at the detox a while, I was moved to a dry-out place that catered mostly to Indians.

One time, this guy, an Ojibway from Ontario, talked with me. I knew he had been trying to get me to think about drying out for real and not just to escape the DT's like I had done before. He told me he had just come from a place where I could go to get help for what was wrong with me.

I looked at him and laughed. I said, "Joe, it ain't what's wrong with me, you know. It's what's wrong with the stinking world. I can sober up, Joe, but for what? Ninety percent of my people are dying a slow death. I can't stand to see what's happening to the ones that ain't."

He sat there and looked down at his feet, then he said real low, like he was talking to himself, "That's what they want you to think. Them ain't the only choices. There is another way. It's always been there. We just got to see it ourselves though. There are some people who help people who are looking for another way to live as an Indian person. You know we don't have to cop out and be drunks and losers. We don't have to join the rats either. There is another way. Slash, there is one place you should check out, if you do nothing else that makes sense. I don't know of any other way you are going to get out of this mess except to go for help to that kind of place. We could take you. There are another couple of guys who want to go from here. Think about it."

I did. I had really liked Joe when he came to the dry-out to visit some of the guys. He was different than some of the workers there, who had a kind of missionary attitude about their work. They were reformed alkies, you could tell. Joe wasn't jumpy and over-happy like them either. Some of that really put me off, like it was a forced act. Almost a desperate attempt to prove that being sober was just hunky-dory.

Joe was quiet and talked easily with anyone. He somehow made you feel good, just by being around him. I felt that he was deeply religious in the Indian way. He had a gentle strength and a peaceful way, that other people seemed to lack.

Once, as he prayed with his pipe for the Thanksgiving meal, he talked with real emotion about being happy to be there sharing with us. You felt his caring even though everyone there was from different parts of the country. It was real. It wasn't a put-on. I wanted to be like Joe. I wanted to feel again, to care, to love.

I decided I would find out if what he was like was connected to that place he mentioned. I had a feeling it did, from the way he talked about it.

I went to that place. I was afraid, but I was desperate. I knew for me it meant life or death.

When I got there with the other two guys, we were given the low-down. We were told that this was a camp where young people could find sanctuary from the concrete jungle. We were told that this was a place where we could learn about Indian ways so we could become strong again. I wasn't sure what that meant, but I knew my only hope was to try to stick with it.

They put us through sweats, every day for ten days. Those were the hardest ten days of my life. Those were the hardest sweats I have ever had to endure. Sometimes after the sweats, all I could do was crawl out and lay on the ground, for a long time so weak and drained I felt like a noodle. I had known that there was a lot of stuff I had to clean out of my system before I would ever be strong again. I prayed hard them times, during the sweats. I stuck close to the main man around the camp, hoping I could draw strength from him not to take off and lose myself again. I knew I couldn't make it on my own.

I stayed at that camp for six long months. During that time, I had a lot of time to think. I also had a lot of time to ask the questions I needed to ask.

There was a medicine man who came to the camp during that time. He had been travelling through to other places where he had to help people who were sick or troubled.

I had never met anyone quite like him. He never dressed up in garb that others called Indian stuff. He wasn't old, probably middle-aged. His hair was a little long and he didn't wear braids. He was a Plains Indian, and looked it.

The day he came to the camp everybody had seemed really excited. The women around the camp cooked all kinds of stuff. All the men who knew him took turns and sat talking with him. The rest of us sat back and wondered what all the commotion was about.

This man was very unassuming, but you could feel the warmth and love everybody had for him. You saw it in the eyes of the people, that this was a very special person. He was quiet and joked a little, while people talked to him about things that were happening around the country and in their personal lives.

He set up a ceremony that night for the people at the camp, to help them in the things they were there for. I went. It was a lot like that night in jail some years ago. What happened to me was the single most profound experience in my life.

Something touched me deep inside and I came out of there a new person. It was like suddenly waking up, like what those people say about being born again. All the questions that were unanswered for years, suddenly seemed so simple. I knew with my whole self that this was what being Indian was all about. From one moment to the other, I suddenly knew I would never despair again, in the way that I did before, no matter how hard things got, because I knew it wasn't a matter of belief. It was more, it was knowing for sure. I realized I would be able to make it then because there was something worthwhile to live for.

When I came out I felt so light and happy, it was a genuine high. For the first time in years, I felt warm inside. I felt like I wanted to hug everybody and shout and dance around. I felt good, so good it's hard to describe.

He talked to us for the next few days that he was there. One of the things he said sticks in my mind all the time. He said, "It's hard to be Indian. Most of you know that by now. Right now you feel good. It's always like that after a ceremony, but you have to realize in order to stay that way you have to keep to this path. It's hard to do that sometimes. Everything pulls you away from it. I don't mean you have to quit the whole society. I mean you don't have to take part in the things that destroy you. The kind of jobs you work at, for instance. The things you get involved in for Indian rights, too. The kind of recreation you get into is important. You see, there are certain things that are good for us, things we need to keep our balance. The drum and songs are important to us. We need to work with those things around us and work under the instructions handed down to our people. That way, we can live good and be a help to them others around us. That speaks louder than any grand speeches of politicians."

He continued, "The next generations, and how we survive as Indians, depends on that. It's something that can't be changed by any legislations or politicians. You young people are the real leaders, whether you know it or not. It is you that will make the biggest changes for people in what you do. Remember this, nobody says it's going to be easy. The responsibility is heavy and you will be tested hard at every turn, but every test will make you stronger."

He seemed to be talking just to me. He seemed to know the things that were in my mind and the questions I had about what to do from here on. I knew then that I would stay to work with these ways a while longer, until I knew more about it. Then I would go home.

I met a lot of people during that time and talked to a lot of people in the same space as me. It was a good time, full of peace and good experiences.

When I finally felt I was strong enough to face the world without falling flat on my face again, I left. By then, I had met a large circle of people involved in the same things, from all around the country. I had met them through the camp.

I found out that there were places like that springing up all across the country. Most of them were not advertised around. A wider and wider circle of people knew about them. At these places there was sameness in the ways things were done. The use of the pipe and sweats were common to all. All kinds of ceremonies and traditional practices were revived. Some of the things were held open to people of all tribes to participate in. Survival gatherings and survival schools, working with those concepts, started up in almost every part of the country.

I went to a lot of places where really old medicine people were. I found out something very important. In every area there were those people who, for some reason, kept to the old ways regardless of what other influences had been. All I had to do was to look and I found them. They were always willing to help you in whichever way they could. It seemed to me a new world had opened up. At the same time I knew it had always been there and had never gone anywhere. I knew then what that old man at that Alberta gathering had spoken about.

I learned many things during that time, about the strength those ways gave the people. I learned about the goodness, the caring and the sharing. Most of all, I learned about me. I learned that, being an Indian, I could never be a person only to myself. I was part of all the rest of the people. I was responsible to that. Everything I did affected that. What I was affected everyone around me, both then and far into the future, through me and my descendants. They would carry whatever I left them. I was important as one person but more important as a part of everything else. That being so, I realized, I carried the weight of all my people as we each did.

I understood then that the great laws are carried and kept in each of us. And that the diseases in our society came because those great laws remained in only very few people. It was what my Pops had meant when he had said, paper laws weren't needed if what you have in your head is right. I saw then that each one of us who faltered was irreplaceable and a loss to all. In that way, I learned how important and how precious my existence was. I was necessary.

I realized then that it had been something that had been missing all my life. And that it was missing from a lot of peoples lives. I saw how people went looking for it in various ways, some good and some bad. Many filled that gap with things that made you feel good for a little while, but was a far cry from finding what I had just found.

It was as though a light was shining for my people. I felt that we were moving toward it faster and faster. There was a rightness about it that the past few years didn't have. Yet I realized, without the past few years, I would not have made it to this point. I knew that as a certainty. I would have ended up like Danny.

Sometimes, as I went from place to place, I wondered how things were at home. I had heard some new young Chiefs had been elected in the Okanagan and they were more moderate in their approach to things. I had heard the Union of Chiefs had reformed under a new leader. I was surprised when I learned that the man was once the head of the national organization.

I had kind of kept up with situations up there, while I made my way around the country. I hadn't been ready to head

home, though. I heard that an inquiry over the pipeline up
North got a lot of support for the Indians concern over the
damage to the environment and their culture. I knew, too,
that a bigger and bigger group of Indian people became very
vocal about stuff like that. Almost everywhere, you picked up
the newspapers, you read about a Tribe that was opposing
this development, or that mining explorations proposal,
because of concern for damage to fishing and wildlife and
people's health. I knew that there was a total abhorrence for
the exploration for minerals like uranium and proposed coal
burning plants among our people. Much of the opposition was
based on a greater concern for the health of the people that
lived near those areas.

Many people who surfaced at such meetings were people
who were aware of their responsibilities as Indian people.
At most of the gatherings I went to there was serious discussion about the responsibility of Indian people to educate the
ignorant non-Indians about our role as human beings on this
earth. I felt I understood so little of what was meant. I was
satisfied to listen and learn.

When I decided to head home again, it was winter time.
Almost two years had passed since I left. I had been down in
Oregon at a camp there. Things got kind of boring for me.
I was attending the same kinds of meetings to "strengthen
ourselves" and going to the same kinds of ceremonies to help
us with our personal problems. I talked to one of the men
there who sometimes came to visit and counsel. I told him that
I thought I was ready to head home. I told him how hard it
had been for me to put aside my drinking and toking, and
that I was halfways afraid it might hit me in the face again
if I wasn't with the circle of people that were a strong support
group. I told him what had happened before and how I had
lost myself even when I thought I was strong.

He looked intently at my face as I talked. When I got done
he nodded and said, "Slash, you know all the things we talked
about. Well, the most important of them is to know you are in

control of what you do. You can ask for help anytime things go wrong. You can help yourself anytime, anywhere. Them Indian ways belong to you; to each one of us. You don't need somebody to pray for you or help you all the time. Most of the time if you live right, you can deal with everything that comes along yourself, no matter how hard it is. As long as you stick to that you'll be okay."

Softly, he continued, "There comes a point when you got to start giving help yourself instead of relying on people to lean on. You got to start to be a support for others. Go home and be what you are supposed to be. A good strong Indian that don't tear people down but builds them up. You'll do okay."

He sat quietly for a while then said, "You know, in every Indian family, it don't matter how modernized the family has become, there is always one who is a keeper of the ways. That person is drawn to Indian ways like a magnet. That person sometimes suffers the worst because of it, but inside that person knows the rightness of it. I can't explain it too good, but I have seen it to be true, no matter where in the country you go as long as there are Indians, it is true. These ones find their way eventually, to the things that they need to help them be what they are intended to be. Some of them don't even know it and spend much of their lives in frustration because things pull them in other directions. You are one of those."

"You'll be okay, though." he added, "You still got some learning to do when you get home. Just remember, don't spend your time criticizing people in their weakness, spend your time instead, getting them up in their thinking. You don't have to act like a missionary. Respecting people and being a good teacher just by your actions is enough. That talks louder than any speeches shouted at the top of the lungs. You'll be okay, you got a good mind and a big heart, and the spirit is in you."

I hitch-hiked all the way home. I got a few rides, but sometimes I walked for miles in the raw cold. I came into the valley from the south end, after having left Omak. The weather had been kinda warm and a soft snow fell. There had been no cars for a long ways. Just the quiet snow and my tracks. I looked back and I saw that my tracks stretched far away into the white, white distance. Flakes fell into my tracks and my tracks were soon gone. I looked ahead and the white snow stretched for miles ahead of me. I had felt the silence, alive around me. I stopped and stretched my arms up toward the soft white flakes that danced around me. I felt the feeling rise inside my head. Like a quiet explosion that spread ripples to all my body. I felt the singing music that the swirling snow danced to. I felt it take hold and I danced to the sound that swirled in white cascades around me, and covered the earth with a promise. A promise that the flowers would bloom again for my people. I knew I was home, really home and my land welcomed me.

I could tell everybody was gone when I walked up to the house. The house was locked and cold looking. I went in and started a fire in the old living room heater. I put some tea on and went to look for Mom's sack of dried meat. Everything seemed so quiet, too quiet. I put some soup on and drank some tea and waited.

I thought about the house and all the things I had learned and done here when I was growing up. I thought about my parents and how they had tried to give us the same teaching that I had to go a long way to find out about. I thought about my brothers and my sisters and my aunts and uncles and old Pra-cwa. Suddenly, all I wanted was to hear Uncle Joe and Old Pra-cwa's talk. I remembered lying under the covers late at night and listening to them tell stories and laugh. I recalled the things they talked about when they talked about protecting our land and our ways. I finally understood how that tied into the problems of our people. I envisioned the house filled with people for the winter dance. I was lonely for my people.

Towards early morning Mom got home with Josie. She had come in before I woke up. She stood there crying softly by the bed when I woke up. Josie stood beside her. She said, "Tommy's come back. Just when we need him, he come back."

I got up and sat on the bed and looked at both of them. Mom sat beside me and put her arms around me and held me for a long time. I didn't say anything. I looked at Josie and she looked at me with a familiar, sad look in her eyes. I knew something was wrong. I couldn't ask but my heart seemed to freeze.

Finally Mom said, "Your Pop, he had a heart attack, Tommy. That's where we were; at the hospital. He's pretty bad. The doctors are afraid of his chances. It's good you come back. It'll do him good to see you. He took to drinking around some, you know, after you left the last time. Things were so bad here with the people all fighting one another. We just don't know what to do."

I got up and stirred up the fire and heated the soup and tea. We talked about what should be done. I told Mom and Josie about the places I had been at and the kind of people I had met. I told them about the medicine people. I told them maybe it would be a good idea to get that kind of help for my Pops.

Mom was kind of reluctant to do that. She didn't trust people from other Tribes when it came to that stuff. But I talked with her and told her about my own experiences with some who I knew for certain worked in a good way with Indian medicine. Finally I said, "Look at me, Mom, they helped me. I couldn't have made it to be sitting here talking to you if not for the help I got from them." So she said, "Go ahead, Tommy, I guess you are the man now to decide about things until your Pops gets better. Whatever will help him is okay, as long as it's good help, not bad."

I got the help my Pops needed. I phoned to the place I knew where the person I wanted was. He and others came up. They did what they needed to do to help my father. Those times were good for the whole family. People came to the house and stayed throughout the week, while ceremonies and sweats were held. The women cooked tons of food and the men went out hunting for fresh meat. The feeling was good and I knew that it was a time of healing for the whole family, not just my father. It was like winter dance time, the way everybody smiled and joked around. Everybody was glad I was back, too.

My Pops was especially glad. He had been brought out of the hospital for the ceremonies, to the complete disapproval of the doctors. He looked old and tired. That time when we met, it was me who held him without saying a word. It was me that took all hurt from him into my own body. When I held him I felt it seep into my arms. I felt it spread throughout my body and center on my chest. I found it hurt to breathe and I felt like letting go and crying in great heaving sobs like a child. But I knew I couldn't do that. I knew I had to take his hurt from him so he could get the healing he needed.

I had learned that it was one of the ways our people had that made us different.

In that simple way, we were able to help one another.

After that, Pops looked a lot better. His eyes sparkled whenever he talked to one of the people who was there to help him and our family. He got better right away. I knew it was a turning point for us.

I stayed home that winter and got all caught up on the things that had happened locally and around the province with Indians. I worked feeding the cows and horses and cutting wood and hunting for the winter dance. I spent a lot of time with Uncle Joe and old Pra-cwa who had arrived to camp a few days and had stayed all winter. He sure was old. He was blind and his hair was snow white, and he had a hard time hearing unless you hollered at him, but none of that stopped his mind.

Pra-cwa talked only in Indian and he told me the whole history of the Okanagan people as he knew it. He told me all the places he had travelled through the mountains and valleys of our land. He had seen change. He had seen the valley change from a land full of deer and good things to eat, to a land cut up and cultivated and turned into towns. He had seen forests cut down and miles of land mined and changed. He had seen the people change, too. He had seen what the government policies had caused. He told me how our people had been, and how they had begun adapting to the changes in their own way, and how that was interfered with because of simple greed and prejudice by the settlers.

He told me how he saw things now, with the new generation of young people and the things that they were doing.

He said, "You see, Tommy, all the time things have been happening, Indians have been trying all kinds of ways to do alright. They forget one thing. They forget that we are a people. Different because of the things that we care about. When we talk about rights we are talking about that. Our rights come from the Creator so our government is the Creator. His laws are for a purpose. We are just a small part of it. Lots of ordinary white people know that, too. Some of them are joining us in trying to protect all we can, but it's hard for them because for so long they have lived under governments that are more interested in keeping rich than respecting them laws. The people end up fighting their own government on lots of stuff. They don't see it but most of them work all the time and hardly get anywhere just to live and have a little free time. I guess that's their problem, till they learn, but us, we don't need to be like that. Yeah, we are going to stay the way we are and we are getting stronger all the time. You younger ones are seeing to that. What has happened in the last few years will go a long ways, even though it don't seem like too much was done. Maybe we lost the fight but what we won was our people back."

I listened to Pra-cwa and thought about how those things were discussed all over the country by Indian people. I thought about the gatherings I had attended where the Elders and medicine people of different Tribes talked about that. I knew Pra-cwa didn't know those people and yet he said the same things they did. I thought about how much farther ahead

I would have been if I had listened to my own parents teach me those things while I was growing up. Instead it hadn't been good enough. I had to look for other solutions. I realized that there were people like me who had all that teaching right at home and had completely missed the point.

I realized then that slowly, painfully, every step of the way making mistakes, we had to rebuild our people. My part was that I had to find out what things were left of the old ways in my own Tribe and make it usable in our modern Indian lives. I had to work with all the old people in any way, to find out them things. It was critically important to our survival as Indians. I just hadn't seen how important before then.

Later that year, after the Union of B.C. Chiefs held their conference in Penticton in the spring, there were some meetings about a place that was used by our people for medicine. I didn't go to the first ones because I had been mostly enjoying going out to the mountains as much as I could. I also spent a lot of time talking to some of the old men in our Tribe. The first meeting I went to about it was a small gathering of young people and a few old people. They were concerned that the medicine place was going to be rezoned so that it could be developed into a tourist attraction. They were trying to figure out ways to stop that from happening. They were trying to find ways to convince the owner to leave the land as agricultural.

I sat and listened to the talk and thought about the same kinds of talks happening all over North America. I thought about the sacred Black Hills in South Dakota. I thought about the other places Indian people were concerned over because of their beliefs and practices. I went home and spoke to one of the old people about it. I asked about the place and what it was used for and whether it was still used.

The old man I talked to told me the place had been known to help many people. He told me the use of the place was tied to the beliefs and medicine ways of our people. He said, "Tom, it's important that the place be protected. But the fact that it was a medicine place which once meant something to our people, isn't enough. It's like an old basket on a museum shelf. You can't preserve our culture that way. It's using them things that's important. In using it, you understand it. That's what our culture is. You protect it by using it. It's the same with that place. What the people are really trying to preserve is our ways. If you are interested in preserving that place then you got to understand that. It's our ways that need to be preserved, then that place can be protected because then it has a purpose to be protected. You got to learn about them things and pass it on to others."

I had known that our ways were important to continue learning because they were good, but I had never really been certain why else except that it was our way. I saw it in a different light then. I glimpsed a small understanding of what the old man had meant. I saw that it was like that with all of the ways of our people. Like our language. We couldn't preserve it by having a linguist come and record it to be put away so it wouldn't be lost. We could only preserve it by using it. It was the same with our values and our rights. We couldn't protect our rights on paper if we didn't practice our rights. I realized then that it was simple. There was no question of whether or not we should or should not do things our way. We just had to do it or lose it.

I understood then that the practice of things separated us from other peoples. I realized then that's what culture is. The things I had seen about my people which were different came from the way things were approached. I remembered how my parents were and how some other Indian people were across the country. The ones who were strong and confident in their ways were different. The way they looked at the world and how they fit into it was different. They understood their part in the whole scheme of things from way in the past to way in the future. I realized that I had some of that understanding but that there were a lot of things I would have to learn about.

I understood then that most Indian people have knowledge of different ways and values and that's what comes into conflict with some of the values that are taught to them in schools and by society as a whole. I realized that schools are meant to teach the young of the middle class the best way to survive their society and to maintain its system. They are not meant to instruct those who do not have the values of that society. So confusion arises inside each of the Indian kids who begin to question which value system they must live by. Some of the ones who have parents that are more assimilated than others, as far as material wealth is concerned, have an easier time at those schools, but they still have a difficult time coping with ordinary living. The conflict usually comes out in the form of social problems, like heavy drinking or other harmful things.

I could see how the ones like me, who had more of those values at home, really got screwed up. When every single thing that meant something good to me was continuously being battered from all sides, I had to fight to justify my existence the way I was. It seemed to be the only way I could survive. I saw then that anger and bitterness was a natural outcome. I saw then why so many of our people first became angry and fought back then finally gave up and became defeated.

That whole year of learning went by fast. I got caught up by going to all the things that happened in the Okanagan and in the rest of the province. Many different reserves talked about Indian control over this and over that. Indian control over education was a big topic. Indian control over our laws for hunting and fishing was another important thing that was discussed everywhere. A new determination grew among all the people with a new kind of awareness and a search for deeper understanding of our culture.

During that spring, a protest over some really strong anti-Indian bills was held in the U.S. The protest was carried out in the form of a long walk. Indians and non-Indians supporters walked all the way across the U.S.A. from California to

Washington, D.C. It was labelled a spiritual walk to inform the people all across the States about the effects of the proposed bills, not only on Indians, but to the public at large. The walk received a lot of attention by groups of Indians in Canada. I saw it as an important pivot point for Indians across the whole of North America. I felt that a new feeling or attitude was surfacing, different from the early seventies. A strong undercurrent of spiritual awareness seemed to be there, rather than the sheer anger and frustration which seemed to be the motivation before. It was much stronger.

The same feeling began to happen around home also. People gathered in groups at pipe ceremonies and other Indian ways of praying. Large meetings were always started with an Indian prayer or a pipe prayer. More of the old dances were held out in the open at those gatherings.

That summer the provincial government announced a fishing ban on the Fraser River because of what they said was salmon stock depletion. From the meetings that I went to, I understood that to the Indian people who lived on the salmon along that river it meant a serious infringement on their right to fish for food. I understood their view was that there were no proper restrictions placed on industrial fisheries and sport fishing and no proper enforcement of laws on industry pollution that destroyed estuaries. It seemed logical that all of that needed to be investigated and acted upon before food was taken from the mouths of people who depended on salmon as their source of protein. It seemed to me that it was a question of corporations having more right to make profits than people to eat food that was provided by the Creator for that purpose. To the Indian people on the river, there was no question. They said they would continue to fish and eat the salmon as long as the Creator provided. They said they would continue to practice conservation in the way that was shown to them, so that there would not be shortages of salmon. It seemed to me that it was clear that it was a responsibility of the culprits to clean up their own acts, instead of trying to blame others for overuse.

Some of the things that happened during that summer were incredible, to me, as far as the lack of understanding by officials who had no idea of the Indians' point of view. The Indian people ignored the fishing ban, so a lot of arrests were made that summer. The kind of violence that was employed to stop them from fishing seemed beyond reason.

At one point an N.D.P. MLA was charged with obstruction of justice, or something like that, when he had attempted to intervene in some arrests of Indians. I read that his reason was that an unreasonable and excessive amount of violence had been used in the arrests. I had heard some pretty scary stories from one of my friends from the Lillooet area. He told me about one day when a whole load of wardens and police sat across from them on the other side of the river and watched them through the long range telescopes on their rifles. Nobody knew whether if or when the rifles would be used.

I was told that the Indian people never used or incited violence; they just continued to fish no matter how many went to jail. That infuriated the fisheries officials to no end. As one Chief from there put it, "Nobody is stealing. We will go on fishing. I wonder how many they can hold in their jails? Can they spare the money to feed all those Indians in jail and house them? Seems to me it would be saner for them to get their heads out of the sand and quit being so aggressive that everything has to be done their way at no matter what cost. For us, we will continue to use the resources that were made for us to use."

At home in the Okanagan, there was a great deal of controversy over the municipality's applications proposing to dump 2-4D into the lakes to help control the weeds that were starting to take over the lakes. Indian people joined with other people who were concerned about the environment in protesting this proposal. All kinds of meetings and shouting sessions were held. The environmental people were concerned that the breakdown of the chemical, after the application, would cause effects nobody yet had any information on.

The Indian people asked questions that I thought made a lot of sense at those meetings. I attended all of them and listened. One Councillor of one of the Bands said, "Lots of you gathered here are only looking at the surface of the problem. You only see two things. One is that there is lots of weeds. The other is how to kill those weeds. You argue about dumping in a bunch of poison that makes the weeds grow so fast they would kill themselves. Some of you are against that because you don't know what that poison will do to people. Some of you have said the weeds feed good on stuff that comes from what you call effluent."

He stopped and looked slowly around and continued, "That's what I want to talk about. I think you're confused. Our lakes are sick. Sick from dumping into them and the rivers all kinds of shit. The fish are sick. We used to get kikinee from the lakes. There used to be lots. Now, the old people warned everybody ten years ago to stop eating fish from these lakes. You see, when you open them up, they got holes burned in their stomachs. Their gills are all sores. The meat is soft and stinks no matter how fresh they are. On the outside, there is white spots and holes in the tail and fins. Maybe they got cancer."

He continued, "One family that was really poor, was eating only kikinee and hardly any other kind of meat. Three of their kids were born with something wrong with them. We don't know if it ties in with what they were eating, but we won't take chances. We have been watching with disgust the lakes get worse since then. To us, the whole idea of putting shit into the lakes, rivers or streams is not only stupid, but a crime. You see, to us, the water is sacred. We all depend on it. It is against our laws to piss or shit or throw garbage into it. We know somebody or something needs to drink from that water to live. Even the animals know this."

His voice rose as he continued, "You are criminals with respect to our laws. To think of dumping poisons into the water is even more criminal. We charge you with these crimes. There already are enough poisons dripping into the water from all those tons and tons of spray you pour on the fruit trees. They'll end up in the lakes at some time. The unborn are in danger, I would say you put them there. You ought to be here talking about how to stop putting your shit into the lakes and planning together how to stop that. That's all I have to say."

I don't think they liked his talk because there were a few embarrassed coughs and then they started the whole argument going again. There were experts on both sides giving all kinds of complicated reasons, for and against.

The whole thing finally reached a head when approval was given to use the chemical. There was a big flurry of demonstrations and rallies when Greenpeace people were called in to help with the protest. Every time there was going to be a dumping of the stuff, people went out in boats and floated around on the lake to stop them from doing it.

The people on the reserve decided to let them go at it. There didn't seem to be any reasoning with them or stopping them at that point. Sure enough they dumped the stuff sometime late during one night or early morning. It had hurt when we heard that. I knew that a lot of white people felt it, too. I knew that some of them were beginning to become real North Americans and they felt that vast unexplainable sadness whenever something like that happened. I realize that they had begun to feel some of the things Indians felt through their ties to the land or the "Mother Earth" as some called it.

I had talked with Walter, one of the most outspoken of the non-Indians about it. He spoke about the ignorance and the real danger that the people were putting themselves in. He had looked out at the lake and tears slid down his face. He looked at me and said, "I'm sorry. Slash, I guess we are a hard people to learn anything. We came from across the ocean looking for a new world because ours was so polluted and overcrowded. We wanted freedom. We wanted to be able to be free as humans and live comfortable, instead of just a few aristocrats owning everything and the commoners always poor. In our search we reached here. I am beginning to see the things you people are up against. Your people could show us a lot if only we had the sense to listen. I hope we start to listen before it's too late."

In different places that summer and fall and on into winter, talks went on over environmental damage and infringement on Indian rights. The feelings of the people were solidifying again. Everybody talked about self-government and self-sufficiency and ways to do them things. Workshops were held all over by the Union of Chiefs to educate the people on the issues before them. It seemed like there wasn't enough time to do all the things that needed to be done.

I went to most of the "gatherings," as they were called. Most were really informal with a lot of time spent talking about Indian ways and how they were different from the non-Indian ways of looking at things. People seemed to be relearning important things from the old people who attended those gatherings. I thought that surprised people the most. It seemed like people suddenly looked at the old ones in a different way than before. Many of the ideas picked up and used by people who were facilitating workshops on Indian Government were from the old ones.

I felt good and solid again, but I made sure that I didn't go to the meetings that were what I called purely politically oriented. I didn't want to have to deal with that stuff anymore. I mean the anger, the bitterness and the frustration that went with it. I wanted to work with positive things. I knew many other people felt the same way. As always, political meetings went on with much of the energy of the leaders spent jockeying back and forth on interpretations of what Indian Government was. Other people were actually busy defining it by practice. I went where those people met and worked.

What was strange was that there was a group of people all on the same wavelength who networked but who weren't "organized." I remember going to a gathering at the Friendship

Center in Kelowna. The meeting was held to talk about
environmental control by Indian people. I listened as one
young woman talked about how important it was for us to
regain control over these things. I had thought to myself *shit
there goes the politics again* but then she said, "The only way
that we can really regain control is for us to really change.
It means that we're going to have to rebuild ourselves; rebuild
our health, mentally, emotionally and spiritually. We're a long
ways from being in control totally over our lives. In fact we
can't even talk about it, except that we know that it is possible
and that it is what we are moving toward."

Her words were powerful, and in that instant I understood
something that had been bothering me for a long time.
I thought about all those "claims" we were making and
all those changes we were fighting for. I thought about
how I had looked at my people and deep down had thought
to myself, "They can't ever get those things. They're too
dependent. Too dependent on D.I.A., welfare, social assistance,
government programs of all kinds."

I saw then that it was true that our people had learned a
system of dependency. For example, even families that do
have the means to, say, repair houses, or to do things for
themselves, they don't. Instead, they wait for the Band office
to do it for them. I saw how it had become a normal accepted
way of thinking, not to be self-sufficient. It had deteriorated
our health to such a degree that it had become a bigger obstacle
for us to overcome than any obstacle outside. I saw then
that an internal change was more important than changing
anything on the outside. I saw another thing that had been
missing before.

It was clear then that the only way I could work to help
that change come about was to set up a model or an example
of myself. I had to be a teacher in that sense. I had to work
with people the way they were, not condemn them. I had to
work with those people who were ready to make changes.
I saw how I had to, wherever possible, depend on my own

resources and what I could gather around me to do things. I had to be willing to sacrifice my time, my money, and my emotions. That was what was important. I knew then that changes would come about, but the price was high. That, was what that one medicine man had meant when he had said, "Indians can't be politicians. They can only be themselves and show example, good or bad. In that way we are all teachers and that is what makes a difference."

I think that was one of the best winters of my life. I think it was that way for the whole family. We all worked together to help bring in the harvest. My mother and father put up the dance again that winter. People from all over came for the four nights of feasting and giveaways. Things were good.

I spent most of my time with the old people. I talked to them and took them around to the meetings and gatherings, to keep good company. I did some part-time work for the Band, too.

I ran into Jimmy while at work one day. I hadn't seen him in such a long time. It was strange how things had turned out for him. He had gotten the education he had wanted. He had a degree or something in Business Administration. The strange thing was that none of the Indian Band Councils hired him.

We talked one night outside of the Council hall where there had been a gathering to talk about some of the things concerning my part-time work with the Band. He had been involved with the same kinds of things, but in a different way. I ran some evening and daytime recreation things for some of the young people. He had been trying to set up some things on a Tribal level that was a planned approach to education and recreation and other things. He had a fancy label for it, he called it Indian social development. He had been consulting for a group interested in setting up a school or something. He said it would take a few million dollars and a few years worth of planning but it sounded okay when he explained it.

He asked me, without even saying hello or anything, "What are you up to, Tom, or should I call you Slash? I hear that you have been doing some stuff with the youth here. Who's paying you?"

I looked closely at him and I saw that he looked really haggard. There were lines on his face and lots of grey in his hair. His middle was really bulgy. He smoked constantly, you could tell, his fingers were yellow. His movements were kind of jerky and he looked really embarrassed. He wouldn't look at me directly at any time while I answered.

I said, "Call me whatever seems okay. Yeah, I'm working with some of the young guys. You know, physical stuff, mostly just to keep them active and I talk to them a lot. Mostly, they need somebody to lean on a bit. Nobody was paying me at first, then the education committee thought what I was doing was good so they decided to give me some money, part-time, to help me out. I'm not interested to work for a wage for anybody. I don't like to sell myself. I work only at things where I see I can be of some good whether it pays money or not. If there is money to help out, fine. Most things I work at don't have no money attached to it but I seem to be able to get along just fine. My needs are simple. How about you? Are you working now in the kind of stuff you wanted to get into? You married or what? Sure been a long time since we talked."

"Yeah," he said real slow, then he turned to me and his eyes were smouldering, he said, "I got a Business Administration diploma. You know it took me four years of hard work to get that together? While I was at the college, I married that lady. What a big mistake. She somehow thought because I was Indian, I could just get money for nothing. Soon as she found out I was on a living allowance and just couldn't afford any of the stuff she wanted, she started going sour on me. I kept telling her to wait until I got out of school, then I would get a high paying job. She left me. She always thought I was dumb anyway, but it screwed me up for a while. As I was saying, I got my diploma, but shit, nobody will hire me. All the Indians are talking about self-government and stuff and they hire white people in the positions I'm looking for. Just because I'm Indian they seem to think automatically I'm incompetent. Our own people are like that. Sure they will hire me for puny jobs, but they hire some ex-D.I.A. goat for the cream jobs. You tell me why, Slash. I'm not the only Indian who's found that out. It seems to be one of the hardest barriers to break through and one of the hardest things to understand. It's also one of the hardest things to deal with. I do good work. I do care, you know, about seeing things run right. Tell me what you think, Slash. Or maybe you don't run into that stuff. Everybody knows right off about you."

I smiled when he said that, "Do they?" I asked, "Maybe you should look at your own thinking, Jimmy. I'm no expert on things, but I told you way back I wasn't the kind to get excited about setting myself up. I never was comfortable with that. I see the world somewhat different because of the point of view my folks gave me. Later I started looking more closely at what they were saying. I found the same answers all over the Indian world. Its clear what we are suffering from is the effects of colonization. One of the effects of it is the way people see themselves in relation to those who are doing the colonizing. Everything that the colonizers do, tells the Indians they are inferior, that their lifestyle, their language, their religion, their values and even what food they eat, is somehow not as good. There is no understanding why that happens, it just does. So it gets transferred in subtle ways by our own people. They get ashamed to look Indian or eat Indian foods or talk Indian. They reject our religion and our values. They attempt to become the same as the colonizers in as many ways as they can, to escape being inferior, or being tainted by it. They don't want to hurt inside, you see. It's the reason some Indians automatically think white men are more competent and smarter than any Indian no matter how brilliant the Indian is or how many degrees or diplomas he has."

I looked at him and searched his face as I continued, "You know what's wrong with that. It isn't true. It causes a great burden of guilt to feel that way. You never know why you feel so shitty inside and why you feel so much contempt for Indians yourself. Some of us over-compensate by heaping ego-building roles on ourselves to prove we aren't the "average" Indian and that we are worthy of praise by the white man. You usually find people like that in some political role. Probably the ones who won't hire you, Jim. But we each carry some of that in us, in one way or another. We are all affected by colonization. Realizing the problem and consciously avoiding some of the most common mistakes is all we can do. But, you know, even the white man does not escape that common problem. They all live under a colonized mentality here in this country. Think about it."

Jimmy looked down at his shoes and said, "Shit, man, you always got some crazy ideas about stuff, but you may be right on this. If you ain't, then there must be something really wrong with the thinking of some of our leaders. They'll never get anywhere with their self-sufficiency ideas. They'll be handing out welfare checks for another few generations unless there is a place for people like me. In fact, unless all of our people are given a chance, any kind of chance. But why does it have to be like that? I played their game. Shit, man, I even believed in it. Now, I don't know. I'm all loused up, you know. Ah, what the hell. I'm going to go down to the Valley for a few beers. Want to come? I feel like slumming. I gotta keep the old image going, you know, in case there is some job for me at the Band office, so I don't go there too often. I usually go to the other bars, where the businessmen go. I like to keep a low profile as far as being seen in public drinking, you know. Gotta prove all of us ain't drunks."

I looked at him and felt really sorry for him and angry with him. It seemed that he just couldn't look facts in the face. He still believed in the myth.

I said, "Jim, the whole problem is a lot deeper than just Band leadership not willing to take the chance of Indians running things and working in the jobs they say Indians aren't qualified for. Staff are just not conforming to the European attitude toward work. The nine-to-five work ethic. If you can get as much work or production out of three days a week or four hours in a day instead of the usual five day week and eight hour day, what's wrong with that? Nothing, except it doesn't conform, you see. Indians adjust their time at work according to output, and D.I.A. programs really requires only minimal output. Everybody gets upset at that and don't hire Indians. Indians aren't lazy because of that. If you were to hire Indians and give them free rein with what could be done in their programs with what is available, you would begin to see some results. Of course, there would be those who would try to take advantage of that but they would get weeded out. Work would go back to the meaning we give it. Meaning, getting something done instead of filling in time for a paycheck under rigid terms and conditions."

I went on to say, "You can strive to be the same as them in everything you do, but you find that there are just too many things wrong with a lot of their system. Much of it goes against natural human rhythms. Look at what the whole anti-establishment movement was about. Ordinary working people would know what I'm saying. They would agree to a certain degree but then they know they would be ostracized by the rest of society. Indians just do it without calling it anything. Even the ones who try to conform in every other way somehow are affected by this. You find that those people will make excuses to slide at least one or two days a week or a few hours at a time, then when they really get tired of it, they just cop out on a binge or something like that. Binging is convenient, but it can end up with the person becoming a bonafide alcoholic. Why can't they just be allowed to adjust their work time without feeling they have to justify it?"

I had his attention, so I continued, "Jim, as I said before, we are slowly learning decolonization. We got to recognize our solutions to some of those social problems are in progress already. We have our own interpretations as to how we

function best. Some of these solutions are highly criticized by
D.I.A. and D.I.A.-oriented leadership, I know. I've been
watching all the Chiefs and administrators and Band staff for a
while."

Jim kept his head down, then in a soft voice said, "Slash,
I'll have to do some thinking. You know something, I was
told you had changed. People feel your strength. It feels good
to talk to you. You make me feel like there's hope even though
the things you talk about are hard. I don't understand everything you just said, but some of the main things got to me.
I guess I'll have to examine my own thinking, like you said.
Let's go hunting sometime, okay? At least I still do that once
in a while."

I smiled at him and said, "Sure, I like the hills. How about
getting together with me when I take some of these boys out?
I sure could use the help."

Spring and summer were pretty hectic for me. I got things
going at home and talked to a lot of young people. I went to
many of the meetings and gatherings that the Union held.
Most were involvement things like the opposition to the Hat
Creek Coal Project.

One group, that was headed by my cousin Chuck, really
moved on the sacred site issue. Active protests to the plans to
rezone the property escalated. I went with the young people
to those hearings and got in on some of the demonstrations.
I also got involved and helped to set up some information
meetings on uranium mining explorations. The Union was
active in all of those things.

It was during one of those meetings, on both the sacred site
and the uranium question, that I met Maeg. We had been
discussing ways to deal with the whole thing because it had
seemed like we were up against a stone wall every which way
we turned.

At that meeting, I noticed this chick who sat with an older
lady, not saying too much. She was really something to look
at although you couldn't say she was pretty. Her eyes were

what struck me right off. A soft intensity about them told me she didn't miss a thing in the whole room. Her hair was thick, brown and wavy. It hung past her shoulders and her skin was smooth and light brown. She hadn't worn any choker of beads or braids. In fact her clothes were just plain, not the usual "radical Indian" or "office Indian" garb. I hadn't been able to tell where she stood from her clothes. She was dressed too plain to have been one of those people who were "into" Indian medicine ways, in a cult kind of attitude.

I watched her. At one point during the meeting I saw her bend her head toward the older lady who sat next to her and they discussed something. I watched her mouth. She spoke Okanagan.

She stood and spoke. " My people," she said, "My mother has a suggestion you might find worthwhile. She suggests that we approach this whole question in an Indian way. We are not aggressors. We must simply resist for as long as we can the kind of destruction we are talking about here. Resistance must mean we will not participate in destruction and that we will inform as many people of our resistance as possible. If we are to be successful to any measure then we have to be sure that we see the whole question we are faced with and deal with all of it in an Indian way. It is the resistance of our forefathers and the continued resistance of our fathers that has left us with something to call ours. It was not negotiating on our rights to this land. They can pass any legislations they want but they know and we know that the land belongs to us unless we sell it out for money. As long as we don't sell it out we still own the land, and we shall retain the right to resist destruction of it and of the people and living things on it. Thank you."

She had power when she spoke. She made it seem so simple, the way she put it. I realized what she had said was her mother's words, but anybody who spoke with that passion believed very deeply what was said.

I talked to her after the meeting. I had to. I went up to her and said, "Hi. Thanks for the talk. The direction of this whole thing has changed for the better. You or your mother was effective in changing the direction of this meeting from anger and violence back to a more powerful direction."

She smiled, and the whole room seemed to warm up. She said, "Thank my mother. Anyways what's your name? I've been watching you watch me. My name is Maeg. Short for Maegdaline. I'm from the south side of the border."

I told her my name was Tom, Slash for short and she laughed. "Really, how did you get a name like that? I think I would like it. See you around. Ma wants to leave now. She's from up here but lives down there with her old man. We come up to these kind of meetings whenever we hear about them."

I hadn't even had time to talk to her about anything and she was gone. I wanted to know a lot more about her.

I asked around about her. Actually, I asked around about her mother. Lots of people knew her. She was a medicine person, very well respected and known for her wise counsel to people. She was from a Band north of us. Maeg was her only daughter and she had two sons that were both living up there. Maeg's father was from up there but died when she was little. With us Okanagans, we all keep track of our people, even if some move away, so it wasn't hard to find out that Maeg wasn't hitched up. I decided to check it out.

All summer, I went everywhere I thought she would be. I talked to her as often as I could. She sure was something else. She understood a lot of things that still I had been trying to find the answers for. She had been brought up by her grandparents after her dad had died, so she could talk our language. She was mysterious and funny.

One time, I went to see her at her home, and she asked me to drive her and her mother to a ceremony further down south. I was glad of the opportunity to get to know her better. During that trip we talked and told each other all the things about ourselves that mattered. I found out that she really was very traditional in her worldview but that her approach to everything was from an everyday practical point.

At the ceremony which her mother was taking part in, she turned out to be very knowledgeable about the medicine ways. I watched her as she stood and helped her mother burn some sage and begin preparations for the prayers. She did everything with a concentration that came from a deep respect and understanding of what she did. She knew all the songs. And when she sang her voice was so clear and so beautiful, it was almost painful.

I had seen many chicks who went to ceremonies and hung around the spiritual camps and gatherings. They all seemed to wear certain clothing and carry themselves with a certain air, a "more Indian than thou" attitude. She wasn't like that. She spoke to me about it, after I brought it up on the way home.

She looked at me and laughed, "You mean how come I'm not wearing turquoise and all the beadwork and moccasins and braiding my hair? Shoot, for one thing, I can't afford turquoise, and all the beadwork and moccasins I make are given away. My Mom has a lot of giveaways. I used to wear my hair a lot longer, but I cut it when my Grandpa died. I found out it's easier to manage at this length so I keep it like that. The most important thing, though, is while I like to look good, I'm pretty careful about how I look to others. It's known you make a statement by what you wear. Indians used to use that very carefully. I don't want to be misinterpreted and appear to be expert or know something about Indian ways that I don't. My Mom uses some things when she is working with the medicine; people all know her by that. I would never put on a false pretension by what I wear. The consequences of that kind of disrespect is sometimes heavy. I dress up in wing dress and braid my hair for pow-wow, then I know what the purpose is and it is acceptable. Understand?"

"Yeah, I know what you mean," I answered, "I used to feel pretty uncomfortable around some of the guys I would see wearing a ribbon shirt, beaded belt and braids and at the same time using drugs or drink. I would ask myself why they would bother wearing that stuff? It seemed like they had to prove something by their clothes. However, something one of the main men in AIM once said makes some sense, too. He said, that those things lock you into remembering who you are, and if you forget, then for sure someone will remind you if only because of what you wear. Some of us need to be reminded and I guess that is the purpose of those things for them."

"Yeah, that's what I mean, if you know, then it's alright for you. For me, it's hard to wear them because of the stuff I associate certain colours and items with," she said. Then she laughed and asked, "Slash, are you married or have you ever been?"

I looked into the rearview mirror at her mother and saw her look straight and hard at me. I said to her mother, "No, I haven't. I was in prison for a while and then when I got out I was on the move for a while. I hit a snag in the city for a while and have spent the last year recovering from that. I don't know how I feel about marriage. Anyway, you ask too many questions, Maeg."

She looked at me and her eyes were deep and serious. "I need to ask. I need to know what I'm getting into. We both know what's happening, so does my Mom. She needs to know."

When we got back to their house her Mom asked me to come in and have tea. She told Maeg to cook some lunch and when I protested she looked kind of sharp at me. I shut up. She looked at me and said, "Maeg likes you. I like you. Maeg will cook for you." What could I say; I liked her, too.

After that we went together. Her Mom did like me. I took Maeg up to meet my Pops and them. She fit in so easily, it was like she belonged. They all took to her. We got to know each other just by going around together.

It had been summer and the world was fine. There had been no heavy stuff happening with the political people, and in many places there were positive steps towards really getting down and practicing Indian government. Indians all over took the government and large corporations and others to task over the environment. A couple of big cases were won, some were lost. On the sacred site, things were at least being put into halt stage while the Indians pursued some avenues to deal with it. Spiritual gatherings were held in many places throughout the province. We went to some of them, whenever I could get Maeg to come up.

In August, we decided to go together to South Dakota to a sundance. I remember every detail of that whole trip. We slept in the car most of the time. Another couple of people went with us, friends of hers and mine. We didn't have much money and one guy with us decided to take his car instead of the vintage Pontiac I had bought for seventy-five dollars.

When we got to the sundance, the whole world was like magic. There was such an intense feeling of power and love at that place. You could feel it as soon as we passed security at the gates where they checked for booze, drugs, cameras and recorders. We watched the dancers that day, while we sat outside the arbor, and felt good with them. In the night, we were in our tent as sounds of the camp drifted around us. We got together and knew we would stay as one whole person. This beautiful place had been a gathering place for thousands of generations, bringing people together, and we shared in that magic.

The next day we asked my friend, the medicine person from the camp that I had been at, to smoke a pipe for us. His eyes sparkled when we told him what we wanted. He looked at me and said, "It's been a long road from the last time I saw you, Slash. You see things are working out for you. Remember, though, there are always heavy tests down the road for everybody. If you know what is right and keep to that, them tests need not put you down. Joining together as one is painful sometimes. It is best to see it as two sides to one whole person. You must remember whenever you hurt your partner, you also hurt yourself. Respect and treat the other the

way you want to be treated, and it will come about in a good
way. You both have a great deal of work just ahead of you.
Stay strong on this path together and you'll do okay."

I took her home after that. We stayed at a youth camp in
the Okanagan for a while. We camped out and what you
could call honeymooned. Her Mom visited a couple of times
to bring her some stuff and to ask her to do some things.
My Mom and Pops were so happy they went up to the youth
camp as often as they could just to see us. They took meat
and vegetables and stuff for the kitchen.

For that whole next two months and into the fall, we spent
all our time together. We went to the gatherings at Fish Lake,
Kamloops and Vancouver. Everyone got to meet her. She
was liked by everyone. She was good at almost everything
you could think of. She could help organize and take control,
without seeming to, at those gatherings. I watched her.
Old people talked with her and she spent lots of time with
them. She liked almost all the same things I did.

In the fall, we started building a house. I told her I wanted
to build it myself and not have any Band monies in it.
She thought that was great and worked out there with me
even when it got really cold. It was just a one room cabin,
really, but it sure looked nice when she got it all fixed up with
rug pieces and curtains and a really nice star quilt we had been
given. We just had a wood stove and had to carry our water.
She laughed about that, saying, "Yeah, we got running water.
I run to the spring for it."

All our people helped out with stuff like chairs and pots and
dishes. It was great. I never knew just how full a person's life
could be just to share it with someone who enjoyed it with
you. I had never felt so strong in all my life.

We walked up to Flint Rock that fall. It had been a long
warm day, when the summer slowly stretches into the warm
colours of the fall and you weren't sure which started or
ended where. Up there, the wind was warm on our faces, we
could see for miles and hear all the sounds of the valley below.

Up there was where the blue grouse strutted around and we saw deer lying in their soft dust beds, catching the afternoon sun. We walked up there and had some dried meat and bannock for lunch.

She came and knelt in front of me. She took my hands and spoke my Okanagan name softly. I had a strange feeling like I did when I heard the dance songs inside my head. I felt like I was made of mist or something and I melted into the scene around me. She said in our language, "We are now more than one. We have become three. Your son will be born in the springtime when the saskatoon flowers bloom. He will be named to your side of the family."

I couldn't speak. All I could do was reach out and pull her to me and rock her while the feeling washed over us. I knew she felt it. Somewhere in my head I saw us from another point of view, just a little above us, like through clear glass. I saw us kneeling and moving with the rhythm that flowed around us in shimmering waves, then we grew smaller and smaller until we were just a speck on top of that mountain and our land was vast and spread out around us, like a multicoloured star quilt.

Throughout that fall and winter, the magic infected people all around us. I carried on my work with some of the young people. Her and I spent a lot of time at the youth camp. We mostly arranged for old people to get together with some of the young people and teach them about various things. It was as if they had waited for this. We helped set up dinners for them and went out with them to collect medicines. Many ceremonies were held and lots of people went to them. It was a time of great peace and learning for our people. That seemed to be going on all over the province, as far as we could tell.

Some politicking went on over the constitutional issue, but we never got involved in the political scene that winter or spring. The leaders had been trying to convince the government that they should be included as equal partners in the talks over whether or not to bring the constitution into

Canada's parliament rather than leave it as an act of the British parliament. A delegation of Chiefs had gone to England but they weren't taken seriously. A delegation attempted to meet with the Cabinet. They were refused.

I monitored the whole thing because it still bothered me. I knew the Chiefs got angrier and angrier about the government's high handed treatment of them. I wondered how the whole issue was going to be approached, but I never attempted to attend any of the political meetings.

It had seemed to me that the important things were already going full blast. Young people from all over, were becoming strong leaders in working with the Indian ways. I looked at that and I knew that was where the real strength to fight anything that society had to hand out was going to come from. Every time we went to a gathering, I saw it in the way things were done. Indian people were coming together, caring for one another. Whenever there was a pow-wow or a potlatch or a gathering, people brought food and helped cook. Things were talked about from politics to the various court actions going on all over the province. Sweats and pipe ceremonies and prayer gatherings were common. A whole different attitude than in the mid-seventies was plainly evident. There were young people who were very aware of what was Indian in approach and what wasn't. They were rebuilding a worldview that had to work in this century, keeping the values of the old Indian ways. To me that was more important right then than anything else. I thought that through this way, there was no bullshit that could get through for very long.

Living with Maeg made the whole world seem so rich at that time. We used to go out to the hills and walk for hours. It was during spring, when the flowers bloomed and new plants were coming up.

We had been up at my Uncle's place helping with the hoeing of the corn when my son started wanting to be born. She said, looking up from pulling some weeds, "It's so simple, planting is, but when you really think of the complicated things that happen to see a seed grow into a corn plant that will itself bear seeds, then you get a little glimpse of the greatness of our Mother the Earth. You begin to see what it means to grow a seed yourself, and one day it becomes a tall person. To be a part of that is one of the most sacred of trusts and yet it is made so simple. To us it is a natural thing, this corn plant growing, but I'm overwhelmed at the whole idea. He's ready now."

She spoke in our language, and her voice was so soft. For those few minutes it had seemed that we flowed into all the things around us. We had no clear edges that set us apart as different from everything; like how you mix paint and spread it on canvas, each color different but all of it just paint in different positions to make up the whole picture, and the picture becomes more than mere paint on canvas.

Our son was born that night. I asked her how she knew it was going to be a son and she said, "I saw it before I even got together with you. I saw you two in a dream. Slash, this boy is going to be important to a lot of people. You have to remember that always, while he is growing up."

I knew she was serious. I understood our people have the ability to see through their dreams. Many of them denied this but almost all have it. I believed it. Maeg just accepted it.

He was dark with lots of black hair, but his eyes were soft brown, like Maeg's. He was the most wonderful thing I had ever seen. Both of us were so overwhelmed, we would just look at him for hours. Sometimes, when I held him and he squirmed around I would get this tight feeling inside and I felt like squeezing him. Those feelings were so strong it was scary. We called his English name Marlon for a man we both respected a lot. His real name would be given to him later by old Pra-cwa at the winter dance.

Pra-cwa was there when we brought him home. So was Uncle Joe and about all the rest of the family. They all had little things like socks and diapers and sweaters and blankets for him. Maeg's Mom brought a baby board decorated with velvet and beads. It was beautiful. Everyone in the family from the oldest on down took turns and held him and greeted him in Okanagan. They said that they were glad he had finally found his way to us.

The long hot days of that summer, we went to different kinds of meetings and pow-wows and gatherings. We usually took along some of the young people to help them to under-stand what was going on. I spent a lot of time painting again. Sometimes Jim used to come up and we worked together or went out with some of the young ones. He really got involved with the whole issue around the constitution. He was then working as manager for one of the Bands.

We spent long hours discussing the whole thing from top to bottom. It seemed like people weren't too sure how to approach the whole thing. He went to all the political meetings where the Chiefs would strategize on actions to convince the government to allow them to be part of the talks along with the provinces. He spent a lot of time trying to convince me that it was important to get involved. He got all gung-ho on the same things I had been into a couple of years before that. I saw that he had to do that. So I talked with him and tried to clear up some of the things that had crystalized for me.

After the Chiefs were locked out of the constitutional talks, he came up and spoke long hours with me about what should be done. He was angry. He said, "I sure wish we could get together in our approach to this thing, then we might have some chance. Even Trudeau said that. The way we are so fragmented in our approaches with all the different political Indian organizations, we'll never get anything done."

I thought about that for a while, then I said, "Maybe the reason they can't all come together in their approach is because there isn't any strength to any one position. Everyone is looking for one compromise solution. For some, there is no compromise, for others there are degrees of compromise but limits, too. I don't see why they have to all agree on any one position. We are talking about different nations here, not just one large conglomerate group called Indians, the way the government would prefer it and is trying to force on us. We can each deal separately according to each nation's preference. What may be acceptable to some may not be acceptable to others. Up in the North where a land base is so crucial and the culture very much in harmony with it, there will be a totally different need. In the south and especially in areas more closely assimilated into the city economy the needs will again be quite different for survival."

"Yeah, I can see that," Jimmy said, "but if we deal with the government like that, we won't have the strength that we would as one body. That's why it's important."

I said back to him, "That's not true, we can all support each other on whatever position each of us takes. It doesn't mean each has to take the same position. The government weakens us by making us fight each other to take one position, as each one wants their position to win out. Each position is important and each has the right to try for it. We should all back each other up. That's what I think."

"Well," Jimmy answered, "I sure hope some of the Chiefs can see that. You know how it is with politics. There are about half a dozen organizations headed by a half dozen or so strong leaders who each are convinced of being right. I guess the government would suggest to them to form one unit or else. The fighting alone would cancel out anything positive coming out. The Indians would sure turn tables if they came out all supporting their various stands equally in co-operation."

Of course, that didn't happen. There were all kinds of meetings and emergency sessions going on, over the constitutional issue and some other side issues.

In B.C. the government announced a seven year moratorium on explorations and mining of uranium. There was an audible sigh of relief from the people in the Okanagan who were well informed about that issue. However, the government announced they were ready to proceed with the Hat Creek thermal power station.

Controversy over Human Resources' policies of taking Indian children and putting them into non-Indian homes, without any say by Band governments, was on-going. There was enough anger over that issue that a caravan was arranged in support to meet with the government.

Maeg wanted to go on that caravan. She said it was important, especially having a child ourselves. We had to appreciate and support what was being done for the other Indian children. I agreed, kind of reluctantly. I wasn't too sure I wanted to get involved with that kind of politicking again. But I could see Maeg's point.

The feelings ran high during that whole caravan, but throughout, there was something more in the air than the point they made about child welfare. I knew the recent actions of the government on the constitutional issue was on everybody's minds.

People were angered and humiliated at the treatment of the Chiefs as the provinces went on bartering what didn't belong to them. All kinds of meetings of officials went on in the Indian organizations, planning what to do. We went to some of the gatherings, rallies to raise money to take a caravan all across Canada on a diplomatic mission to the government. There seemed to be almost an obsession with getting Trudeau to listen and involve the Indians.

Maeg and I helped out and had a good time during the planning of that caravan. I was mainly there because she thought it was important. She said, "This is a people's mission. We care for our rights and our land and we have a child. Maybe more than that, we have to clear the future for him. Nobody is looking out for our rights so we all have to do what we can. Maybe we'll be successful or not but at least we will have tried. Slash, I'm Okanagan even though I lived most of my life south of the border. I care. That's why I'll go on that express and carry a sign that says, "CONSTITUTIONAL RIGHTS FOR OUR CHILDREN."

"I care," I said, "More than you think. I'm just not sure this is the right way to do things. Something not quite right nags at me when I even think of joining the caravan to Ottawa. I know everybody wants to draw public attention to the thing, and we need to sway public opinion on the question of whether or not Indians should be consulted on the constitution. I know everyone is deeply concerned that non-Indians just do not realize the inborn need to practice our ways. Our rights are really that, no matter how each Tribe or individual interprets it. I know the real fear is that it will all be wiped away if we are not included in the talks. But somehow, I feel very uncomfortable about the whole thing."

She said, "Well, maybe we should go on that caravan to Ottawa, and maybe you will find out what it is. Marlon is still small enough. It will be no great hardship. We aren't tied down."

"Okay," I said, "I guess I should talk with some of the old people about what's bothering me."

I didn't get a chance to talk to any of the old guys at all. We got caught up in the fund raising and the preparations for the whole thing. More and more Maeg used her organizing ability. It was needed, I knew that, and she did it in such a way nobody could see she was directly responsible. I helped as much as I could and cared for Marlon when she was busy. My part was to coach the young people, who would be acting as security, to get a feeling for what they would be responsible for. Some of the older guys I knew from a few years back, "Bro's" did some tactical training. People had been so busy doing all kinds of things, it had been almost impossible to keep track of what everybody was doing.

The Union assembly, that fall, was heavily attended. People from all over the province flocked to the meeting. All kinds of things went on for ordinary people to take part in. An Indian food auction and an Indian fashion show was held. Different Tribal groups performed dances and entertainments. A pipe ceremony was held every day during the assembly. A feeling of great strength and determination throughout the whole thing enveloped the people. Many people resolved to support the caravan in different ways. It was clear that there was a mandate from the people.

I was still uncomfortable with the whole idea, but I couldn't seem to put my finger on what the reasons were. I decided that I should just put it out of my head and give my full support. I ran into Chuck, my cousin, during the rounds that I made to recruit some of the younger guys to act as security. We talked about the whole thing. It was almost a repeat of a few years earlier, except that this time I didn't argue with him. I tried to hear what he said and make some sense out of it.

He said, "So, Slash, you're looking for warriors again. What happened the last time around? Seems like we always come full circle every five years. How do you feel about things now? Are you still angry and ready to kill, or have you become pious and full of the spirit like everybody else?"

His eyes were accusing and his voice was filled with sarcasm, but there was a gentleness to his movements, too. His hand rested lightly on my shoulder. He had cut right to the center.

I smiled at him and said, "Nah, I'm helping this caravan. It needs all the help it can get. I'm not angry anymore, and you were right last time and you'll be right again this time. Let me tell you what I think. I know there is something wrong, but I can't really be sure what it is. Maeg is convinced I'm just a worrier. She's working really hard to help get the thing together. I'm really on this ride for her and for Marlon. I know I should believe in it strongly, or not go, but I can't say what's wrong, even when I think and think about it. Can you tell me? You seem to have a way of clearing the crap from the truth."

He laughed, "You have changed, Slash, I'm glad to see that. There is hope after all. What's wrong is the wrong motivation for the damn thing. Indian people are against patriation. Period. Some of them can't sort out the difference between that and being against it because Indians aren't included in the talks. They're going to Ottawa to give Trudeau shit for not letting them in on the talks. Can't you see how absurd that is? If they were going to Ottawa saying, "Bullshit to any constitution but our own, for each of our Indian Nations," the feeling would be much different. Eventually, they will say that anyway, no matter what happens. The only thing is, it could happen a lot sooner. Does that set you straight? Watch things and see if I'm not right. Go on that trip and plant the idea at least. Your head space is okay now. You won't lose your grip."

He looked kind of sheepishly at me and said, "Sorry about the reference to being pious. I know what kind of help that has been to you and a lot of people, but there are a lot of people who are abusing Indian ways. Using it for a lot of things it wasn't meant for. I hate that kind of bullshit worse than them that don't believe in it because they think it's black magic."

"Yeah, I feel the same way when I see it happening. I guess everybody's got to approach it from different angles though. I'll think about what you said on the constitution issue. I'll bet that is why I can't seem to generate too much enthusiasm from the people I thought would most likely take to the idea. I can clearly see your point but I still can't see any way for the people to come to that realization. I will go on that express and talk about that idea as much as I can," I answered.

We went on that caravan. It was different than the one that I had gone on when I was first on the move. A feeling of closeness amongst everyone was strongest. There were a lot of, what I would call, the grass roots people. Everything was informal and friendly. Singing and drumming and storytelling went on continuously. Political talks were kept up to inform the people of new developments. People were picked up all along the way. A whole train was chartered for the purpose, so it was easy to keep track of everyone.

I remember being tired and keyed up all the time, but Maeg seemed to just shine. She packed Marlon around dressed in his little ribbon shirt and moccasins, and everybody played with him and talked to him.

Once during the trip, the train was stopped supposedly because the police believed that the train was rigged with explosives. The whole episode was tense with them getting aboard to go through everything.

I went up to one of the head security guys and said, "You believe them?"

Dave answered, "It could be for real. Just think of what an opportunity. Kill a whole bunch of us at once. It makes sense."

I said, "No. What makes even more sense is they aren't concerned about our safety. They're just checking to see if we are armed. That's why they're going through everything."

He looked at me and laughed, "Damn, Slash, you're probably right."

So, nothing came of the whole thing. I guess they satisfied themselves. All they found was a lot of drums and people's pipes, and other items used for Indian ways.

It was natural for them to assume that this was just a media attention trip, and there was no real need to pay attention to it and they didn't. Trudeau was off on an important talk to some other country by the time we got to Ottawa. "His" Indians weren't important enough to worry about. Everyone was angry about the cold shoulder they got from him and became more determined to force him to meet with them.

After a series of meetings in Ottawa, some of them decided to go on to New York to the U.N., to seek the support of some of the other countries on their position. I had talked with a few people about some of the things that Chuck and I had discussed, but when I did, they looked confused.

Dave put it into words when he asked, "How are we going to guarantee our rights if they ain't in the constitution? Isn't that what this whole trip is for? Whose side are you on?"

"I'm on our side," I said, "That's why I'm saying the things I'm saying. If I weren't, I wouldn't be here either, but there is a difference if you really think about it. What I have come to realize about half-ways through this is the people on this trip are saying one thing and the Indian politicians are saying another. Think of the song that everybody sings, the so-called Constitution song. It clearly says, "We don't need your Constitution, B.C. is all Indian land. We don't need your Constitution, hey yeah hey." How much clearer can it be? We don't need anybody's constitution, what we have is our own already. We hold rights to the land and to nationhood. We just need to have it recognized. We want to keep it. They are trying to make us hand it over by telling us that we have no choice. That's a lot of bull. They want us to believe it and are coercing us into negotiating with them by pretending to write us out of the whole thing, unless we negotiate, so that we will negotiate for whatever we can get. It's a typical big bully method. You deal with us or we'll just take it away anyway, kind of thing. Don't you see? What they stand to gain out of the whole deal is Indian land with all its resources, without incumberances to stop this pipeline or that mine or that thermal plant."

I wanted him to realize that Indians are the only people standing in the way of some of those things. I asked, "Why do you think there was a moratorium called on uranium explorations? Why do you think Berger recommended a ten year stop to any further development until land claims was settled? It's what they are doing right now. Settling it. They will buy out the land and the billions of dollars worth of resources on it for as little as they can. Then after that they will "give" you rights in some areas of it within provincial regulations for conservation, if it doesn't interfere with other important things like mining and forestry. But they will hold off agreeing to any of these rights until they buy out all the land claims. They'll continue to 'negotiate' on rights until that is done. Then they'll give us whatever they choose because our greatest weapon will be in their hands."

I went on to say, "What I think is, our people really want to have our rights recognized with our ownership over the land understood. That is what we mean by settlement of land claims and rights. That's not what the government means. They mean extinguishment and sell out. I, for one, am against that. If they never settle the land claims question, that's fine with me. It still belongs to us. It leaves something for our descendants. Someday they will achieve their rightful inheritance if things are left that way."

Dave sat there for a while and thought about what I just said. "Then we should be telling them what the song says; we don't want their constitution. We will never negotiate away our land or anything on it, and the only settlement that we will accept is recognition. We could be compensated for what they have already removed and sold off of our lands without a treaty. If they don't like that, they can tell us no or whatever they like, but we will still have legal rights to the land, and we won't give that up. We don't have to do a damn thing. They have to come to us. We can wait another hundred years or whatever. They will still have the same wrong doing over them. I see it clear. We gotta try to reach some of the others on this, or they will agree to negotiate for constitution rights and sell out our lands in settlements in the meantime. God, Slash, that's scary. We got to convince some of the leadership."

"I don't think you will, I tried to talk to some of them. They think I'm crazy. One guy just laughed and said nobody will give us any rights at all if we don't fight for some. I heard even Trudeau said something like that about land claims. The people are afraid and they can't seem to see through that. No matter what the government tries to force on us, we don't have to agree. Otherwise it is coercion and that is not supposed to be practiced by any civilized nations. We have the right to not agree on their terms. It is our land, until we are defeated in war or sign any agreement such as a treaty with them, or we give them their right on it by selling it to them. That would be absurd without a Nation to Nation treaty, because we would not be guaranteed anything. Our bargaining power is our ownership of the land. If we sell that before we bargain, what is our hope for a fair treatment for our rights on that land?" I answered him, all fired up now that it came clear.

Later, however, people just got real quiet when we talked about it, like they resented being told that. It was like what we said was against what they tried to do on that express. People became angry with me and those who listened to me. I was treated like an outcast.

Maeg and me went home after that. I knew many of the people went on from there to New York, to set up some talks with other Nations who would support them in their bid to be included in the talks. It got stronger and stronger support from other countries of the world.

I was against that idea, but Maeg was still caught up in the whole thing. She said to me, "Slash, I think it's important we do get some rights into the constitution. We will have a real rough trail ahead of us if we don't. We can't survive assimilation on such a large scale, and in so short a time, if we are forced to be treated equally with the rest of Canada. Equal rights is no rights, as you well know. That's what we will face if we don't try to secure some aboriginal rights. Extinction, ethnocide, genocide; it is a reality right now. How will it be in ten years? With or without our land base on the reserve, which we'll lose to taxation. There will be a few very rich Indians and many poverty-stricken and landless slaves to the labour market. We must get some special rights guaranteed, and maintain our land bases, free of taxation. Your way doesn't guarantee anything but opposition and resistance, and a maybe that someday our descendants might be able to get a better deal. Your way guarantees years of bitter struggle. That is what them leaders do not want for our people. We have been beaten over the heads too much already. This way we will get some measure of control and not be left out in the cold. It may end the years of struggle and suffering. Canada is here to stay. All our leaders are trying to make sure of is that we join Canada in a way that is not too harsh for our people. What you are proposing will only cause more strife and bitterness.

We will lose out in the end, because it is unreasonable.
It's unrealistic."

She looked almost ashamed to have said what she did.
I knew it cost her a great deal to have said it. She loved me,
and I knew she wouldn't do anything to hurt me, so obviously
it had meant a lot for her to come out and disagree with me.

I said to her, "Maeg, I will never interfere with what you
are doing, but from now on you can leave me out of it, okay?
I can't go along with supporting anything that will compromise
what I know to be at the center of all that I believe in. I agree
it is a big and dangerous responsibility in the face of a country
like Canada. I agree they would probably take away everything they can, but, to me, that is preferable to us giving in
and selling out the heritage of our descendants. That shame,
I cannot agree with. What if our ancestors did that, like some
of them bead and trinket treaties? At least them old people
had no clue about what the colonizers were up to. We don't
have that excuse. We'll end up with beads and trinkets anyway
if you really think about it. You will see when the negotiations
start. You will see how clever they will be at convincing you
of rights that are empty. You will see how they will settle
claims, not for true value but on terms and conditions that
will strip off any real value in today's economy. Finally, and
worst of all, you will see the defeat of our people when they
realize what they have done."

After that, we didn't talk too much about it to each other.
It was too painful to me to know she couldn't understand.
She kept up her work with the rest of the people who were
organizing things. Throughout that winter, she went to
meetings and potlatches and fund-raising things. They raised
money to go to England and Europe to launch a court case in
Britain and to lobby support to stop the patriation unless they
were included in the talks.

Winter turned into spring and things looked worse and
worse for any hope of rights to be written into the constitution.
Indians got angry over not being allowed to meet with the

government. To me it looked alright. I stayed home and worked on things that needed to be done around home. I worked with the young people and talked to some of the old people.

Chuck was right. The old people around the Okanagan who were involved in Indian politics were angry with the leaders. They accused them of not listening to the Elder's direction. I, myself, accused them of not hearing the Elders, even though they did appear to listen to them respectfully. I tried to help out and got the old people to the meetings and interpreted for them in a clear way for anybody to understand. But, it was difficult. The old people didn't want to go to meetings that supported the quest for inclusion in the constitution. They were against it, period. They did not participate.

That summer, Chuck and Jim, who worked with the Tribal Council which had a newly established administration, decided to set up an information forum on the subject. They tried to inform the people and our Chiefs of the position some of the Elders took. Our Chiefs didn't participate in the Constitution Express mainly because they felt the lack of support from their people, but didn't understand it.

The forum, which was called a historical symposium, centered on what the old people said on the first day. The second and third day was set up to get a representative voice from as many points of view on the question as possible, from the most assimilationist to the most radical. So much was covered during that time, it was unreal. Some of the most powerful speakers in the whole of North America were brought together. It was an educational experience.

I had hoped that people from the leadership of the constitution would be there to get an objective look at some of it. As it turned out, they weren't there, except for one or two. A planned sit-in at D.I.A. started on the same morning the symposium did. A lot of people we had hoped would turn up went to the sit-in instead of getting that information. I resented that. I knew that many leaders thought that we were working against them to undermine the support of the Elders who were so strong before. Many of them still could not get over their stereotyped image of us as AIM radicals. Even Maeg went to take part in the sit-in, since it was organized by the aboriginal women's group. The ones who were at the symposium were there mostly to speak. They were intent on getting support on their own point of view. They didn't hear anything else.

From that point on, I felt hopeless about the whole thing. I became very frightened to see what was happening. It seemed like we were slowly sinking and people were grabbing at anything that looked promising, except the truth.

The Tribal Council decided to follow up on some of the suggestions made at that symposium and sent a brief to Geneva concerning our position. One of the Elders accompanied it to a conference organized by the International Treaty Council. The conference was on aboriginal rights for indigenous peoples.

The constitution express organizers went into a frenzy of fund-raising after the sit-in was over. They did get a promise that there would be an investigation of D.I.A. wrong-doing.

Maeg was home only a few days out of every week after that. I sure missed her when she was gone, but she seemed to be doing okay.

Marlon had just learned to walk and I kept him home with me most times. We went to Old Pra-cwa's place to visit. Or we would go to my parents and help with the gardens. My Pop was just crazy over Marlon. So was Pra-cwa. Pra-cwa had given him his name at the dance that winter before, when he was six months old. He was called Little Chief in our language after my great-grandfather. My Pop and Pra-cwa and all the old people called him that.

Sometimes they would ask me about Maeg, but they usually didn't mention it too much. They had known she was busy working as one of the organizers. They all respected her a lot and never questioned that. They also knew why I wasn't with her at them things and how painful it had been for me.

I missed her so much, I hurt sometimes. When she came back all tired and worn out and all keyed up the way things went, I tried to calm her and take her mind off it. I rubbed her back and held her on my lap and rocked her gently and sang Indian songs that she liked. I talked to her about the things that went on locally and took her for long walks up to the hills we both loved. She sang for me sometimes in her beautiful, clear, haunting voice and it echoed over the hills and down the valleys.

In the early fall, when the last warm days stretched shadows over the land, we camped out for four days. We picked huckleberries at Tulameen. Those four days were like a dream. Everything was right, everything good. The wind was soft and the sun warm. The nights were crisp and coyotes' shrill cries mingled with owl calls. We were so close to each other in a way it's hard to describe. The whole world was far away. The politics were gone. Just her, me, Marlon and the hills, the beautiful earth, with everything there for her and me. I hated to go back home when we left.

The next month, she went to London and then on to Europe with the Constitution Express she had been helping to organize. I knew she was needed. People could depend on her. At the same time I wanted to beg her not to go. I wanted to tell her of the resentment from some of the people toward the express and warn her that it might be harmful. I didn't want to see her suffer consequences for something she couldn't understand. It was hard for me not to follow her. I thought of Mardi and the time I had made a similar decision. I was scared that Maeg might get hurt or something, but nothing happened. She kept sending postcards. I kept up on all the news that happened over there.

Some of her notes were real tense. One said, "There is a lot of heavy internal stuff going on. Ragged nerves, I guess. People really feel the strangeness and it has an effect that isn't good. Things not too good overall."

I had read something about a seeming split of the lobby force, especially after the announcement of the new constitutional accords eliminating aboriginal rights. Most of the people had come home after that and held Canada-wide demonstrations. Things just got worse and worse. It seemed like there was no hope for anything to the Constitution Express people.

To me it was good news. I thought that it would stop the whole thing on negotiating our rights away. It would give us strength and determination to do what we finally must. We had to be patient and strong because what finally must happen surely would.

Maeg finally came home just weeks before Christmas. I was so happy I was silly. I knew she felt the same way. We spent that Christmas in a great flurry of visiting and feasting. All my family was glad she was back. She was thin and defeated looking, and she wouldn't talk much about it. She kept her ear on the situation all the time and I knew she was worried. I couldn't tell her I was glad that the constitution talks were failing.

After all the demonstrations in ten major cities, Canada relented and recognized aboriginal rights in a half-hearted manner. Some of the premiers were still reluctant, it was obvious from their statements in the press. The constitution amending formula passed Parliament; Indians would be included. They would negotiate for their rights. Maeg was glad.

I felt like the world had come to an end. The worst had happened. I knew for people like me it meant only one thing. We would finally have to take a real stand to resist this or our children would have nothing. Nothing but equality in a slave market to the corporations. I feared for our future then. I saw some dark days ahead. I knew, finally, our real defeat could be just around the corner.

Many of our leaders would be lining up to get compensation on their lands. That would be the worst devastation of all. Our rights would be empty words on paper that had no compassion for what is human on the land. I saw what money and power could do to our gentle people and I felt deep despair. Nothing much would remain after that to fight for. Nothing to heal our wounds in the fighting. We would no longer know freedom as a people. We would be in bondage to a society that neither loved us nor wanted us to be a part of it. We would truly be second class citizens instead of first class Indians.

I was angry at those who had let it happen. Pushed for it to happen. They didn't ask me or the rest of the ordinary reserve people. If they had asked and listened, they would have heard the answer, especially from the old ones. But, nobody had asked, listened or heard.

Early in January, there was a potlatch held somewhere up in the north of the province. People who were a part of the Constitution Express were invited to get together and be honored. Maeg went up. She asked me to go. I couldn't. I felt too much resentment to go. Not against her, but against the whole thing. I knew they were already all tired and felt defeated. There was a feeling of confusion that had slowly spread amongst them. Maeg had told me about it. They didn't need me to add to it.

She said, "It's as if something is eating away at everybody. But nobody can be sure what exactly it is. Like when you know something is wrong but you don't know what it is."

I looked up with interest. "Is that right? Well, maybe its not too late after all. Maybe the seed is starting to sprout finally. Maybe it will grow. God, I hope so. You know, through all these years, we have made it, to avoid the worst. Like something was looking after our interests even when we didn't think so. Somehow things fouled up for them and they were never successful in taking our rights and our land. Maybe it'll happen again. Maybe our prayers are being listened to. Maybe enough people will see it in time."

She looked at me, smiled for the first time in a long while and said, "I haven't the faintest idea what you just said, but,

I have the same feeling. I'm going to go to this gathering to tell them of some of the things you have said to me, then, I'm going to concentrate on being home. It's finally beginning to make some sense, after I have had time away from all the heavy politics to examine it. Maybe that is what is happening to everybody. I'll be back in a couple of days. I think I'll leave Marlon. He doesn't like to travel. I wish you would come. You know, a lot of people have a deep respect for you, even though they don't understand all you say."

I said, "No, I don't want to go. I don't want to spoil the party. My place is here. Here is where the real fight will be. You go and enjoy yourself. Don't even for a minute worry about Marlon. We'll be waiting for you when you come back."

I was happy at her words. I loved her. Marlon needed her. She was the center of my world. During the days while we waited, I played with Marlon. I talked to him in Okanagan. I told him all the things that he would wake up to.

I told him, "You, my little man, are named Little Chief. Someday you will grow to be strong and straight for your people. I promise you I'll do all I can to see that through. You are our hope. You are an Indian of a special generation. Your world will be hard but you will grow up proud to be Indian. That will make you different than some of us. If I keep to the Indian path and protect your rights the way Pra-cwa explained, you will be the generation to help them white men change because you won't be filled with hate. That's why the prophesies say yours is a special generation. I'll go through anything to see that come about. You are the part of me that extends in a line up toward the future."

He listened with his big soft eyes so serious on me.

I didn't think anything could go wrong. It seemed like I had the whole world in my hands, and I was so strong I could face anything. My Pops had told me once that when you reach a point when you feel like that, you're due for a hard fall. I didn't think so. What could go wrong?

Sure things looked bad for Indians on the whole as far as

the constitution was concerned, but what had started about fifteen years ago had grown. It would never be put down until Indian people did what they had to, not only for their survival but for the survival of what is human in an inhuman world. It was inevitable. It seemed worthwhile to put up with some hard times for that.

Two days later, Maeg came home in a box. A car had hit theirs and killed her and two of her friends.

The days that followed were dark and dream-like. I didn't think or move or even cry. I just sat. I was like that at the funeral. My despair was complete.

Yet I could hear, from somewhere from out there a little boy's voice that whispered, "Papa, I'm a Little Chief."

Somewhere from out there something pulled at me and I had to wake up to what was real. I wondered how I would make it to get up one more time. I was so tired.

Epilogue

Tonight, I sit here up at the Flint Rock and look down to the thousands of lights spread out in the distance where the town is creeping incessantly up the hillsides.

Across the Okanagan valley the sun begins to set. Blazes of mars-red tinged with deep purple and crimson brush silvery clouds and touch the mountain tops. The wind moans through the swaying pines as coyotes shrill their songs to each other in the gathering dusk. Long, yellow grasses bend and whip their blades across cactus, sand and sage.

I feel old and I think I have seen many things for a young person. I have made my stand and chosen my path and I decide to tell my story for my son and those like him because I must. My reason is simple. Under the cruel blows of the harsh one some call destiny, many of our people have shuddered and fallen. Few have accepted this teacher and taken her gifts. To those that do, defeat is a stranger and pain an everyday reality. Some shall call them leaders.

Let Me
kiss your footprints
in the grass.
I have been a warrior
because I suffer.
Let me pray:
     Though a tree falls and dies
     or dies and falls
     let its flowers
     not perish
     but spread and scatter
     in the chill dance
     that is kin to sky.
Let
me
open my way
among grasses,
I carry your seed.
The wind will wipe out
little traces of you.